HAUNTED HIBISCUS

Tea Shop Mystery #22

LAURA CHILDS

BERKLEY PRIME CRIME
New York

BERKLEY PRIME CRIME
Published by Berkley
An imprint of Penguin Random House LLC
penguinrandomhouse.com

Copyright © 2021 by Gerry Schmitt & Associates, Inc.
Excerpt from *Twisted Tea Christmas* by Laura Childs copyright © 2021
by Gerry Schmitt & Associates, Inc.
Penguin Random House supports copyright. Copyright fuels creativity, encourages
diverse voices, promotes free speech, and creates a vibrant culture. Thank you for buying
an authorized edition of this book and for complying with copyright laws by not
reproducing, scanning, or distributing any part of it in any form without permission.
You are supporting writers and allowing Penguin Random House to continue to
publish books for every reader.

BERKLEY and the BERKLEY & B colophon are registered trademarks and BERKLEY
PRIME CRIME is a trademark of Penguin Random House LLC.

ISBN: 9780451489708

Berkley Prime Crime hardcover edition / March 2021
Berkley Prime Crime mass-market edition / February 2022

Printed in the United States of America
5 7 9 10 8 6 4

HAUNTED
HIBISCUS

1

Dark clouds bubbled across a purple-black sky, then lifted gently, like a velvet curtain in a darkened theater, to reveal the top two floors of a dilapidated old mansion.

"That's it," Theodosia said. "The place they dubbed the Gray Ghost."

"I can't say it looks particularly charming," Drayton said. "In fact, it's slightly off-putting."

Theodosia gazed at a corner turret that was bathed in green and purple lights. At one time the home had whispered wealth and taste. Not anymore. Now the exterior, the balustrades and finials, even the third-floor widow's walk displayed the battering it had received from a century of Atlantic hurricanes, salt-infused sea air, and industrial-strength humidity.

"Haunted houses generally aren't that attractive," Theodosia said. "But at least this one's being put to good use."

It was the week before Halloween, and tea maven Theodosia Browning and her tea sommelier, Drayton Conneley, were strolling down Tradd Street in Charleston, South Carolina, heading for the old Bouchard Mansion. It was a property that had recently been bequeathed to Drayton's beloved Heritage Society.

"The Heritage Society wasn't all that happy about inheriting this old place," Drayton explained. "But it was donated by one of the last remaining Bouchards. Written into his will. And you know our fearless leader, Timothy, is loath to turn down any sort of gift."

"Still, I love how your curators and marketing folks figured out how to make the most of it," Theodosia said. "What an amazing idea to create a literary- and history-inspired haunted house. And then to launch it the week before Halloween?" She gave a little shiver of anticipation. "It's a fabulous concept. People will be standing in line." They rounded a tall hedge of crepe myrtle and arrived at the front walk where at least five dozen people were clustered, waiting to get in. "Actually, people *are* standing in line."

"Opening night," Drayton said as they shuffled up the sidewalk with the rest of the visitors. "So I suppose folks are curious."

"I sure am," Theodosia said as she gazed at the old place. Yellow light spilled out from tall, narrow front windows; inside looked to be a beehive of activity.

"You remember Willow French, Timothy's grand-niece?" Drayton asked.

"Oh sure, I've met her a few times."

"She's here tonight, signing her new book."

"Willow's written a novel? That's wonderful."

Drayton pursed his lips. "It's not exactly a stunning piece of literature. Rather an anthology titled *Carolina Crimes and Creepers.* Supposed to be a mixture of true crime and some of our low-country legends."

"You mean, haunted legends," Theodosia said, feeling another tingle. Even though she didn't believe-believe in spirits and ghosts, it was fun to pretend that Revolutionary War–era ghosts and headless pirates still stalked Charleston's narrow cobblestone alleys. Besides, there were plenty of folks who *did* believe in ghosts. Case in point, there were four different ghost tours that guided visitors to the Old City Jail, Provost Dungeon, and Unitarian Church Cemetery. As well as to a twisted old hanging tree where dozens of pirates had been executed.

Drayton glanced up at the dilapidated mansion where a swirling projection of ghosts and witches moved eerily across an outside wall. "Haunted, yes," he said.

The low country and Charleston in particular were a hotbed of legends and lore that included ghosts, hauntings, boo hags, spirits, apparitions, and spectral goings-on. Everyone who lived in Charleston knew about the haunted theaters and mansions, Lavinia Fisher, the Headless Torso, and the Weeping Woman of St. Philip's Church. And there were dozens more creepy tales that had been passed down through generations.

As they walked through antique wrought-iron gates, a ghoul with a green-painted face and a bolt through his neck tapped Drayton on the shoulder. "Tickets?" he rasped.

Drayton fumbled in his jacket pocket. "As a matter of fact, I do."

"This is going to be amazing," Theodosia said. She was already three steps ahead of Drayton and loved what she was seeing. Edgar Allan Poe lounged on the front portico; Washington Irving's Headless Horseman lurked in a window. And she was pretty sure she could see Lady Macbeth sweeping past the guests who were already inside.

"You're liking this, yes?" Drayton said when he caught up with Theodosia.

"Yes!"

Possessing a keen sense of adventure, Theodosia was in her mid-thirties and the owner of the Indigo Tea Shop on Church Street. She was also blessed with expressive painterly blue eyes, a fair complexion (it helped to be religious about sunscreen), and a riot of auburn hair that she worried sometimes looked slightly untamed.

Drayton, on the other hand, was sixtyish, dapper, a true Southern gent, and the model of conservatism. He was always appropriately dressed (tweed jacket and bow tie tonight) and had a personality that could veer from genial to slightly stiff. Drayton's idea of an exciting evening was attending *La Traviata* or holing up in his private library to read his beloved Dickens.

"I think this place is terrific," Theodosia said. She was excited and feeling a little bit giddy. "Who doesn't like Halloween, after all? Who doesn't enjoy a good haunted house, even if it is all costumes and theatrics?" She reached out, letting her fingertips brush against the rustling full-length satin skirt of a masked woman.

"Ah," Drayton said, catching up to her. "From the legend of Madame Margot." Then he took her arm and said, "Come on, let's go find Willow."

Willow French was young and pretty, with honey-colored hair that framed a smiling face. She was clearly in seventh heaven from all the attention she was receiving tonight. Seated at an antique library table, she smiled brightly as she autographed books and thanked everyone in her immediate vicinity for showing up.

The authoring business must be good, Theodosia decided. Dozens of people waited in line for a signed copy, Willow's table was stacked with double towers of books, and cardboard cases full of books filled the small parlor where she was seated.

"Willow," Drayton said, greeting Timothy's grandniece with a wide smile and a nod of his head. "I see our favorite author is in residence tonight."

Willow glanced up, recognized Drayton immediately, and grinned from ear to ear. "Uncle Drayton!" she shrieked.

Theodosia gave Drayton a sideways glance. "*Uncle* Drayton?"

"That's how Timothy has always introduced me to his grandniece," Drayton said in a low, soft voice. "As though I'm a member of the family."

And it was abundantly clear that Willow *did* consider Drayton part of the family, because now she skittered around to the front of the table, arms flung wide, ready to give him a most exuberant bear hug.

Willow squeezed Drayton, uttered another high-pitched squeal, and, after a few giggles, eventually released him. "I was hoping you'd show up," she said breathlessly. Standing barely five two, with shining eyes and an impish expression, Willow looked even younger than her twenty-four years.

"I wouldn't have missed this for the world," Drayton said. Then, hurriedly, "You remember Theodosia, don't you?"

"Of course. You're the tea lady," Willow said, immediately reaching out to give Theodosia a quick hug as well. "Hey, thanks bunches for coming."

"This is a big night for you," Theodosia said as she returned the hug. "I understand it's your first major book signing."

Willow nodded. "I've been to a couple bookstores, but am I ever loving this. I wondered how my book would go over here, but it's been gangbusters so far. Sales are good with lots of friends dropping by to say congrats. One of the bigwigs from the Charleston Library Society even stopped by my table to tell me she'd ordered twenty copies from my publisher, who I hope is wandering around here someplace."

"I couldn't be happier for you," Theodosia said.

"We're delighted," Drayton echoed. "And of course we both want signed copies."

"I've got first editions that I can personalize for you." Willow hurried back around the table, sat down, and grabbed two books from a box on the floor. She flipped them open and grabbed a squishy marker pen. The large moonstone ring on her left hand flashed as she signed both books with a flourish.

"Has Timothy stopped by yet?" Drayton asked.

Willow nodded. "Oh yeah, he's around somewhere."

"I don't think Timothy was all that keen on this haunted house idea," Drayton said. "But judging from the crowd that's turned up tonight, I must say it's . . . Well, speak of the devil!"

Timothy Neville ghosted into the room like a character out of *King Lear*. He was an octogenarian who was not only the power behind the Heritage Society, but also a board member of the Charleston Opera Society, occasional violinist for the Charleston Symphony, collector of antique pistols, and proud possessor of a stunning mansion on Archdale Street that was furnished with equally stunning paintings, tapestries, and antiques. Interestingly enough, all that knowledge and power were contained within a small man who was barely one hundred forty pounds and had a bony, simian face, yet possessed the grace and poise of an elder statesman.

"Looks like your haunted house is a rousing success," Drayton declared.

Timothy favored Theodosia and Drayton with a thin smile. "I wouldn't have dreamed this up in a million years. But my staff . . . all I can say is they're blessed with vivid imaginations."

"But in a good way," Theodosia said.

"Did I hear there was some some sort of property dispute?" Drayton asked.

Timothy gave an offhand wave. "Another of the Bouchard

relatives tried to contest the will, but my attorneys assured me it was ironclad. This place, such as it is, remains ours, lock, stock, and barrel."

"That's wonderful," Theodosia said. She was marveling at the crowds that continued to pour in. And then, as Drayton and Timothy continued in conversation, she managed to slip away. She definitely wanted to get a good look at the various literary characters in their elaborate displays.

And she wasn't disappointed. The folks at the Heritage Society had done a masterful job.

Edgar Allan Poe had his own writing studio—really, more of a dark garret—complete with quill pens, inkwell, antique desk, threadbare rug, old leather-bound books, and even a stuffed raven sitting on a perch.

Wearing a silver-gray floor-length corseted dress, Lady Macbeth stalked her way through the old mansion carrying a silver candlestick. Dr. Jekyll and Mr. Hyde had their own laboratory set up as well. And Sherlock Holmes had a wonderful study, complete with books, a messy desk, and a coatrack that held his tweed overcoat and deerstalker hat.

As Theodosia gazed into a mirror that reflected an image of Dorian Gray, she decided that she'd better get a signed book for Haley as well. Haley, her compadre and young chef at the Indigo Tea Shop, was a good friend of Willow's and would appreciate having one of the first editions.

But when Theodosia eventually wound her way back to the small parlor, Willow was no longer seated at her table.

Stepped out, I suppose, Theodosia thought to herself. *Maybe I'll pop back later in the week. I know Willow plans to do a couple more signings.*

"There you are," Drayton said.

Theodosia whirled around. "Have you seen Willow? Do you know where she ran off to?"

"She's probably being introduced around by Timothy," Drayton said. "He's busting his buttons over her. Or perhaps she's taking a break." He smiled. "Could have picked up a touch of writer's cramp from signing so many books."

"Tonight's been a real success for Willow. Really, for the Heritage Society in general," Theodosia said as they walked through the main parlor, then stepped outside onto the wide porch. A chill wind had sprung up, and she was suddenly cold. As she buttoned her jacket, they continued out into the front yard.

"I'll be the first to admit that I thought a literary haunted house was a half-baked idea," Drayton said as they walked past a horde of people anxiously waiting to get in. "But this was rather . . ."

A loud, collective gasp suddenly rose up from the moving crowd, drowning out the rest of Drayton's words.

Puzzled at the burst of noise, Drayton shook his head and said, "What?" just as a woman's high-pitched scream rose like some kind of ungodly yodel and pierced the night air.

Both startled and curious, Theodosia spun around just in time to see something—could it be a body?—dangling out the window of the third-floor tower. She grasped Drayton's arm and pulled him around as well. "Drayton, look up there!"

"My heaven!" Drayton exclaimed in a shaky voice, as all around them the cacophony of screams and shouting continued to build and build until the noise seemed like an explosion.

"It's some kind of illusion!"

"How terrifying!"

"Oh no, it's really happening!"

"Help her! Somebody please help that poor girl!"

At first glance, Theodosia thought it had to be part of the entertainment, some special effect that had been rigged to frighten people. A woman's body, dangling from a rope, motionless and frozen in the harsh purple and green lights.

But that would be too terrible, wouldn't it? And this looks positively . . . real.

And then the body twirled slowly and horribly, twisting around so everyone could finally see the dark-purplish tinge to the woman's face, the dead sunken eyes, the long blond hair whipping frantically in the night wind.

That's when a rocked-to-the-core Drayton suddenly clutched at his heart and gasped, "Dear Lord, it's Willow. Someone's hanged her to death!"

2

❧

While dozens of stunned visitors whipped out their cell phones en masse and flooded Charleston's 911 system with distress calls, Theodosia short-circuited the lot of them. She immediately called Pete Riley, police detective first grade, trusted first responder, and boyfriend extraordinaire.

Riley picked up on the third ring. "Well, hello there," he said in a leisurely tone of voice. He had caller ID, so he knew it was Theodosia. What he didn't know was how upset and terrified she was.

"Riley, I need you to come quickly!" Theodosia said in a tight voice. She tried not to sound crazed or hysterical, just focused every part of her being on holding it together.

"What's wrong?" Riley knew Theodosia well enough to realize there had to be some sort of emergency.

"At the haunted house . . . the one the Heritage Society is sponsoring, there's been a . . ."

"Hold a sec, will you?"

"Riley!" Now Theodosia did cry out in frustration. Why

had he cut her off like that? What could be so all-fired important? Especially now when she needed him the most.

A few seconds later Riley was back on, his voice crackling with alarm. "I just received an emergency text from dispatch. Theo . . . are you calling from the haunted house on Tradd Street?"

"Yes!"

"Then stay put. I'm on my way." And just like that Riley was gone.

Drayton stared at Theodosia with alarm in his eyes. "While you were talking, the police just . . . They're already here. Two officers ran upstairs to see if . . ." Drayton's words ended in a guttural choke, as if he'd run out of air. Then, "Did you get ahold of him? Riley? Is he coming?"

Theodosia breathed out slowly. "He's coming."

"We need to find Timothy," Drayton said. "To tell him . . ." He touched a hand to the side of his head. "Gracious me, what do we tell him? *How* do we tell him?"

At that exact moment, a sharp, strangled scream rose up from inside the haunted house.

"I think he already knows," Theodosia said.

The EMTs arrived next. Hauling a gurney and emergency packs, they charged into the house and up the stairs to the third floor. Then three more squad cars came screaming in, the officers immediately rushing into the haunted house to try to round up visitors and herd everyone outside.

"Timothy," Drayton said as they watched the frightened visitors pour out. "He's still in there. What must he be feeling? We've got to go in and help him!"

Together, Theodosia and Drayton fought their way through the surging, almost hysterical crowd. They pushed back up the front walk, reached the porch, and then slipped inside. They found Timothy standing in the parlor where Willow had been signing books only minutes earlier. His face was twisted in anguish, his narrow shoulders hunched. He looked as if he'd just been sentenced to death.

"You people need to go outside," an officer barked at the three of them.

"The woman . . . she's his grandniece," Drayton said.

The officer's face fell. "Oh," he said, stepping away.

Theodosia, Drayton, and Timothy stood there, too stunned to even speak to one another, as yellow-and-black crime scene tape was strung all around them and more officers arrived.

Finally, Detective Pete Riley came flying through the front door.

"Riley!" Theodosia cried as she rushed into his arms.

"You saw it happen? You've been here the whole time?" Riley asked her.

Theodosia nodded, savoring his warm embrace. Then she took a step back and gazed at him. "It was awful. I thought maybe . . ." Tears formed in her eyes. "I guess I don't know *what* to think."

Riley just nodded. He was used to dealing with distraught people. Used to investigating homicides and serious crimes. At age thirty-seven, he was one of the up-and-coming detectives on Charleston's police force. A tall, intense man with an aristocratic nose, high cheekbones, and cobalt blue eyes. Theodosia, of course, simply thought of him as Riley, her Riley. He called her Theo, and she called him Riley. It was as simple as that because it suited them.

"What's going to happen now?" Theodosia asked.

"This whole place is a crime scene, so we're going to follow standard procedure," Riley said. "We'll detain as many people as possible and get statements from them. At least that's what the boss ordered."

"The boss?" Theodosia said.

"Tidwell."

"You've already talked to him?"

Riley nodded. "He's on his way over. Should be here any minute."

Theodosia glanced at Drayton and Timothy. "I should stay here with them. Maybe I could . . ."

"No," Riley said. "Let's get you outside right now before things get really ugly." He walked Theodosia to the front door and down the steps into the large front yard. Harried-looking officers wielding pens and clipboards were hastily asking questions and writing down the names of as many witnesses as they could round up.

"What are you going to do?" Theodosia asked Riley.

Before Riley could answer, a large, bulky man strolled out of the shadows and into the garish green light. It was Detective Burt Tidwell, the head of Charleston PD's Robbery and Homicide Division. He was as wide as a soccer mom's van and as touchy as a puff adder.

"Riley," he growled.

"Yes, sir."

"After we conduct a thorough search of this so-called haunted house, I want you to go over and search the victim's apartment," Detective Tidwell said in his trademark baritone. Hesitating for a moment, Tidwell cast a quick, almost sardonic glance at Theodosia and added, "That's if you're not too busy here."

"I'm on it, sir," Riley said. He snapped to attention as Tidwell pushed past them, his large belly protruding from between the lapels of his ill-fitting tweed jacket. Though Tidwell was irascible, overweight, and overbearing, he was undeniably the finest investigator on the force. As a leader who inspired utter confidence, his men would probably leap into a volcano for him. They'd probably follow him into the pit of hell.

Theodosia watched, fascinated, as the crowd parted for Tidwell as if he were a visiting dignitary. She'd butted heads with the crusty Tidwell before. And though she didn't always get along with him, didn't always see eye to eye, she did respect him.

Theodosia turned back to Riley, put a hand on his arm, and said, in an urgent voice, "Let me go with you."

Riley half smiled as he shook his head. "I can't do that."

Theodosia was not about to take no for an answer. This was far too important.

"Please," she said. "For Timothy's sake. You'll be haphazardly looking through all his grandniece's personal belongings. And I'm positive it would be a great comfort to Timothy if someone he knows and trusts went along with you."

"No can do. We can't have civilians poking around and contaminating a crime scene."

"You think that's a crime scene, too?" Theodosia asked. The idea hadn't occurred to her. Now the notion of checking out Willow's apartment seemed almost tantalizing.

"I suppose I won't know until I get there," Riley said.

Theodosia stared at Riley, a combination of nervousness and excitement sparking in her eyes. "I'm not exactly a civilian, you know. I've been down this road before."

"I get that. It's just . . . tonight, no. It's simply not possible." Riley brushed his lips across Theodosia's forehead and was gone. Strode deftly through the crowd and back into the haunted house.

Five minutes later, Drayton emerged. He had a hangdog, defeated look on his face.

"They threw me out," he said to Theodosia.

She touched a hand to his shoulder. "Timothy's talking to the investigators?"

Drayton nodded. "Trying to anyway. He's awfully upset."

"They'll see he gets home safely," Theodosia said. Then, "There's nothing we can do for him here."

"I suppose you're right," Drayton said. "But I still

wanted to . . . Oh no, will you look at that?" His eyes drooped heavily as he glanced out toward the street.

Theodosia followed Drayton's gaze and saw that one of Willow's books had been discarded in the gutter, its spine broken, pages fluttering crazily as they were ripped out, one by one, by the chill wind that was now battering in from the Atlantic.

3

With sad and heavy hearts Theodosia and Drayton left the crowd of gawkers behind and wandered aimlessly down Tradd Street.

"I wish there was something we could do for Timothy," Drayton said. "The poor man wasn't just upset; he was desolate."

"There is something," Theodosia said.

"Hmm?"

"We can be his friend. Try to help him in any way possible."

"Of course." Then Drayton's conservative bent kicked in. "Up to a point, that is. We can't exactly solve a murder."

Theodosia was about to say, *Why not?* Then she changed her mind and said, "But there is something we have to deal with immediately. Like, tonight."

"What's that?"

"We've got to break the news to Haley. She and Willow are pretty good friends."

"*Were* friends," Drayton said. "I'll give Haley a call soon as I get home and try to tell her as gently as possible."

They stopped at the corner of Tradd and Meeting Street under a wrought-iron lamp made to resemble a turn-of-the-century gas lamp. Pale-yellow light filtered down, giving their faces and everything around them a slightly ethereal look. Wind whipped at trees; faint tendrils of fog drifted in from Charleston Harbor.

"That's kind of you to volunteer," Theodosia said. "But maybe I should . . ."

Drayton shook his head. "No, you need to head on home. There's always a chance Pete Riley will call you and we can learn something new. Some information, something crucial that might shed a bit of light on this terrible tragedy."

Theodosia thought about this for a few moments and decided that Drayton was right. Riley would probably be on his way to Willow's apartment in a few minutes, so that might produce some key information. And even though Drayton was just as bewildered and angry as she was, he was basically the calm, rational one right now. He wasn't a hot reactor like she was. If Theodosia had her way, she'd be back at the haunted house, creeping through the attic, searching for clues.

"I suppose you're right," Theodosia said. It really killed her to go on home and leave the senseless murder of Willow in the hands of the police. But she did stand down.

At least for now.

Theodosia's little home in the Historic District was a welcome sight tonight. It was a perfect Queen Anne–style cottage complete with slanting shingled roof, leafy vines crawling up the brick exterior, small turret, and rounded front door. Cute as a gnome's home.

As she stepped through her front door, Earl Grey came hurtling toward her.

"Hey, fella," Theodosia said. All fifty-five pounds of him thumped hard against her, almost knocking her off-balance. Then she knelt down and gave her dog a hug, touched her face to his soft muzzle, and found quiet comfort.

Earl Grey wasn't just a rescue dog; he was also a well-mannered tea shop dog (allowed in on special occasions) and a trained therapy dog. With his gentle and friendly Dalbrador demeanor (half dalmatian, half Labrador), he loved to interact with seniors in special care facilities as well as children in hospitals.

Theodosia dumped her hobo bag on the buffet as she and Earl Grey bounced from her living room to her dining room and then out the kitchen door and into her small backyard.

Gazing up at the sky with its scatter of stars, Theodosia inhaled the night air. The evening was cool and getting colder with the faint salty scent of the Atlantic Ocean riding on the breeze. There were night sounds, too. Leaves tumbling across dry grass, scritching and scratching, bare branches rubbing together like dry bones.

Summer's truly gone, Theodosia thought to herself. *All Hallows' Eve creeps in this Saturday night, and winter's chill is just around the corner.*

"C'mon, boy," she called to Earl Grey. He was snuffling around the base of a pine tree that Drayton had artfully clipped and snipped to create a supersized bonsai. "Let's go back inside."

Theodosia and Earl Grey stepped into her kitchen. It felt warm and cozy after the evening's chill, and the sweet, slightly outdoorsy aroma of fresh wood lingered in the air. Her new Carolina pine cabinets had finally—*finally*—been installed. And they looked absolutely wonderful, even if she was still waiting for some brass knobs and pulls that were being handcrafted by artisans who, like monks working an entire year on a single manuscript page, were taking their own sweet time. She paused to admire her new kitchen cabinets—yes, they really were lovely—then grabbed a bottle of Fiji water from her fridge.

In the dining room, Theodosia paused as a wave of sadness suddenly washed over her. She stepped to the Sheraton buffet, where she'd tossed her purse, and pulled out the book Willow had autographed for her less than an hour ago.

Carefully, almost reverently, Theodosia set the book upright on the dining room table. How bizarre that Willow's book would be a compendium of hauntings and strange deaths. Giving a little shudder, Theodosia wondered if the book had been some sort of harbinger of doom.

But no, that wasn't possible. That would be way too freaky.

Perhaps if she kept the book in a special place and treated it as a sort of talisman, thought only positive things . . .

Theodosia's cell phone shrilled inside her jacket pocket, practically scaring her to death. She grabbed for it, fumbled around, then was finally able to answer.

"Riley?" she said. She was fighting to remain calm even while anticipating the latest breaking news.

"Theo?" Riley's voice sounded faint and a little bit hoarse. As if there were millions of miles between them instead of just a dozen or so city blocks. Like their cell phone signal was randomly bouncing from satellite to satellite.

"Yes!" Theodosia said as her words bubbled out. "Are you at Willow's apartment? What did you find? Anything that might help shed a light on . . . ?"

"Sweetheart . . ." Now Riley's voice sounded thick and a little strangled. As if he was trying to clear his throat but couldn't quite make that happen.

"What is it?" Theodosia asked again. A nugget of worry

blipped in her brain. "Is something wrong?" For whatever reason, Riley didn't sound like himself. His chipper professional demeanor just wasn't there.

"I don't want to upset you," Riley said. Now hesitation was evident in his voice.

To Theodosia, Riley's words weren't just heavy with caution; they were flashing bright-red warning signs.

"You *are* upsetting me," she said. "In fact, you're scaring me. Did something happen at Willow's apartment? Please, tell me what's wrong."

"I will. But first you have to make an excellent promise to me. I don't want you to come running over here because . . . Wait one, Theo. Hang on a minute."

"*Riley*," Theodosia said in exasperation. Then, "Okay, I'll . . ." Her voice trailed off as she heard a hollow *thunk*. Riley had set his phone down. Or maybe he'd dropped it. It was obvious something major was taking place. Maybe he'd stumbled upon some critical piece of information? Maybe he'd already figured out who Willow's killer was?

Theodosia stood in her dining room, tapping her foot, staring at Willow's book, waiting for Riley to come back on the line, all the while growing more and more restless.

"Riley, what's going on?" Theodosia finally shouted into the phone.

There was still no reply.

Where did he go? Should I be worried? Nope, too late for that. I'm already worried sick.

Theodosia perked up when she heard faint voices in the background. It sounded as if more people had arrived at Willow's apartment, if that's where he was calling from. Okay then, Riley must have found something important and brought in a crime scene team. She allowed herself to relax. Additional law enforcement felt like a positive step.

There was a bump and a scrape, as if Riley's phone was

being handled roughly. And then someone who clearly wasn't Riley was suddenly on the line and speaking to her.

"Hello?" came a man's voice, deep and resonant. Official sounding. "Is this Theodosia? Do I have that right?"

Warning bells jangled in Theodosia's brain. Her heart pulsed even faster. "Yes. Please tell me what's going on. Who . . . who is this, please?"

"My name is Ellis Starkey, and I'm one of the EMTs that came to Detective Riley's aid."

"You came to his aid?" Had she heard him right? Perhaps not. "I'm confused. What sort of aid are you talking about?"

"Ma'am," said Starkey, "there's been an OIS."

"An OIS?"

"An officer involved shooting. Detective Riley has been shot."

Theodosia would have dropped the phone if she hadn't been so utterly gobsmacked. As it was she kept it gripped tightly in her hand as she scrambled for her car keys, slung her purse onto her shoulder, and raced outside to where her Jeep was parked. She left her house lights on, the door unlocked, and Earl Grey staring after her in doggy amazement.

Jumping into her trusty Jeep, lights and seat belt almost forgotten, she cranked the engine over and took off as if her life depended on it. Or Riley's did.

She blasted down King Street, past the City Market, then blew through a stop sign and turned onto Calhoun. From there it was just a few blocks to University Hospital at the Medical University of South Carolina. She'd weaseled the information out of Starkey and knew for a fact that this was where the ambulance was transporting Riley.

"Where's the ER entrance?" Theodosia muttered to herself as she tapped her brakes to slow down and fought to make her brain function a little more clearly. Scanning the unfamiliar buildings, she hesitated, then said, "Okay, I see it. Now I need a parking spot."

Theodosia found a spot a half block away, then jogged back to the ER entrance and flew through the electronic doors.

"Pete Riley," she shouted to the woman who was sitting behind the reception desk. "He was just brought in here. Where is he?"

The receptionist, an older woman who was wearing a blue smock that said WILLA DEVORE, VOLUNTEER on a lapel pin, consulted her computer. "Riley," she said. "Randolph, Riley . . . yes, here he is." She looked up. "Police officer?"

"Detective," Theodosia said. As if it mattered.

"GSW," the receptionist said.

"What?"

"Gunshot wound. The ambulance brought him in eight minutes ago. Well, more like nine."

"Great. Where can I find him?"

"You can't. At least for now anyway. You'll have to sit tight."

"Why is that?" Theodosia asked.

"Because the ER docs are with him right now. Evaluating him. Taking care of him."

"Making sure he's stable?" Theodosia asked. She was shaking now.

"Are you a relative?"

"Girlfriend."

"If you'll just take a seat, we'll let you know when you can see him. Or at least speak with one of the ER docs."

"Great. Okay," Theodosia said. But she didn't take a seat. Instead she paced back and forth, looking at her watch, then at the receptionist, then at the door that led back to the ER bay. She was tempted to rush it and try to find Riley, but she didn't.

Ten more minutes crept by, then fifteen minutes. A few more people trickled in, mostly friends and relatives worried about injured friends and relatives. Theodosia felt so frustrated she was ready to jump out of her skin.

Then Detective Burt Tidwell walked in and her brain bonked into hyperdrive. Now she had a mission.

Before Tidwell even made his approach to the reception desk, Theodosia was in his face.

"Do you see what you did!" Theodosia cried. "Do you? You sent Riley over there all by himself and what happened? He got shot! I should have gone along with him . . ."

"And you might have been shot as well," Tidwell said. His tone was restrained, his attitude maddeningly casual.

"No. That's not what would have happened. We would have been a lot more careful."

"You don't know that."

"Neither do you!" Theodosia shouted back.

"You're upset," Tidwell said.

"No kidding."

"Please," Tidwell said. "Just calm down and wait here while I see what's going on."

Theodosia crossed her arms and got out of the way. But she did not sit down. Or calm down for that matter.

Tidwell had a whispered consultation with the receptionist, then came over to talk to Theodosia.

"A doctor will be coming out to talk with us," Tidwell said. "Give us a prognosis."

"Good." She tapped a foot. "When will that be?"

"Anytime now."

But it was a good half hour before a tired-looking doctor in blue scrubs finally emerged from the ER bay. He glanced at Theodosia and Tidwell and said, "I'm Dr. Benjamin. You're the ones waiting for news on Mr. Riley?"

"Detective Riley," Tidwell said as they both popped out of their chairs.

"What can you tell us?" Theodosia asked.

"He's been stabilized and is in good condition," the doctor said. "Because he's relatively young and physically fit, his vitals and respiration are excellent. He's not injured too badly even though the bullet went through his left arm." The doctor indicated a spot on his own upper arm. "Right here. He doesn't need surgery, but he does need some, um . . . repair."

Theodosia swallowed hard and whispered a prayer.

Theodosia and Tidwell waited together for another forty-five minutes, barely speaking to each other, until, finally, mercifully, they were told they could go up to the fourth floor where Riley was now resting in a private room.

"Riley." Theodosia tiptoed to his bedside and gazed down at him.

Riley turned and smiled up at her. His face was pale, but he looked comfortable enough with pillows and white blankets fluffed all around him.

"Hey, kiddo," he said.

"Hey, kiddo, yourself," Theodosia said. "I've been worried sick about you. How are you feeling?" She wanted to cry but tried to smile instead.

"Mostly just sleepy," Riley said. Then he noticed Tidwell, who was standing with his back pressed up against the wall.

"Sir," Riley said. "Sorry about this. I guess I forgot to duck."

Tidwell crept closer to Riley's bed. "What happened, Detective?"

"I went to the victim's apartment, walked in, and before I even had a chance to look around, someone fired on me."

"You mean they *shot you*," Theodosia said.

"You had no idea anyone was there?" Tidwell asked.

"I'd literally just turned the key in the lock and opened

the door," Riley said. "Hadn't even hit the light switch. Maybe I . . ." He stopped and shook his head.

"Maybe you what?" Tidwell asked.

"Maybe I interrupted a burglary?" Riley said.

"Or an ambush," Tidwell said. "Were you able to get any kind of look at the shooter?"

Riley grimaced. "Unfortunately not. Too dark." He touched his wounded arm, threw a sheepish look at Theodosia, then turned his attention back to Tidwell. "What happened at the murder house?" he asked. "Did you run the scene? Were there cameras that might have picked something up?"

"There were no cameras," Tidwell said. "We checked. But all these questions can wait until you've had a good night's rest and are feeling some better. For now, we'd best just say goodbye."

Tidwell stepped back, allowing Theodosia to have a private moment with Riley. And then, seconds later, they were back outside his room walking down the corridor and into the elevator.

Theodosia didn't have much to say, though she was fuming inwardly.

When they reached the waiting room, Tidwell said, "He was lucky."

"He was not lucky!" Theodosia cried.

"No, it could have been much worse," Tidwell said in his maddeningly cool and observant voice.

"You think?"

"Rest assured, we will deal with this."

"Will you really?" Theodosia snapped. Then immediately regretted her flare-up. They were on the same side here, and she hadn't meant to be quite so sharp and accusatory. If Tidwell wasn't deeply concerned about one of his own detectives getting shot, then he wouldn't be standing here looking just this side of devastated.

Tidwell was clearly hurt by her words. "You don't expect I'd let one of my best detectives get shot and do nothing about it, do you?" Now his manner was both serious and brusque. "This will be handled expeditiously and swiftly, I assure you."

"But which case will get top billing?" Theodosia asked. "Willow's murder or Riley getting shot?"

"I promise you they're both equally important," Tidwell said as they walked out the front door of the hospital and into the cool air. He glanced at the dark street. It was late, ticking toward midnight now, and there was no one else around. "Where are you parked?"

Theodosia waved a hand. "Over . . . there."

She wanted to be alone right now. To let the cool night air wash over her like a refreshing balm and maybe help her sort things out. But Detective Burt Tidwell thought otherwise.

"I'll walk you to your vehicle," he said. Like most law enforcement personnel, he referred to it as a vehicle rather than a car or Jeep.

"That's not necessary," Theodosia said.

"Listen to me." Like a dancer executing a sharp pirouette, Tidwell stepped in front of her and stopped in his tracks, bringing Theodosia to an abrupt halt as well. He was a large immovable object that was suddenly peering down at her, a mix of concern and determination evident on his face.

Theodosia paused, afraid of what Tidwell was about to say, knowing full well that he was going to say it anyway.

"Please do not attempt to insinuate yourself into this investigation, Miss Browning," Tidwell said, fixing her with a hard gaze. His beady eyes were pinpoints of darkness, and his ample jowls shook as if to punctuate each sentence.

"Please don't be paternal," Theodosia said.

Tidwell's mouth twitched. There, she'd struck a nerve.

But seconds later, he was back, his voice and manner sharp as a serpent's tooth.

"I warn you, Miss Browning. Don't you dare get involved in any of this."

"Right," Theodosia said.

But the only thought that ran through her brain like chase lights on a theater marquee was, *I'm already involved. So why on earth wouldn't I stay involved?*

4

❧

Drayton and Haley stared at Theodosia in almost total disbelief.

Finally, Drayton managed to choke out a single word. "No." Then, with a visibly shaking hand, he tried to place his teacup back in its saucer, spilling some of his prized Fujian oolong tea in the process.

"Yes," Theodosia said. "As a matter of fact I've already been to the hospital. Stopped there first thing this morning."

"Riley's going to be okay?" Haley asked. "I mean, even though he was shot?" She looked both nervous and scared as tears sparkled in her eyes.

"He's doing about as well as can be expected," Theodosia said.

It was eight thirty Monday morning, and the three of them were seated at one of the small tables in the Indigo Tea Shop. Theodosia had just dropped her bombshell. Obviously, Drayton and Haley already knew about poor Willow being murdered, but they hadn't heard about Pete Riley getting shot. Needless to say, her tea shop cohorts, really her two best friends, had reacted strongly to her stunning news.

Now Haley dropped her head in her hands, her long blond hair falling forward like a curtain around her face. "First Willow, then Riley. Why is this happening? What's going on?"

"I don't know," Theodosia said.

"It's some sort of bizarre crime wave," Drayton said.

"It's more than that," Theodosia said. "There has to be a powerful motive that's driving all this."

"I can't imagine what that might be," Drayton said.

Haley lifted her head and stared damp eyed at Theodosia. She was young, in her twenties, their chef and baker extraordinaire. Always an optimist, ever trusting, Haley was a joy to be around. Now she struggled to hold her emotions together.

"Willow was engaged to be married, you know," Haley said.

Theodosia looked startled. "Willow was? Really?"

Haley nodded. "The wedding was coming up soon. In a matter of weeks."

"That makes it all the worse," Drayton said.

"Willow had even asked me to make her cake topper. For her wedding cake," Haley said.

"I'm so sorry," Theodosia said. "I know you two were good friends."

"We were," Haley said. Then, casting a sideways glance at her, she said, "Are you going to get involved with the police? Help investigate this craziness and try to figure out what happened? Figure out *why* it happened?"

"Theodosia shouldn't get involved," Drayton said hurriedly. Though Drayton could be strong-willed and tough as nails when he wanted to be, he tended to err on the side of conservatism and moderation.

Theodosia didn't have that particular problem.

She lifted both hands and spread them apart in a *Why wouldn't I?* gesture. "I'm already involved," she said simply.

"Where was Riley shot?" Haley asked.

"Like I explained, he was at Willow's apartment conducting a follow-up investigation on . . ."

"No. I mean where exactly on his person?" Haley asked.

"Oh. His left arm," Theodosia said.

"Ouch," Drayton said.

"Two crimes," Haley said. "One person murdered, one seriously injured. So what are you going to do about it?" she asked again, this time ramping up her intensity, staring at Theodosia with searching, hopeful eyes. "I mean *seriously.*"

"She's going to let the fine detectives of the Charleston Police Department do their job. After all, Pete Riley is one of their own," Drayton said. "Willow's murder, this attack against Riley are going to be of top concern to all of them."

Haley shook her head slowly. "Sure, the police are good, they're *supposed* to be good. But my money would still be on Theodosia."

"I don't think her getting involved is a particularly prudent idea," Drayton said. "We're all a little too close to the situation." He reached over and patted Haley's hand as if the conversation was hereby closed.

It wasn't.

"But Theo has to do *some*thing," Haley said, gazing at Theodosia. "Don't you?"

"I've been warned not to," Theodosia said.

"Tidwell is a very prudent man," Drayton murmured.

Haley squirmed in her chair. "But Willow was my *friend.* Riley's your *boyfriend.*" She clenched her small hand into a fist and pounded the table, making her pink-

and-gold teacup clatter and jump in its saucer. "You have to get to the bottom of this!"

Theodosia sighed. "Perhaps you're right."

But first things first, because there was a tea shop to get ready. Haley disappeared into their postage stamp–sized kitchen to tend to her morning baking while Theodosia bustled about the tea room. She put out cups and saucers, sugar bowls and cream pitchers. Then she added small tea lights in glass holders. Floradora Florists had delivered bundles of orange mums, yarrow, and bittersweet earlier this morning, so Theodosia cut and arranged the blooms and greenery in ceramic vases and placed one on each table.

Even though Theodosia worked with a heavy heart this morning, fussing about her tea shop still brought her enormous joy. The Indigo Tea Shop was located on Charleston's famed Church Street and had been the culmination of almost a year's worth of work and planning. Theodosia had lovingly refurbished the little cottage with its leaded windows, pegged floors that uttered an occasional squeak underfoot, and small stone fireplace. She'd shopped endless antiques shops and tag sales to find vintage teacups, teapots, glasses, and silverware. And it had all come together in the end. She'd wooed Drayton away from his culinary teaching position at Johnson & Wales University and found Haley through a simple help wanted ad. That had all happened a few years ago. Now the tea shop was a Church Street jewel and the three of them worked as a well-oiled team, delighting their friends, neighbors, and visitors with a dazzling array of fine teas, baked goods, amazing lunches, and special events.

Theodosia lit the last of the small white candles, then stepped back for an appraising look. The place really did look lovely. Candles flickered, polished wood gleamed, and the brick walls that were hung with grapevine wreaths and antique prints made the place look cozy and inviting. Overhead, the more recent addition of a small French glass chandelier added sparkle and a wash of soft light. There were additional vintage touches as well. Toile café curtains, a blue-and-persimmon-colored Persian rug just inside the front door, two antique wooden highboys that held retail items such as tins of tea, mugs, tea strainers, fancy sugar cubes, jams, jellies, honey, and bunches of lavender. To a visitor's eye, the Indigo Tea Shop was a delightful amalgam of vintage, antique, and country French decor.

"Perfect," Theodosia said under her breath as she stepped over to the front counter. Drayton was busily brewing tea, looking like an alchemist at work in his laboratory.

"Of course it's perfect," Drayton said as he scooped Assam into a Chinese blue-and-white teapot. "We're the finest tea shop in all of Charleston."

Theodosia had to smile as she lifted a single eyebrow. "Hyperbole from you, Drayton? You're always so modest."

"Not when it comes to our tea shop," Drayton said. "I've turned over a new leaf—a tea leaf, if you will. From now on I'm going to toot our horn as much as possible."

"Our favorable review in *Tea Faire* magazine really got you wound up, didn't it?"

"So much so that I think we should launch that Tea of the Month Club we talked about."

"Just tell me what November's blend is and I'll list it on our website," Theodosia said.

Drayton was a master at blending new teas—he'd come up with dozens over the years—but now he suddenly looked hesitant.

"Well, I wasn't thinking *that* far ahead. I didn't know I had to create a brand-new house blend Johnny-on-the-spot."

"You're always so inventive. I'm sure you'll do fine."

"Maybe oolong tea with bits of plum," Drayton said. "Call it Autumn Splendor."

"Works for me."

"But for now . . ." Drayton poured a cup of fresh-brewed tea and slid it across the counter to Theodosia. "I want you to try this organic Assam. It's got good body and a whisper of maltiness—guaranteed to pick you right up."

Theodosia took a sip. "It's delicious."

"Do you feel picked up?"

"Not exactly."

"Still feeling down because of last night?"

Theodosia nodded. "Who wouldn't be?"

"Do try to look on the bright side," Drayton prompted. "Riley is going to make a full recovery. You said so yourself."

"Still, someone caused him a great deal of pain." Theodosia took another sip of tea. "Then there's the matter of finding the person or persons who murdered Willow."

"We're back to that, are we? Let me ask this . . . are you looking for justice or seeking revenge? Because revenge isn't exactly your cup of tea. In fact, it's totally out of character for you."

"Maybe so, Drayton, but Willow's body is lying on a slab in the city morgue right now. And Riley . . . well, I've never had anyone that close to me be so savagely attacked."

"Point taken," Drayton said. "So. I have to ask. Are you going to investigate?"

"Let's just say I'm going to look into things."

Drayton pursed his lips. It wasn't the answer he was hoping for.

"I know you're thinking about Timothy's feelings—and of course Riley's recovery—but please don't forget we have an extremely busy week ahead of us," he said.

"They're all busy."

"Not like this. Need I remind you we have the Sherlock Holmes Tea tomorrow, then our pumpkin and spice tea as well as our afternoon catering gig for the Edgar Allan Poe Symposium on Wednesday, and then the Enchanted Garden Party on Saturday?" He paused. "I hate to even bring this up, but there'll probably be a funeral shoehorned in there as well."

"I'm sure there will be," Theodosia said. Her brows pinched together at the thought of it. So sad, such a tragic situation. "I've also got Delaine's Denim and Diamonds Fashion Show on Friday."

"Please tell me you're attending as a guest and not doing m'lady's bidding by serving tea and scones."

"It could be a little of both," Theodosia admitted. "Delaine and I still need to put our heads together and talk."

They both got busy then as the bell over the front door *da-dinged*, signaling the arrival of their first customers of the day. Theodosia seated their guests, took orders, ran them back to Haley, and served pots of tea. Thirty minutes later, the tea shop was almost full, the air redolent with the aromas of smoky Lapsang souchong, slightly muscatel Darjeeling, and malty Assam. What Theodosia liked to think of as aromatherapy for tea lovers.

By midmorning, things had settled down. Customers were enjoying Haley's orange scones, butterscotch muffins, and lemon-lavender bread. Drayton was packaging up take-out orders as well as call-in orders from the local B and Bs. Theodosia was answering phones and taking luncheon reservations.

"We're good," Theodosia said as she swung by the counter to pick up a pot of black currant tea for table six. She wasn't feeling as rocky as she had an hour ago. "We've got this."

And that's when it all went *kaboom*.

That's when the door whapped open with a thunderous peal and Timothy Neville lurched in. His face was pale, his Burberry trench coat flapped open on the normally unflappable Timothy, and his shoulders were hunched forward as if he were carrying a terrible burden.

"Oh dear," Drayton said under his breath. "Timothy looks upset."

Theodosia was of another opinion. "No, Timothy looks completely devastated."

And he certainly was.

Theodosia rushed to greet Timothy at the door. "Timothy, are you here for tea? Can I . . . ?"

"We need to talk," Timothy said, cutting her off sharply. It was the same brook-no-nonsense voice he used when he was chairing a Heritage Society board meeting.

Theodosia glanced about the tea shop. Her customers had all been served and taken care of so, yes, she could probably spare a quick five minutes.

Sprinting ahead of him, Theodosia led Timothy to the small table by the fireplace where they'd be able to talk in relative privacy.

Timothy lowered his thin frame into one of the captain's chairs and drew a deep breath. Theodosia slipped into the chair across from him.

"Tell me," she said. She could see that Timothy was so upset he was practically shaking. In fact, she'd never seen him this upset. Despite his age, Timothy always comported himself with a certain strength and dignity. Now suddenly, with the murder of Willow hanging over his head, he looked like a man consumed with rage and bitterness. But also one who seemed battered and beaten.

"I made a solemn promise to my nephew Byron that Willow would be perfectly safe here in Charleston. That I would watch out for her. And now you see what's happened . . ." Timothy's voice broke and ended in a choking sob. He was unable to continue.

Drayton to the rescue.

"Excuse me," Drayton said. He was suddenly front and center at their table, a tea tray in hand. "I don't know if you're interested, but I just brewed a pot of Darjeeling." He set cups and saucers on the table and poured tea into them, all the while talking in a soothing voice, giving Timothy the necessary time to recover. "This Goomtee Garden Darjeeling is an assertive tea, just the thing to revive and invigorate."

Timothy reached out, grabbed his teacup, and took a long sip. "Thank you," he croaked.

"But you're not just here for tea, are you?" Theodosia said. "Or to listen to our condolences."

"I came because I desperately need your help," Timothy said.

"Because of Willow," Drayton said.

Timothy nodded, then switched his gaze to Theodosia. "And because you were there."

"You see?" Theodosia said to Drayton. "Timothy needs our help."

Drayton gazed at them over his half-glasses. He didn't look happy.

"Perhaps," Theodosia said, "I could start by interviewing the people from the Heritage Society who were there last night."

"That can easily be arranged," Timothy said.

"I mean like today, this afternoon," Theodosia said.

Timothy gave an eager nod. "Yes. Fine. The sooner the better." He seemed slightly more relaxed now that he knew Theodosia was on board.

"Do you know who'll be spearheading Willow's . . . mm . . . the investigation?" Drayton asked. He'd just caught himself. He was about to say *murder* investigation.

"Detective Tidwell assured me he'd be taking charge," Timothy said.

"The big cheese himself," Drayton mused. "Well, Tidwell's got his work cut out for him. A publicly staged murder and a vicious attack on one of his own detectives have probably ignited a hornet's nest at police headquarters."

But Theodosia was barely listening to Drayton. Her focus had turned to the Heritage Society and its people who were working at the haunted house last night. Perhaps one of them had seen or heard something and might be able to offer a bit of insight?

"Is the Heritage Society still holding the Edgar Allan Poe Symposium this Wednesday?" Theodosia asked. She wondered if it might be put on hold, considering the circumstances.

"I'm afraid we've committed considerable time and energy to the event, as have the speakers we engaged," Timothy said. "So we're going full speed ahead."

"Maybe that's good," Theodosia said. "It gives us another chance to talk to people on Wednesday, though I can't imagine . . ."

The front door banged open yet again as a tall, almost scarecrow-thin man rushed into the tea shop. He glanced about hurriedly, spotted Timothy, and screamed, "They told me I'd find you here!"

5

❧

"Ellis?" Timothy said, flopping against the back of his chair in surprise. "Ellis Bouchard? What are you doing here?" Timothy seemed shocked and completely unnerved by this intrusion.

Without answering, Bouchard sped over to their table and launched into a ferocious diatribe.

"You see what happened at that horrible, so-called historically accurate haunted house that your curators and publicity people thought was such a marvelous idea?" Bouchard screamed. "A woman was killed!"

"That was my grandniece," Timothy said with great emotion.

"But it happened in *my* family's estate," Bouchard said. His long face twisted in anger, and his wiry gray hair seemed to fluff up every time he screamed.

"Excuse me," Drayton said, interrupting the man and hoping to temper his outburst. "We haven't been properly introduced. You are . . . ?"

"Ellis Bouchard," the man answered with an almost feverish assertion. "I'm a direct descendant of Beau Bouchard, who built the Bouchard Mansion back in 1872. His fifth cousin. As a matter of record, I was in line to *inherit* that house!"

"I'm sorry but we've been through this," Timothy said, his voice turning sharp as a knife's edge. "That house has been fully deeded to the Heritage Society."

"A haphazard mistake," Bouchard countered.

"No mistake," Timothy said. "My lawyers assure me that the document—the will—is perfectly legal."

"Still, I find it a great travesty of justice," Bouchard said.

Several customers in the tea shop had overheard Bouchard's blustery words and were beginning to wonder what was going on. Curious heads turned and voices murmured nervously as they stared across the tea room at Timothy and Ellis Bouchard.

"Please. Sit," Theodosia said to Bouchard. She meant to be polite, but it came out sounding like a command.

Sensing her seriousness, Bouchard took a seat at the table.

"Good," Theodosia said. "Thank you. Perhaps now we can discuss this in a more civilized manner."

"There's nothing to discuss," Bouchard said. "I was cheated."

"The will was deemed legal," Timothy countered. "As far as I'm concerned, the matter is closed."

Bouchard held up a finger and shook it in Timothy's face. "Why do you refuse to believe there are two sides to this story?" His face had turned a blotchy red, his voice rose, and he seemed poised to launch into another angry diatribe.

That was it for Theodosia. She'd had enough.

"I'm sure we'd all like to hear your side of the story, Mr. Bouchard," Theodosia said. "But now is not the time nor place."

Bouchard's eyes widened in surprise. "Whaaat?"

"So if you'll . . ." Theodosia's hands fluttered in a *Move along* gesture.

"Excuse me, are you asking me to leave?" Bouchard said.

"If you would," Theodosia said, still being scrupulously polite. "I think that's best for everyone involved."

Bouchard stood up. "All right, fine, I'll leave. For now. But, mind you, Timothy Neville, this isn't over by a long shot."

And with that Ellis Bouchard turned and stomped out of the tea shop.

Timothy's shoulders slumped forward. "Oh dear," he said. "On top of everything else, now I have to contend with *him*."

Once Theodosia had reassured Timothy she'd drop by the Heritage Society this afternoon, she hurried out the back door, almost tripping over a stray cat in the alley, and drove her Jeep to University Hospital. She was desperate to see how Riley was doing.

But when she arrived, she found him lounging in bed, watching TV—*TMZ*, seriously?—after having eaten an early lunch. His tray held the remnants of a small sandwich, a cup of fruit cocktail, and some chocolate pudding. None of it looked particularly appetizing. Maybe she could bring him something nice and tasty tomorrow?

Riley saw Theodosia standing in the doorway and gave an expectant grin. "You're a vision," he declared. "Albeit one that keeps reappearing."

"It's hard to stay away," Theodosia said. "I'm so worried about you."

"Please don't be." Riley reached for the remote control and snapped off his TV set.

"Concerned, then." Theodosia moved closer to his bed.

"Well, thank you kindly, ma'am."

Riley looked tired, played out. As if he'd just run a marathon or crewed his heart out in a yacht race. Or got shot. And Theodosia thought he seemed thinner lying there under the covers. She wished she'd brought him something good to eat, like a slice of quiche and an orange scone.

Riley was smiling at her, trying to make small talk, attempting to downplay his injury as well as the circumstances surrounding his attack. Theodosia would have none of it.

"I want to know exactly what happened last night," she said.

Riley gazed at her. "I already told you, Theo. I may have been in pain last night, but I think I was still fairly cogent. And when you stopped by this morning . . ." He reached his good arm up and scratched his head. "Did I miss something? Didn't we talk then?"

"I only had time for drive-by kisses and hugs," Theodosia said. "Not a whole lot of conversation. But now . . ." She sat down in a green vinyl chair and slid it closer to his bed. "Now I want to hear a minute-by-minute, play-by-play account of what *really* happened."

"So you can sneak in behind Tidwell's back and run your own shadow investigation?"

Riley had pretty much hit the nail smack-dab on the head, but Theodosia managed to maintain a mild expression. She didn't want to let on just how close he was to the truth. "I just . . . want to understand what happened."

"It's as simple as that?"

"Yes, because I care about you." Theodosia wondered how much of this Riley was actually buying. Maybe, possibly, he'd open up a little more if he was in a slightly drugged and altered state. She studied his nightstand. Did she see any drugs there? Nice strong painkillers? Nope. Not really. Too bad.

"Theodosia," Riley said. "I can read you like a book,

and I know you've got a powerful attraction to danger. So I want you to promise me that you won't get involved in what's probably going to be a complicated and dangerous murder investigation."

"I'm not just filled with outrage over Willow's murder," Theodosia said. "Let's please not forget the breaking and entering and shooting of a law enforcement officer—namely you." Riley was trying to downplay the whole thing, and it frustrated her no end.

But Riley didn't seem to care about the mounting charges. "Just promise me you'll keep your distance?"

"A safe distance, yes," Theodosia said. She reached out, took his hand, and squeezed it. "I'm curious as to how it all went down, okay?"

Riley sighed. He was stuck in bed, practically immobilized by a huge bandage on his arm. He wasn't going anywhere. So . . . he supposed it wouldn't hurt to tell her some of it.

"I'll tell you only because I know you don't have the resources to launch a full-scale investigation," Riley said with a crooked grin. "Sure, you might sniff and snoop around, ask a few probing questions, but I seriously doubt you'll come up with anything concrete."

"You're probably right," Theodosia said, smiling to herself because she had an ace up her sleeve. She knew the police were duty bound by all sorts of rules and regulations—search warrants, subpoenas, procedures, protocol, and the like. Pesky little details that she didn't have to bother with. Which meant she could snoop, dig, and ask questions to her heart's content.

"Okay, here goes," Riley said. "I arrived at Willow's place on Logan some ten or twelve minutes after I left you . . ."

"Wait. Willow's place—is that a house or an apartment?"

"It's both. Willow lived in a one-bedroom apartment that had been carved out of a Charleston single house."

"Okay," Theodosia said. "So you had a key. You walked into her apartment and saw . . . what? What was your first impression?"

Riley touched a hand to his forehead as if trying to remember. "It was crazy—completely unexpected. Even in the dark it looked as if the apartment had been ripped apart. Chairs overturned, books pulled from shelves, boxes everywhere, papers scattered all over. The place was a disaster zone, as if an F5 tornado had ripped through it."

"So you're standing there, starting to take it all in . . ." Theodosia stopped, hoping for more information, anticipating that Riley would helpfully fill in the blanks.

He did.

"The only clear space I saw was the top of a small white desk. Where I'm now assuming a computer had been parked. Yeah . . ." Riley nodded to himself. "It was only a few seconds, but I remember seeing a printer, but no computer. Just a tangle of wires."

"So somebody broke in, ripped the place apart, and stole Willow's computer." Theodosia figured this had to be significant. She didn't know why exactly, but it was something to keep in mind.

"Yes, but the missing computer didn't mean anything to me at the time. Because . . ." Riley's face twisted as if he'd experienced a sudden uncomfortable flashback. "It was dark in there and warm, as if the heat had been jacked way up. Then I felt, more than I actually saw, a quick flash of motion. I guess it was someone's hand reaching around the corner from the bedroom. And then all I remember is a loud bang and a sudden sharp pain in my arm. Not terrible, more like a quick sting from a wasp. But suddenly I'd lost my balance and was falling. And it felt as if it took forever, like a slow-motion descent into a deep, dark well. Then I remember my head cracking against the floor and feeling this enormous jolt of pain."

Dear Lord. Must have been awful. Theodosia practically squirmed in her chair. She felt uncomfortable just hearing about it.

Riley continued. "I tried to pull myself up. Actually, I kind of sat up halfway. And then I heard the clatter of footsteps."

"Whoever shot you was running away," Theodosia said.

"They were gone—*poof*—like the wind," Riley said. "But they left the door standing wide open, so there was a shaft of light coming in from the hallway. That's when I looked down and saw a bloom of red on my jacket sleeve." He closed his eyes, then opened them. "And the pain started coming in waves."

"So you called 911." It was a statement, not a question.

"And then I called you," Riley said. He favored her with a crooked, slightly nervous smile, as if the memory of getting shot was still a little too fresh, a little too vivid. "And here we are."

"I'm sorry," Theodosia said. "So sorry I called you about Willow, so sorry you were sent over there and basically walked into a trap."

"Yeah, well, it's not . . ."

Theodosia stood up, leaned over, and kissed him before he could finish his sentence. Off to her left, a monitor beeped loudly.

Driving back to the Indigo Tea Shop, Theodosia thought about Riley's story. Again and again, she parsed through it, trying to glean some bit of information or clue. The shooter had to be the same person who killed Willow, right? Yes, it made sense, it tracked. So this killer had come to the haunted house and lured Willow upstairs—which meant that Willow possibly knew her assailant. And then she'd fought with him as he looped a noose around her neck and tossed her out the turret window. In front of . . .

Dear Lord, how awful.

Theodosia struggled to quiet the terrible images in her head as she drove along. Hands shaking, she tried to stay in her lane, tried not to run any red lights.

And after killing Willow . . . what then? Obviously, the killer hotfooted it over to Willow's apartment to steal her computer. But why would he do that? What was on her computer that was so all-fired important?

The more Theodosia thought about Willow's murder and Riley getting ambushed, the angrier she got. Until finally, when she drove down the cobblestone alley behind the Indigo Tea Shop, she was buzzing and humming like an angry bee. Pulling up at the back door, she jumped out and ran inside.

"Ho, you made it back in time for lunch," Drayton said when he saw Theodosia striding down the hallway. He sounded pleasantly surprised.

At the same instant, Haley popped her head out of the kitchen. "How's Riley?" she asked. "Is he doing any better? Feeling okay?"

"I'd have to say he's some better. The doctors are still giving him antibiotics via an IV. But he thinks he might be released tomorrow or the day after," Theodosia said.

"Good news indeed," Drayton said. He returned to his command post at the front counter.

"It is," Theodosia murmured. She was still thinking about the strange tale Riley had told her. *Who was this maniac?* she wondered. And how could she begin to get a bead on him?

Still in a fog, Theodosia stepped into the kitchen and glanced around. A pot of soup bubbled on the stove, and wedges of cheese and loaves of fresh bread sat on the cutting board. It helped pull her back to the here and now of a busy lunchtime.

"What did you come up with for our lunch offerings?" Theodosia asked, knowing Haley was always highly creative and clever with her menus.

"I made it easy-peasy for today," Haley said. "Because I didn't know when you'd be back. Or *if* you'd be back. So. Shrimp and corn chowder, cheddar cheese and asparagus quiche, and everybody's favorite, a ploughman's lunch."

Theodosia nodded. A ploughman's lunch was traditional English fare. As its name suggested, it was commonly eaten at lunch and was most often associated with English pubs and village inns.

"What good stuff are you putting on your ploughman's platter?"

"Soda bread, a thin slice of meat pâté, small chunk of Stilton cheese, and a Scotch egg. As a lucky strike extra I managed to score a couple jars of Branston Pickle."

That finally brought a smile to Theodosia's face.

"The perfect accompaniment," she said. Branston Pickle was a sweet and spicy condiment sauce with a chutney-like consistency.

Haley nodded. "I know, it's so gosh darn authentically British."

"And for dessert?"

"Apple pudding."

Theodosia stepped out of the kitchen and saw that two tables were already occupied. The rest of the tables were beautifully set up for lunch. Crystal glasses filled with water, fresh teacups and saucers, knives and forks, and bright-yellow napkins tucked into silver napkin rings.

She glanced over at Drayton. "You did all this?"

"Along with my other tasks, yes," Drayton responded. He seemed oddly pleased that Theodosia had noticed his handiwork.

"Thank you, the tables look wonderful. I didn't know I'd be gone so long."

"It wasn't a problem." Drayton drew a deep breath. "I take it you checked with Haley regarding the menu?"

"I have and it sounds perfect," Theodosia said. "What teas are you recommending?"

"I'm glad you asked," Drayton said. "I have this marvelous rooibos that should complement the quiche. Now for the ploughman's platters, I'm thinking a nice white tea. White teas have the highest level of antioxidants and are often considered the healthiest of teas . . ."

And Drayton was off and running, entertaining Theodosia with a virtual litany of teas and tea lore until the front door flew open and at least a dozen guests came spilling in. Then they were both caught up in the genteel hubbub of seating guests, pouring tea, taking orders, and running food out from the kitchen.

Finally, some two hours later, Theodosia was able to take a breather. That's when she finally pulled off her long black Parisian waiter's apron, grabbed her jacket, and, her auburn hair flying like streamers in the breeze, dashed down the street to the Heritage Society.

6

❧

The Heritage Society was one of Theodosia's all-time favorite places. Set smack-dab in the middle of the Historic District, it was an enormous gray stone edifice that looked almost like a medieval castle. There were various galleries filled with maps, antique etchings, coin collections, Early American silver, and sculpture. Walls were covered with tapestries as well as paintings by Jeremiah Theus, Anna Heyward Taylor, and Arthur Rose. Many of the period rooms contained Early American furniture by Sheraton and Hepplewhite. And there was a library that was filled with books and oak tables and chairs, and that smelled of old leather-covered books and possibly just the hint of tobacco and fine whiskey.

Theodosia didn't have time for any of that today. She hurried down the long central corridor to Timothy Neville's office, knocked on the door, then opened it and peered in. It was empty. No Timothy. She paused and gave a lingering gaze into the interior anyway. Timothy's office was a combination library and mini museum that always fascinated her. His shelves contained antique books and precious antiquities that included rare coins, Greek statues, American pottery, and even a jewel-studded crown that had once belonged to a long-exiled Hungarian prince. It was all quite wonderful.

Still, Theodosia needed to find Timothy posthaste. Yes, she had her marching orders concerning staff interviews, but she needed him to rally the troops. Which was why she popped next door to check with June Winthrop, Timothy's longtime administrative assistant.

June was fifty-something, smart as a whip, and coolly efficient. She could balance the budget (and trim it mercilessly if need be), knew every board member and major donor by first name, and would finish your sentence if you weren't careful.

Today June wore a camel-colored cashmere twinset with a string of pearls. Real deal pearls, Theodosia suspected. She also had a photographic memory and a knack for ferreting out any object that might be missing or misplaced from the Heritage Society's vast collection.

If Timothy ever became incapacitated, Theodosia figured that June could run the whole enchilada without missing a single step.

"Timothy's in a meeting," June told her in her usual brusque, superefficient manner. "But he said to go ahead and conduct your interviews." She picked up a sheet of paper, studied it for a moment, then handed it to Theodosia. "This is a list of the staff members who worked on the haunted house."

"Great. But who were the ones who were there last night?"

"I put checkmarks next to their names," June said.

"Will people know why I'm . . . ?" Theodosia began.

June gave a brisk nod. "They've been briefed."

"Great. Thanks."

Claire Waltho, one of the Heritage Society's curators and a recent hire, was first on the list. So that's where Theodosia started. She found Claire in the Palmetto Gallery supervising an installation of black-and-white photographs. Claire was mid-forties with short curly hair, a friendly smile, and warm brown eyes. Theodosia had met Claire twice before and found her to be a smart, knowledgeable curator, especially when it came to antique prints and photographs. Now Claire was studying the position and height of a framed photo her assistant had just hung. When she noticed Theodosia lurking in the doorway, she stopped what she was doing and came over to greet her.

"Timothy said you'd be dropping by," Claire said. She didn't sound nervous, just busy.

"I'm doing a quick sweep today, talking to everyone who was at the haunted house last night," Theodosia explained. "Trying to gather any ideas and impressions that people might have."

Claire raised an eyebrow. "Impressions of what happened last night?"

"That or if you saw anything a little out of context . . . or someone acting suspiciously."

"It was kind of a madhouse," Claire said. "Our first night with all the literary and historic characters interacting with visitors. And then, of course, Willow and her book signing . . ."

"Nothing struck you as strange or unusual?" Theodosia asked.

"The whole evening was strange. But I know what you're asking, and I can't for the life of me think of a single thing that was out of place. I mean, right after Willow was murdered, when the police were questioning everybody, I racked my brain to see if I remembered a discordant note of some kind. And I didn't."

"I understand you were one of the people who helped conceive and design the haunted house."

"One of several, yes," Claire said. "Now I wish . . . well, I wish we'd left that old mansion, the Gray Ghost, well enough alone." She pursed her lips together as if she wanted to say more. Finally, she did. "It has a reputation, you know."

"I didn't know that," Theodosia said.

"It's supposedly *really* haunted," Claire said. "Not just made-up haunted."

Theodosia relaxed. This was nothing new to her. "According to the Charleston Visitors Bureau, so are half our hotels and B and Bs."

"Ah, I suppose you're right."

"Besides, we don't need an exorcism, we need an investigation."

Claire smiled at that.

"Will the haunted house attraction be open again tonight?" Theodosia asked.

Claire looked sad and a little apprehensive. "I'm afraid so. We contracted with a number of professional actors, so we need to honor those agreements. And then there's the awful truth that the Heritage Society needs the income that'll be generated."

"Because donations and pledges are not as forthcoming as they have been in the past."

"Donations are seriously down," Claire said. "Ask anyone who works here about pinching pennies. The truth is, we're using everything we can muster to keep the lights on, pay staff, and continue to offer a full complement of speakers and special events."

"None of which comes cheap," Theodosia said. She was enough of a businessperson to know that a place like the Heritage Society carried an enormous overhead.

"That's putting it lightly," Claire said.

"So how many people were involved in getting the haunted house all spiffed up and visitor ready?" Theodosia asked.

"All told, maybe a dozen?"

That jibed with what Theodosia had on her list.

"Okay, I want to ask you sort of a tricky question. But I can guarantee your answer will be treated with the utmost discretion."

"Uh-oh." Claire furrowed her brow. "What is it you want to know?"

"Of all the people connected to the haunted house, can you think of anyone who could have been involved in last night's fiasco? Maybe not a mastermind, but someone who had a bone to pick with either Willow or the Heritage Society?" Theodosia thought it unlikely, but some twisted soul might have wanted to cast a bad light on the organization.

"Nobody," Claire answered immediately.

It wasn't the answer Theodosia was hoping to hear.

"I know you don't want to make any false accusations, and I don't blame you," Theodosia said.

Maybe if I came at this from a different angle?

"I have to work with these people, you know," Claire said, a little defensively. "I can't just throw somebody under the bus because I don't like them."

"I understand. But is there anyone who might have acted a trifle strange or jittery?"

This time Claire thought the question over for more than a single second.

"When you put it that way, I *can* think of one person," Claire said. "Ellis Bouchard."

"Interesting you should say that," Theodosia said. "Because I had the not-so-great pleasure of meeting Mr. Bouchard this morning at my tea shop. Okay, so why do you think he could have been involved?"

"I personally don't think he was. But Bouchard has been stewing over that house like a rabid dog gnawing a bone, telling everyone that it's his rightful inheritance."

"Has anyone been listening to him, taking him seriously?" *Taking his side?*

"Not that I know of," Claire said.

Theodosia thought for a few moments. "From what I could see, it's not that great a house."

"It's in terrible disrepair. The roof leaks, the plumbing is shot, and no matter how many times you air it out, the place still smells musty. But the land it occupies is worth an absolute fortune." Claire hesitated, as if she wasn't sure she should reveal more. Finally, she said, "And Ellis Bouchard is apparently flat broke."

Here was an interesting sidebar that made Theodosia's ears perk up.

"Do you know that for a fact?"

"He told me so last night," Claire said.

"Bouchard was there last night?" Theodosia hadn't noticed him. Then again, she'd not met him yet.

Claire made a rueful face. "Bouchard was babbling to anyone and everyone who would listen that the three apartment buildings he owns are all in foreclosure. So I think the man is truly desperate."

And desperate people do desperate things, Theodosia thought.

"Okay, Claire, thanks so much for talking to me," Theodosia said. "If you think of any—"

"Claire?" a voice called from the hallway.

They both turned to find a man staring in at them. He had ginger hair, wire-rimmed glasses, and a small mustache. A tweedy jacket topped his bagged-out brown corduroy slacks.

"Do you have a moment?" the man asked.

"Of course," Claire said, waving him in. "Theodosia, do

you know Allan Barnaby? He's the senior partner at Barnaby and Boise Publishing. His company published Willow's book."

"Nice to meet you," Theodosia said. As she shook hands with Barnaby she studied him carefully and decided he carried the earnest, academic look of a middle-aged English professor. Probably being a publisher put you in that same ballpark.

"Theodosia owns the Indigo Tea Shop over on Church Street," Claire explained. "She was also at the haunted house last night and witnessed the entire debacle."

"You were?" Barnaby looked stunned as he peered at Theodosia. "I understand it was your basic Grand Guignol horror show. People screaming their lungs out and poor Willow just dangling there for everyone to see. They said the lights lent a horrid purplish tinge to her face."

"Terrible," Theodosia agreed. She hated to even dredge up the memory.

"It was garish, yes," Claire said. From the way she shrugged her shoulders and rolled her eyes, Theodosia could tell she hated talking about it. Hated recalling the grisly details.

"Do you know . . . are the police close to arresting someone?" Barnaby asked. He searched their faces. "Have you ladies heard anything at all?" He looked both shattered and hopeful.

"Not a word," Claire said.

"Nothing yet," Theodosia said.

Now Barnaby looked slightly confused. "I understand from the article I read in this morning's *Post and Courier* that a police officer was shot last night in the line of duty?"

"It was a police detective," Theodosia corrected. "He'd gone to Willow's apartment to have a look around and, I guess, stumbled on her killer."

"How awful. I hope the detective is going to be okay," Barnaby said.

"I have it on good authority that the detective will make a full recovery," Theodosia said.

"Good to hear," Barnaby said.

Theodosia gazed at Barnaby. "I bought a copy of Willow's book last night. *Carolina Crimes and Creepers*, the one your firm published."

"I'm sure you'll find it highly entertaining. Willow is . . . was . . . an excellent writer." Barnaby stopped and looked suddenly stricken. "Bless me, now I have to refer to her in the past tense. How perfectly awful."

Theodosia tried to lighten the conversation. "How many books does your firm publish in a year?"

"Last year we put out ten books. This year we're aiming for fifteen." Barnaby seemed momentarily pleased. "We may be a small Southern press, but we have excellent distribution and several of our authors have garnered good reviews as well as some rather prestigious awards."

"Small independent presses are enjoying a resurgence now, aren't they?" Theodosia asked.

"They are indeed," Barnaby said. "Of course I'd always hoped Willow would do a follow-up book."

"You mean more low-country legends and lore?" Theodosia asked.

"Willow barely scratched the surface with this current book, and the market is certainly ripe for more tales," Barnaby said. "Willow was an extremely gifted writer who could bring words to life. We'd even noodled around the idea of having her write a history of the Heritage Society and maybe include some of the essays that the curators have written for the various catalogs."

"You can imagine how excited we were about that," Claire said.

"That would be wonderful," Theodosia said. "Had you talked seriously about that type of book? Maybe drawn up a contract with Willow?" She was thinking about the stolen computer. Had there been a manuscript sitting inside it?

"No, no, we had nothing in writing," Barnaby said. "Willow was still processing the idea. I don't believe she was even at the research stage. Of course now . . ." His voice trailed off. "Perhaps we'll find another writer?" He shook his head. "Such a sad state of affairs."

7

Theodosia found her next employee, actually an intern, sitting in the library, her nose buried in a half dozen books as she scribbled out copious notes. Sybil Spalding was young—Theodosia guessed around twenty-two or twenty-three—with long dark hair, a smile that revealed a rather charming chipped front tooth, and an inquisitive demeanor.

"So you're looking into Willow's murder?" Sybil asked. She was definitely more enthusiastic than nervous.

"I'm making a few minor inquiries as a favor to Timothy Neville," Theodosia said as she sat down at a large oak library table across from Sybil.

"Oh wow," Sybil said. She seemed impressed.

"And because the detective that got shot at Willow's apartment is a close friend of mine," Theodosia added.

"Wow again," Sybil said. "Is the detective guy okay? Is he going to recover?"

"We think he'll be fine," Theodosia said.

After minor surgery, recuperation, and several months of physical therapy.

"Claire tells me you were instrumental in helping put the haunted house together," Theodosia said.

"Working on it was a blast," Sybil said with great enthusiasm. Then her smile slowly crumpled. "Until last night, that is."

"Tell me about your role in the haunted house."

"My task was to research all the clothing worn by the various literary figures. We wanted to put together costumes that were historically accurate yet still had kind of a wow factor, an element of showmanship. You know, so the visitors would be entertained as well as impressed."

"Is that what your internship here at the Heritage Society is about?" Theodosia asked. "You're working in the clothing and costume department?"

"I am right now, but my particular interest lies in antique linens and fabrics."

"There's a good collection here, yes?" Theodosia remembered a show from a few years ago where the Heritage Society had featured antique linens and fabrics. She remembered being impressed by a three-dimensional gros point style from Italy and a delicate rose point lace from Belgium.

"Oh my, is there ever a great collection," Sybil said. "Just working with the French and Italian lace here is like taking a giant step into the past. It's even springboarded me into my new hobby—collecting antique lace handkerchiefs."

"There are a lot of them still available?"

"There are if you know where to look."

"What do you do when you're not interning here?" Theodosia asked. She was curious about this smart, talkative young woman.

Sybil gave a wry smile. "Right now I'm employed part-time at a dry cleaner's, working with delicate fabrics. Interning here is fun, but I also need to pay the bills, if you know how that goes."

"I certainly do."

"So you say you're asking questions about the haunted house? About that awful murder last night?" Sybil said.

Theodosia repeated her spiel about looking into things for Timothy, then asked a few questions about her duties last night.

"Oh, I was pretty much stuck in the back room," Sybil said. "Fitting costumes onto the performers, making any necessary tucks or repairs, then acting as a kind of gopher for the various curators."

"Just out of curiosity, did you detect any false notes last night?" Theodosia asked.

Sybil frowned. "I'm not sure what you mean."

"Someone who seemed nervous or agitated?"

"Oh, you mean somebody I'd point a finger at?" Sybil asked.

"When you put it that way . . . yes."

"Nobody," Sybil said. Her upper teeth nibbled at her lower lip. "Not a single soul."

Theodosia's third interview was with Elisha Summers. She was also a newly hired staff member who worked in the conservation department.

Theodosia found Elisha in the cavernous basement of the Heritage Society working over an oil painting of a small fishing boat struggling through high seas. She was daubing paint over a spot that had been patched and then re-gessoed.

When Theodosia asked her about possible suspects, Elisha said, "Nobody I can think of. But let me noodle it around."

Theodosia sighed. "If you would that'd be great." And she thought, *Strike three.*

Theodosia continued to pick her way through the Heritage Society and talked with four more curators, all people she was well acquainted with and who were near and dear to Timothy. She didn't suspect any of them, and, unfortunately, they didn't offer any insights, either.

Feeling as if she'd seriously struck out, Theodosia walked back to Timothy's office and knocked on his door.

"Come in," Timothy called out.

"It's me," Theodosia said. As she entered his office, she noted that Timothy sounded slightly more chipper than he had this morning.

Timothy was seated behind his enormous rosewood desk with a sad-looking man sitting across from him in a plum-red leather chair with hobnail trim.

"Theodosia Browning," Timothy said, getting right down to business, "I'd like you to meet Robert Vardell, Willow's fiancé."

Theodosia's heart immediately went out to the young man. "Oh, Mr. Vardell, you have my sincere sympathy." She crossed the Aubusson carpet and quickly shook his hand.

"You were a friend of Willow's?" he asked.

"A friend of a friend," Theodosia said, settling into the chair next to him. "And of course I've known Timothy for ages."

Timothy managed a small smile. "Though our ages do differ." Then he cleared his throat. "Robert has come up with, what we believe, may be the prime motive for Willow's murder."

"Seriously?" Theodosia said.

She'd been interviewing people like crazy, trying to extract answers—hunches, really—and not getting much in return. It had been painful for everyone involved, like pulling teeth. And just like that Timothy and Robert Vardell had come up with an actual motive? She couldn't wait to hear it.

"What?" Theodosia asked. "What is it?"

"Willow owned a stunning pair of yellow diamond earrings that she inherited from her great-grandmother," Vardell said.

Theodosia was already nodding, could see where this was leading. "Let me guess, Willow was wearing them last night and now those yellow diamonds are missing?"

"They are according to the coroner's inventory we just received," Vardell said. He glanced at Timothy. "We're quite positive Willow was wearing the diamond earrings last night."

"Our general theory is she was murdered because of them," Timothy said. "The earrings are extremely valuable."

"Five carats total weight and quite rare," Vardell said. "The yellow diamonds were . . ." He stopped and glanced at Timothy again.

"Go on," Timothy urged.

"The thing is, the diamonds have a unique provenance," Vardell said.

Theodosia slid forward in her chair. This was grisly, but it was also slightly fascinating. She knew that *provenance* was kind of a fancy term for the history and ownership of an object, generally a rather expensive object. "Tell me," she said.

"They were part of the Tereshchenko diamond collection," Vardell said.

Theodosia shook her head. "I've never heard of that." She'd heard of the Hope Diamond, the Krupp Diamond, even the Cullinan Diamond. But never anything about Tereshchenko diamonds.

Vardell cleared his throat and began. "Back in the early nineteen hundreds, Mikhail Tereshchenko was a member of the wealthy Russian aristocracy and also served as foreign minister of Russia. Unfortunately, when the Russian Revolution swept the hearts and minds of many of his countrymen, he found himself on the wrong side of history."

"What happened to him?" Theodosia asked.

"In 1917, just before the czar and his family were executed, Tereshchenko was arrested at the Winter Palace, stripped of his title, and hauled off to prison," Vardell said.

"Leon Trotsky took over as his successor," Timothy added.

"I see," Theodosia said. "And Tereshchenko's diamonds? What became of them?"

"They ended up being his ticket out of prison," Vardell said. "Out of Russia."

Theodosia nodded, thinking, *He was one of the lucky aristocrats that got away.*

"The largest and most famous diamond in his collection, the Tereshchenko Blue Diamond, was later cut by Cartier. But there was also the Hibiscus Diamond, a forty-nine-carat yellow diamond," Vardell said.

"Holy cats," Theodosia said under her breath. Then, "Hibiscus like the tea?"

"Exactly. Anyway, Tereshchenko escaped to Norway in 1918 with most of the diamonds sewn into the lining of his sealskin coat," Vardell said.

"And then?" Theodosia asked. She was fascinated by this bizarre tale.

"Most of the diamonds didn't surface again for several decades," Vardell said.

Theodosia gazed at the two men. "But you both believe Willow's diamond earrings were part of that collection?"

"I'm certain they were," Timothy said. "Right before the outbreak of World War II, the Hibiscus Diamond surfaced and was purchased by a Parisian jeweler named Guillard who cut it into smaller stones. My sister, Adelle, lived in Paris at the time and acquired several of those smaller diamonds." He nodded at Theodosia. "She would have been Willow's grandmother."

"And the diamonds were passed down to Willow," Theodosia said.

"Quite so," Timothy said.

"What a remarkable story," Theodosia said.

"There's more," Vardell said. "Willow also inherited a matching pendant."

"Where's this diamond pendant now?" Theodosia asked.

Vardell shrugged and made a *Who knows?* gesture with his hands. "We think it's probably gone. Stolen from her apartment last night."

"Which accounts for the shooting," Theodosia said. She thought for a few moments. "Does Tidwell know about this?"

"We just spoke with him some twenty minutes ago," Timothy said. "After Robert received the inventory list from the"—Timothy's lip curled—"the coroner. That's when we realized the diamonds were missing."

"That's quite a story," Theodosia said. She glanced sideways at Robert Vardell. He looked haggard and drawn, as if he'd spent the last six months chained in a dungeon.

"It's a story we don't want leaked," Vardell said.

"Theodosia here is looking into things for me," Timothy said.

Vardell cranked his head sideways and peered at Theodosia as if he were slightly nearsighted. "You are?"

"Theodosia's had experience with this type of situation before," Timothy said.

"Well . . ." Vardell seemed at a loss for words. "That's good, I suppose. The more help we get the better. I must confess, in speaking with Detective Tidwell I wasn't entirely impressed by his abilities."

"Tidwell plays it close to the vest," Theodosia said. "But please don't discount him for a single moment. He's smart, lucky, and tenacious. Give him one tiny sliver of a clue, one bit of grist, and he'll chew on it for hours. Probably come up with something, too. He's broken many difficult cases."

Vardell still looked doubtful. "But how bizarre is this case? A murder in front of—what?—four or five dozen people? At a haunted house the week before Halloween? It sounds almost . . . ritualistic." He paused. "And then the shooting of the police detective at Willow's apartment."

Theodosia was trying to examine all the different angles as she gazed at Vardell. "I have to ask . . . have you been threatened in any way, Mr. Vardell?"

Vardell practically jumped out of his skin. "Me? No! Who would threaten me?"

"Perhaps the same person who murdered your fiancée?" Theodosia said.

"Listen to Theodosia," Timothy insisted. "Don't discount her questions. Or her ideas."

"Okay," Vardell said. He touched a hand to the side of his head and said, "Okay," again.

"Please think carefully," Theodosia said. "Have you encountered any problems in business lately? By the way, what is your business?"

"I'm in finance," Vardell said. "I work with Metcalf and Solange, a private equity fund."

"Interesting," Theodosia said. "Have you had any unhappy clients?"

"The market goes up, it goes down. Sometimes our clients' moods mirror that fluctuation," Vardell said.

"Money or loss of money can make people behave quite irrationally," Theodosia said.

"But not in this particular case," Vardell said with conviction. "I'm positive the diamonds were clearly the reason behind Willow's murder. She was the target." He gave an emphatic nod that indicated he wanted to close off any more questions concerning his business.

"I hate to ask," Theodosia said. "Are plans underway for a funeral?"

"Still pending," Timothy said. "But if hard-pressed, I'd probably guess it will happen this Thursday morning."

"Will you hold the service here? At the Heritage Society?" Theodosia asked.

Vardell shook his head. "I've been in touch with Willow's family, and we're of like mind that the service should be simple and dignified. A small evening visitation and then, the following morning, a graveside service at Magnolia Cemetery."

"That's probably for the best," Timothy said. His eyes were suddenly red and watery; he looked like he was about to cry.

Vardell stood up so quickly his knees popped. "And I need to take care of a few things." He turned to Theodosia, who had also stood up. "It was good meeting you."

"I'm sure we'll meet again," Theodosia said.

Vardell turned to Timothy. "Timothy, I'll be in touch."

"Of course," Timothy said.

Once Vardell had left, Theodosia sat back down.

"I have a slightly impertinent request," she said to Timothy.

"What's that?"

"I'd like to take a look inside Willow's apartment."

"I'm afraid the police have it sealed off."

"That's fairly standard. But if I go in I promise not to disturb anything."

Timothy sat for a moment, gazing at her. "From what I've been told, the place has already been ripped apart. So I don't believe one more look-see would hurt anything." He reached down, slid open the bottom drawer of his desk, and pulled out a small blue suede clutch purse. Digging into it, he found a ring of keys and handed it over to Theodosia.

"Thank you," she said.

8

Drayton fairly pounced on Theodosia when she returned to the tea shop late in the afternoon.

"Did you learn anything?" he asked. He was standing behind the front counter and leaning forward, the better to catch Theodosia's attention.

"Not a whole lot," Theodosia said. She looked around and saw only a table of two guests seated against the back wall.

Good, things are nice and quiet. Makes it easier to talk.

"Nothing at all?" Drayton's nervous hands reached up to smooth his yellow bow tie.

Haley heard them talking and came rushing out from the kitchen.

"What's going on?" she asked. She wiped her hands on a red-and-white-checked tea towel, looking about as serious as one could look with a smudge of flour on her cheek. "Did you figure anything out? Please tell me you solved Willow's murder."

"I'm afraid not," Theodosia said. "All I really did was interview a few people at the Heritage Society, people who'd worked on the haunted house."

"And?" Haley said. She was ravenous for details.

"And most of them are as baffled as we are," Theodosia said.

"They had no ideas at all? There were no accusations, no pointing of fingers?" Drayton asked.

"Not yet anyway," Theodosia said. She knew that might come later, after everyone had a chance to digest her questions. After they started to wonder if one of them could be the guilty party.

"No forward progress at all?" Haley asked. "Rats. I'm disappointed."

"Actually, I did manage to uncover a couple of interesting wrinkles," Theodosia said.

"Like what?" Haley said.

Drayton held up a finger. "Wait. Wait until I cash out this last table and pour us all a cup of tea."

Theodosia and Haley set out cups and saucers while Drayton took care of their last two customers. Once goodbyes had been said and the front door latched, he carried a teapot over to their table and poured out cups of fresh-brewed Earl Grey tea.

They each took a fortifying sip, then Theodosia drew a deep breath and told them about meeting Robert Vardell in Timothy's office and hearing Vardell's strange tale about the Tereshchenko diamonds. She also told them about Timothy and Vardell's hypothesis that Willow had been murdered on account of her Hibiscus Diamond earrings.

"Hibiscus like the tea?" Drayton asked.

Theodosia smiled. "That's exactly what I said."

"So the earrings are missing, presumed stolen by last night's killer," Haley said. "Is the matching pendant gone, too?"

"We don't know," Theodosia said. "It's possible the

killer went to Willow's apartment last night to ransack the place and search for the pendant."

"Maybe he couldn't find it and got desperate," Haley said.

Theodosia nodded. "Hit the panic button and fired a shot at Riley."

"There's your motive right there," Drayton said, slapping a hand down on the table, making his teacup jump in its saucer. "Money. Envy. Greed!"

Theodosia took another sip of tea. "It does seem likely."

"So it wasn't just a whack job," Haley said slowly. "It must have been someone who was familiar with Willow. Knew she owned those diamonds."

"That seems like the most logical explanation," Theodosia said. "Someone who coveted her earrings and also knew about the matching diamond pendant."

"And poor Riley had to go and stumble onto this crazy killer. And get shot for his trouble," Drayton said.

"Do you think the killer found the diamond pendant and escaped with it?" Haley asked.

"Hard to say. When Riley barged in, he might have interrupted the killer's search," Theodosia said. "Maybe the killer dashed off without it and the pendant is still there."

"Holy cats," Haley said. "What a mess."

They sat there for a few moments, thinking, sipping their tea, digesting Theodosia's words. Outside, the shadows were lengthening. It would be getting dark soon.

Drayton cleared his throat. "You said you stumbled onto a couple of interesting wrinkles. What else did you find out?"

"While I was poking around the Heritage Society I ran into Willow's publisher, a man by the name of Allan Barnaby."

"Never heard of him," Haley said.

"Was he at the haunted house last night?" Drayton asked.

"I think he must have been. Seems to me I remember Willow making some reference to him. Anyway, this Barnaby fellow claims he was in talks with Claire and some of the other curators about publishing a complete history of the Heritage Society," Theodosia said.

Drayton's brows shot up. "First I've heard. That idea's never been brought up at a board meeting."

"Is this Barnaby a suspect?" Haley asked.

Theodosia shook her head. "I've got no reason to think he's involved."

"What about Vardell, the fiancé?" Drayton asked.

Haley frowned. "Yeah, what about him? Did this Vardell guy seem truly heartbroken? You know it's always the husband or boyfriend who comes under suspicion. At least that's how it works in the Lifetime movies."

"I'd have to say Vardell seemed genuinely devastated at losing Willow. The only sour note came when I asked about his business and he cut me off rather abruptly," Theodosia said. "Then again, he does work in finance."

"He may just be a private person," Drayton said. "And profoundly shaken up by Willow's death."

"Maybe," Haley said. But she said it hesitantly like she didn't believe it.

"There's one more thing," Theodosia said.

"What's that?" Haley asked.

"Claire Waltho—you know Claire, she's one of the curators—she told me a bit of gossip about Ellis Bouchard," Theodosia said.

"Let me guess," Drayton said. "Claire told you that Bouchard is insanely angry at Timothy and the Heritage Society."

"Actually, Claire told me that Ellis Bouchard is flat broke," Theodosia said.

"No!" Haley cried. Then, "Broke as in no money?"

Theodosia nodded as she continued. "Clare said that Bouchard's rental properties are all going into receivership."

"So Ellis Bouchard might have had a motive for killing Willow," Drayton said.

Haley's eyes narrowed. "He could pawn those diamonds and walk away a rich man. Pay off his creditors in a heartbeat."

"Not so fast," Theodosia said. "You're making an awfully big leap on simple hearsay."

"Theodosia's right," Drayton said. "Why would Bouchard continue to make a pest of himself, draw so much attention to himself, if he'd committed such a heinous crime?"

"Duh, maybe he's throwing up a smoke screen?" Haley said.

Theodosia shook her head. "You never know."

Haley went into the kitchen to finish up for the day while Drayton wandered back to his domain behind the counter to carefully arrange his tea tins. At one time his floor-to-ceiling shelves of tea had been organized by country of origin. Now he had his black teas on the upper shelves, white teas in the middle, and green teas on the lower shelves. Of course, it was still a colorful mosaic of tea tins that could change on a whim.

"Are we set for the Sherlock Holmes Tea tomorrow?" Drayton asked Theodosia. Besides being a compulsive organizer, he was a prepper of the first magnitude. Menus, special events, and timetables all had to be carefully worked out before he could relax and feel comfortable.

"Haley's got the menu figured out, I'm handling the decorations, and we've got Miss Dimple coming in tomorrow to help," Theodosia said. "I don't know what else we can do."

Drayton shook his head. "Halloween week—not my favorite time of year—is always so darned busy."

Theodosia watched Drayton as he poured hot water into a Brown Betty teapot and began timing whatever it was he was brewing.

"What have you got there?" Theodosia asked. She had

planned to restock her gift shelves, not taste test any new teas.

"Hibiscus tea," Drayton said as he poured out a steaming cup for her. "*Haunted* hibiscus. I thought it might help stimulate your imagination. Get you thinking about those missing diamonds."

"I'm already burning up brain cells thinking about those diamonds. The thief—Willow's killer—has to be someone in dire financial straits."

"Like Ellis Bouchard?"

"He might just be a wild card. Wrong place, wrong time. Though he did seem awfully unbalanced when he rushed in here this morning."

"And unbalanced people do unbalanced things," Drayton said.

"He's a possibility, but I'm guessing there's someone else out there."

"Unless the killer has the diamonds in his hot little hand and has already blown town," Drayton said.

"There is that," she said. "But my hope is he's still hanging around."

Theodosia carried her cup of hibiscus tea over to the highboy and set it down on a nearby table. Then she went into her office, grabbed a large carton that UPS had delivered that morning, and muscled it back out to the tea room.

With so many event teas coming up, it was definitely time to add new gift items to her shelves.

Luckily, the tea cozies Theodosia had ordered had finally arrived. There were three dozen in all—quilted fabric cozies in solid colors, bright florals, and blue toile, as well as knitted tea cozies shaped like teapots, beehives (complete with knitted bees), floral baskets, kitty cats, stocking caps, and one that resembled an orange-and-white tropical fish.

Theodosia moved her teapots, jars of jam, and tins of tea around like pawns on a chessboard, making room for the new tea cozy display, all the while letting the findings of the day slowly percolate in her brain.

Eventually, Drayton came over to check on her display.

"That cat tea cozy," Drayton said. "It's very cute."

"Take it, then."

Drayton held up a hand. "I have dozens. But you already know that."

"You probably have at least fifty or sixty teapots, but that doesn't stop you from buying new ones."

"But now I'm only interested in antique and truly exquisite teapots," Drayton said. As if extreme good taste excused his mania for collecting.

"Like the Royal Copenhagen Flora Danica teapot you just bought at auction?"

"That was a once-in-a-lifetime opportunity."

"I'm sure it was," Theodosia said. She'd learned to never question Drayton's fervor for a new but hard-to-find teapot. Then, "I have a favor to ask." She was still on her hands and knees, scrunched in front of the highboy.

Drayton peered down at her over his tortoiseshell half-glasses. "What's that?"

"I want to snoop through Willow's apartment tonight, and I'd like you to come with me."

"Me?" Drayton was taken aback. "What would I bring to the table?"

"More like to the investigation," Theodosia said. "But to answer your question, you're an interested, involved party. And, when all is said and done, a fair to middling amateur detective."

"I'm guessing we'd be looking for the missing diamond pendant?"

"And we'd hopefully find it." Theodosia stood up, dusted her hands together, and turned to face him.

"I thought the police had Willow's place completely sealed off."

"A few strips of yellow plastic tape shouldn't stop us," Theodosia said.

"No, but a locked door might."

Theodosia reached into the pocket of her slacks, pulled out a ring of keys, and dangled it in front of Drayton. The keys clinking together sounded like tiny chimes.

"Ah," Drayton said, breaking into a smile. "I should have known better than to underestimate you. Where there's a will, there's a way."

"No," Theodosia said, her mind once again flashing on a disgruntled Ellis Bouchard. "Where there's a will, there's a relative. Trying to contest it."

9

❧

The Charleston single house on Logan Street where Willow had lived was completely dark when Theodosia and Drayton pulled up to the curb. They'd waited until eight o'clock at night to make their move. Early enough so they wouldn't garner suspicion from the neighbors, late enough that most people were already home and hunkered down.

"Nobody home," Drayton said, peering out the side window of Theodosia's Jeep. "Not even the landlord."

"I'd say that's to our advantage," Theodosia said.

They climbed out of the Jeep and stood on the sidewalk looking at the dark silhouette of the house. Typical of Charleston single houses, it was three stories tall, one room wide, and several rooms deep. This particular dwelling was a clapboard Victorian version with a two-story side piazza complete with fancy wrought-iron railings and Doric pillars.

The neighborhood was comprised of several other single houses, and those appeared to be fairly quiet as well. There were no kids out playing, no dogs barking, nobody taking their evening constitutional. A few blocks over on Ashley, a fairly well-traveled street, they could hear cars whooshing by and the occasional honk of a horn.

"You still want to do this?" Drayton asked.

"Yes."

"But you're hesitant."

"I'm a little freaked-out because this is where Riley was shot," Theodosia said.

"You want me to go in while you stay out here?"

"No, I'll be okay." Theodosia was touched by Drayton's offer. And yes, she was nervous, but it was something she wanted to do, something she felt she *had* to do. Time to muster up a little faith and fortitude, she decided.

They walked up the front walk, followed a cobblestone path around the side of the house, and opened the screened piazza door. Once they stepped inside there were two entry doors. The first one led to Willow's apartment.

Theodosia stuck the key in the lock and turned it without hesitation, then heard a faint click as the latch opened.

Okay, this is it.

When the door swung open she reached in, batted her hand around, found a switch, and flipped on the overhead light.

The place was exactly as Riley had described it. Complete and total chaos. There were cardboard boxes everywhere, some half-filled, some taped shut. Papers and magazines were scattered all over; books had been pulled from their shelves and piled haphazardly. You could barely see the furniture. Two goldfish peered out from a large oval-shaped bowl that sat on a small table.

"Witnesses," Drayton said, pointing at the fish.

"Too bad they can't tell us what happened here," Theodosia said.

Then Drayton's eyes roved over the mess. "Sweet dreams, you think an intruder caused all this commotion?"

Theodosia walked into the living room and looked around, studying everything carefully. Then she made a slow, deliberate pirouette as her eyes continued to scan the room.

"No," she said finally. "I don't believe the killer—the intruder—did this."

Drayton's head bobbed as he did a double take. "Excuse me, Theo, have you suddenly turned psychic?"

"Just being observant."

Drayton postured with one hand on his hip. "Then would you kindly explain who created this awful jumble?"

"Take a careful look." Theodosia kicked an empty cardboard box with her toe. "You see the printing on the side of this box? Cardiff Moving. I'm pretty sure Willow was packing up all her things so she could move. That's why this place is so crazy and catawampus."

"Moving," Drayton said, slowly digesting the word. "You mean to a new home?"

Theodosia shrugged. "If Willow was getting married in a matter of weeks, she and her fiancé had probably found a new place to live."

"You mean together," Drayton said.

"Yes, together. That's generally how it works." Theodosia wondered if the killer-intruder had also been startled at encountering such a mess. Or maybe he'd just been hell-bent on finding and snatching the diamond pendant.

"So what do we do now?" Drayton asked.

"We stick to our plan and look for the diamond pendant. And see what else we can figure out. If there's any sort of . . . clue. How about you take the bedroom while I poke around out here?" Theodosia said. "Okay?"

As Drayton disappeared into the bedroom, his voice floated back to her. "I'll do my best."

Theodosia gazed at the hodgepodge and wondered where to start. Maybe look in the desk drawers? She crossed the room, kicked aside a stack of magazines, and plunked herself down in Willow's desk chair. Still wondering about the missing computer, Theodosia pulled open the top drawer of the desk. There was nothing much inside except for the usual jumble of pens, pencils, paper clips, notepads, and miscellaneous wires, cords, and earbuds.

Theodosia had just pulled open a file drawer when Drayton called out to her, "Got an upturned jewelry box in here."

That sent her scrambling into the bedroom, where Drayton was gazing at the top of Willow's dresser. There was the decidedly feminine scatter of lipsticks, compacts, combs, brushes, perfume bottles, and a fancy saucer that held spare change and a few pieces of costume jewelry. In the center of it all was a jewelry box. It was a large red leather box with gold trim that had been haphazardly left on its side as if it had been thoroughly ransacked. All of the drawers had been pulled out.

"Did you look inside?" Theodosia asked.

Drayton shook his head. "I thought you might do the honors."

Theodosia grasped the jewelry box and carefully righted it.

"If I owned a stunning set of jewelry," Theodosia said, "I'd probably keep it in something like this. In the very top drawer." She pulled the top drawer all the way out to reveal—nothing. Just an empty drawer lined in red velvet.

"I'm guessing our killer got his hot little hands on that diamond pendant after all," Drayton said.

Theodosia hastily searched through the rest of the jewelry box drawers. They contained rings, a couple of gold bangles, a few silver chains, and a charm bracelet. But no stunner of a Hibiscus Diamond pendant.

"We should look in the freezer," Drayton said.

"You think Willow kept her ice on ice?" Theodosia asked as they headed into the small kitchen.

"It's been done before."

"Sure, but mostly in B movies," Theodosia said.

But when they opened the freezer compartment, there was nothing there but a small carton of praline gelato and two low-cal frozen dinners.

"No pendant," Drayton said. He was disappointed that his idea hadn't panned out.

"Unless it's stuck in the gelato. Is it?"

Drayton grabbed the gelato, removed the lid, and showed it to Theodosia. "Not even a scoop taken out of it."

"While we're in here . . ." Theodosia said, looking around.

She hunted through all the kitchen cupboards as well as the drawer beneath the stove, but all she found were cans of soup, dried pasta, boxes of cereal, plates, glasses, and pots and pans. Coming up empty, she turned to face the living room again. "All we can do now is root through the rest of this stuff."

Drayton nodded. "Got it. Maybe if I . . . paged through the books? There could be a hidden compartment."

"Couldn't hurt."

Theodosia went back to the file drawer in the desk, deciding that's where Willow probably kept her personal papers. She found bank statements, monthly statements from T. Rowe Price, credit card receipts, and a few paid bills. But no papers to indicate Willow might have a safe-deposit box somewhere.

A file marked WEDDING caught Theodosia's eye. She pulled the folder out and casually thumbed through it. Sure enough, all the paperwork related to Willow's upcoming wedding. A copy of an order for flowers at Tropics Florist, a bakery receipt for a six-layer wedding cake from Coco Bella Bakery, notes on her reservation for a reception at the Avalon Hotel, and lots more that Theodosia didn't have the heart to look at.

"Oh, Drayton, this is awful," Theodosia moaned. "This poor girl's wedding was only five weeks away."

Drayton looked up from a stack of books. "Everything will have to be canceled, I assume."

Theodosia returned the file and was about to close the drawer when she noticed a stack of brochures sitting in the bottom. She hesitated a moment, then pulled them out. They were recent brochures and catalogs from the Heritage Society. One for their Carolina Gold Show, another for their Audubon Show.

How interesting.

"Was Willow a member of the Heritage Society?" Theodosia asked Drayton.

He looked up, glasses halfway down his nose, making him look slightly owlish. "Not that I'm aware of."

Theodosia held up the catalogs.

"Look at these, Drayton. I think Willow might have been doing research on the Heritage Society after all."

"You think she was planning to write its history?"

"Maybe. I'll have to ask Timothy if he knows anything about this."

"Please do."

As Theodosia closed the file drawer her eyes fell upon an address book. "How quaint," she murmured, since everyone she knew, with the possible exception of Drayton, kept their contact list on their cell phones. But as she opened the address book two note cards fell out.

What are these?

The first, strangely enough, was from Ellis Bouchard. It was a short handwritten note reminding her that the house on Tradd Street was reputed to be haunted by his great-aunt Abigail, hence the nickname the Gray Ghost.

How interesting, Theodosia thought. Perhaps Willow had been working on a second book about Charleston hauntings and Bouchard wanted to make sure the old homestead was included?

"Take a look at this, Drayton."

Drayton crossed the room, took the card Theodosia held out to him, and scanned it quickly.

"From Bouchard. Strange," he said. "Awkward, really."

"Maybe we need to conduct a séance and ask Great-Aunt Abigail exactly what happened," Theodosia said.

"Heaven forbid." Drayton handed the card back to her. "What's that second note you've got there?"

"This one is even more bizarre."

"Why? What's it say?" Drayton asked.

"It's a handwritten note that says, and I quote, 'And so being young and dipped in folly, I fell in love with melancholy. My dear Willow, I will never forget you.'"

"Excuse me," Drayton said, "but that first part is a direct quote from Edgar Allan Poe."

"I thought I recognized the words. They're a little . . . ominous."

"Is the note signed?" Drayton asked.

Theodosia's eyes scanned down. "By someone named Henry Curtis. You recognize that name?"

"No, but I think we might want to locate this Mr. Curtis. Talk to him."

"I think we should do more than that," Theodosia said. "I think we ought to sit him down and give him the third degree." She sighed and took a final look around. "Time to go?"

"I'm taking those poor fish with me," Drayton said. "Otherwise they're not going to get fed."

"That's very kind of you, but please don't tell them about Willow."

Drayton raised a single eyebrow. "You think it would matter to them?"

"Yes," Theodosia said. "I do." Theodosia believed that sentient beings, even tiny golden fish, could detect vibrations in the universe—that they somehow felt a blip when their world had changed. And what had taken place here last night had been a whopper of a blip.

10

❧

Theodosia dropped Drayton off at his home, then headed over to University Hospital to see Riley. It was still early—well, maybe not that early—it was nine o'clock, but she doubted that Riley would be asleep yet. Unless of course he'd been given a sleeping pill.

As luck would have it, he hadn't.

"Hey there," Riley said when Theodosia entered his room. Then his smile faded and an accusing note crept into his voice. "You're dressed all in black. Does this by any chance mean that you completely ignored my advice and went on a creepy crawl somewhere?"

Oops, Theodosia guessed her black jacket, slacks, and boots might be a dead giveaway. She probably should have stopped at home and changed first. Put on something cheery.

"Well, you're right. I have been doing a little snooping," she said. It didn't feel right to lie to Riley; he looked so helpless in his hospital bed.

Riley pulled himself up straighter. "You went to Willow's apartment, didn't you?"

Doggone, the man is good.

"I did," Theodosia said.

Riley waggled an index finger at her. "Bad idea. What have I been saying to you all along?" He didn't give her a moment to answer. "I said don't get involved, it's too dangerous."

"It's hard not to be involved. To not care about what happened," Theodosia said.

Riley looked vexed. "I know, I know. It's your extreme sport. Some people jump out of planes, some dive with hammerhead sharks. You get drawn into murder investigations."

Theodosia gave him a faint smile. Everything he'd said was true. Then, "Do you know about the diamonds?" She figured she'd toss out that little factoid, plunge right into the deep end.

"Yes, I know about the missing diamonds. Tidwell filled me in when he stopped by earlier." Riley gave her a questioning look. "Wait a minute, is that what you were looking for tonight? The diamond pendant?"

"How do you figure that?"

"Okay, this is going to sound terribly redundant, but I *am* a detective first grade and I *have* worked investigations before. You do remember me telling you that?"

"You don't have to be sarcastic about it," Theodosia said.

"Then tell me what *will* work with you?" Riley answered back. "What do I have to do to get you to stop meddling?"

"I wish you'd stop worrying about me and just concentrate on getting better."

Riley flapped a hand to indicate his sterile, boring surroundings. "I've got nothing better to do than lie here in this stupid adjustable bed and worry about you."

"Please don't." Theodosia moved closer to his bed. He was starting to guilt her and make her feel awful.

Riley put a hand up and swiped his forehead. "I think all this back-and-forth is giving me a headache."

"I'm sorry." Now Theodosia felt even worse.

"We keep going around and around," Riley said.

Theodosia gazed at him for a long five seconds. Then she leaned forward and took his hand. "Talk to me. Tell me what you're thinking."

He groaned. "Oh man."

She pulled back and frowned. "You sound as if you're in pain. Do you want me to call a nurse?"

"No, I want you to—" Riley stopped abruptly and pursed his lips. "I don't know *what* I want anymore."

"But you want this crime to be solved."

"Of course."

"Then work with me. Let me help. Bounce things off me."

Riley stared at her. "Bounce . . ."

"Let's go back to the very beginning," Theodosia said suddenly, hoping to get him talking. "Try to re-create Sunday night at the haunted house."

Riley's brow wrinkled. "I'm not sure I'm following you."

"So it's opening night and people have arrived for an evening of fun and fantasy. But the killer is probably there, too, ghosting around. Willow sits in the parlor autographing books, until suddenly she's not. For some reason she leaves her table right in the middle of her big opening-night gig . . ." Theodosia stopped and stared at Riley. His eyes were half-closed as if he were visualizing the situation right along with her. Would he take up the narrative? Theodosia prayed that he would.

"The killer is watching Willow," Riley said slowly. "But mostly he's got his eyes on the diamonds. They represent escape and power to him, a way out of trouble, a means to a better life."

"How does the killer lure Willow away from her table?" Theodosia whispered. "How does he get her to go upstairs with him?"

Riley thought for a few moments. "Somehow they know each other. They've crossed paths before, so Willow feels safe. The killer says something to her, makes some kind of impassioned plea or excuse that gets Willow upstairs. Once she's there he's able to control her completely."

"How does he do that?" Theodosia asked.

Riley opened his eyes. "The way most criminals control their victims. Threatened her, probably held a gun on her."

"What kind of slug did the doctors take out of your arm?" Theodosia asked.

Riley stared at her. "A forty-five."

"So that's what our killer-shooter was carrying," Theodosia said. She felt a thrill at having a sliver of inside information. Now, could she do something with it? Could she take it to the next step?

"But there was a loose end," Riley said.

"The pendant," Theodosia said. "He was greedy and wanted the pendant, too. Because that's the real biggie."

"She wasn't wearing it," Riley said. He stared pointedly at Theodosia. "You never did say—did you find the pendant when you were searching tonight?"

"No."

"I wonder if the killer had already found it?" Riley said. "Just before I showed up at Willow's apartment."

"I'm guessing he did. And then, of course, he also grabbed Willow's computer—her laptop. To make it look like . . . something else?"

"Yes, but it's entirely possible that the killer's name was somehow on Willow's computer. Perhaps there were e-mails or notes that the killer needed to erase. Best way to do that is to grab the whole thing and destroy the hard drive," Riley said. "Beat it to death with a ball-peen hammer or dump it in a swamp somewhere."

"Besides the diamonds, do you think Willow's murder had anything to do with a book she was writing?" Theodosia asked.

"I don't know. Was she working on another book?"

"According to people at the Heritage Society, Willow might have been noodling one around."

Riley thought for a few moments. "That sounds like . . . not a good reason to murder someone." He was quiet for a few moments, ruminating, then he turned his gaze back on Theodosia. "You're a femme fatale," he said. "You worked your wiles on me and tempted me into talking. I told you way more than I should have."

"But doesn't it feel good?" Theodosia asked. "Don't you feel like we're getting somewhere?"

Riley offered her a crooked grin. "I'm afraid the jury's still out on that."

Earl Grey was waiting for Theodosia when she arrived home.

"Sorry it's so late, buddy," she said. Snapping a leash on Earl Grey, she walked him down the back alley and around the block, allowing for plenty of mandatory sniff time.

Back home, Theodosia locked the door, double-checked it just in case a boogeyman was hanging around, and made herself a cup of lavender tea. She placed the teacup on a silver tray along with a Fortnum & Mason ginger biscuit for herself and a dog biscuit for Earl Grey. Then she walked into her dining room, grabbed Willow's book, and gave Earl Grey the high sign that it was time for them to head upstairs for the night.

Theodosia was more than comfortable with the notion of being an old-fashioned girl, and the upstairs of her home reflected that sensibility. Her second-floor suite, consisting of a bedroom, walk-in closet, and tower alcove, had been lovingly and carefully furnished. A pale-blue Oriental rug was soft and easy on bare feet and paws. A billowy down comforter had turned her bed into a virtual cloud. Laura Ashley wallpaper—the Forsythia Seaspray pattern—adorned the walls. A vintage dressing table held an old-fashioned brush and comb set as well as a Jo Malone candle, bronze leopard statue, rose-patterned ceramic box, basket of costume jewelry, box of stationery, and her journal.

Her tower room, her retreat, was furnished with an over-stuffed chair, footstool, small lacquer table, antique bookcases, and a Tiffany lamp. Well, Tiffany-style anyway. Timothy Neville was the only person she knew who owned an authentic Tiffany lamp.

Curling up in her easy chair, Earl Grey eating his biscuit while stretched out on his L.L.Bean dog bed (one of three in the house), Theodosia opened Willow's book, paged through it, and began to read.

The story she chose was "The Mystery of Alice Flagg," the tale of a young woman who had a secret admirer. Unfortunately, her brother, a strict and straitlaced doctor, thoroughly disapproved of Alice's choice in men. So poor Alice, for her sin of falling in love with this miscreant, was kicked out of her own house, contracted malaria, and eventually died. Upon her death, a wedding ring on a blue ribbon was found tied around her neck.

Theodosia shook her head and closed the book. That's all she needed, another tale of a would-be bride who ended up dead. Not the kind of stuff that was conducive to sweet dreams.

Then again, her head was still spinning from nightmarish images. Poor Willow dangling from the end of a rope. And though she hadn't actually witnessed Riley lying on a stretcher, a terrible red bloom of blood working its way through the thin white blanket the EMTs had hastily thrown over him, she could still see it vividly in her imagination.

And then there was the angry face of Ellis Bouchard. The devastation on Robert Vardell's face.

So much to think about.

Almost too much. She hoped it wouldn't give her nightmares.

11

Theodosia stood at the counter, watching Drayton pull a tin of Fujian silver tea from his floor-to-ceiling shelves. He studied it, frowned slightly, as if something wasn't quite right, and put it back on the shelf. He stood on tiptoes, searched his shelves again, and pulled out a tin of Harney & Sons Chinese Silver Needle tea instead. Even though the Indigo Tea Shop didn't open for another twenty minutes, and customers pretty much chose their own blend of fresh-brewed tea, Drayton liked to be ready with a couple of steaming pots. For emergency purposes, he always said.

"Who do you think is our prime suspect?" Theodosia asked him.

Drayton set his tea tin on the counter and stared at her. "That's a fine opening line for a Tuesday morning. Who do *you* think it is?"

"Right now I'm thinking Ellis Bouchard."

"Interesting," Drayton said. "Yesterday you weren't so sure."

"I know. But I've given it some more thought, and I think Bouchard really was in a desperate situation with his real estate holdings. He was nervous, worried sick about losing his properties, until one day he noticed Willow's diamonds."

"Where do you suppose he saw them?" Drayton grabbed a blue-and-white teapot and added three scoops of tea as well as the traditional pinch for the pot.

"Maybe he was hanging around the Bouchard Mansion while the haunted house was being set up. Maybe he ran into Willow at the Heritage Society. She could have dropped by to visit Timothy. Or she was doing research in their library," Theodosia said.

"It all sounds a little far-fetched," Drayton said.

"But not impossible."

"No, it's not."

"What's not?" Haley asked. She was suddenly standing there, looking inquisitive and holding a tray heaped with fresh-baked treats.

"It doesn't seem possible, but those are the most aromatic scones I've ever smelled in my life," Drayton said. "What magic have you wrought, dear girl?"

"Cream scones and lemon poppy seed scones," Haley said. She was suddenly in a peppy mood, thrilled by Drayton's praise. "The lemon ones are really good 'cause they're made with freshly squeezed and zested Meyer lemons."

"And I see muffins, too?" Theodosia said.

"Those are my double dare chocolate chip muffins," Haley said. "I used cinnamon and pasilla chile–infused chocolate to give them an extra zing." She shifted her tray onto the counter. "But I know you guys were talking about Willow's murder. And possible suspects. I know you're trying to help, and I really appreciate it."

"Theodosia's doing her best," Drayton said. "Even though she's been warned to stay away from the investigation."

"Are you getting anywhere?" Haley asked Theodosia.

But Drayton jumped in to answer for her. "Theo will let you know when she has some concrete facts."

"But do you . . . ?" Haley began again.

"Really, she'll let you know," Drayton said.

Haley nodded sagely at this second interruption and pointed a finger at Drayton's blue-and-white teapot. "You know, Drayton, there are electric tea brewers that are Bluetooth enabled and can send a message to your phone when the tea is ready."

A look of horror spread across Drayton's face. "What?" he squeaked.

"Or you can do it the old-fashioned way," Haley said. She gave her hair a quick flip and grinned at him as she headed back to the kitchen. "Just making sure you're on your toes."

"That girl. She'll be the death of me yet," Drayton said.

"She's just worried," Theodosia said. "We all are."

They were an hour into morning tea when the front door opened and Miss Dimple came rushing in. Drayton was suddenly grinning like the proverbial Cheshire cat.

"There she is," he exclaimed. "Our crackerjack bookkeeper who doubles as my right-hand tea expert."

"I hope I'm not late," Miss Dimple said. She glanced around the busy tea shop as she slid out of her brick-red coat. "Theodosia said ten. Is it ten yet?"

"On the button," Drayton said.

"Thank you so much for coming in to help us," Theodosia said. She took Miss Dimple's coat from her and hung it on the brass coatrack that stood in the entry.

"Are you kidding?" Miss Dimple peered at her with glowing eyes. "This is a treat for me. Gets me out of the house. You can only spend so much time playing with your cats and watching *One Life to Live*."

Miss Dimple was eighty-something and still going strong. Feisty, warmhearted, and barely five feet tall, she was plumpish with a cap of pink-tinged curls. She had a breathy little voice and used quaint phrases such as *oh my stars*, *cheese and crackers*, and *whoopsie daisy*. Miss Dimple was also a very capable bookkeeper for the Indigo Tea Shop and filled in as server a few days a month. Today was one of those days.

"So did I hear you right? You're having a Sherlock Holmes Tea today?" Miss Dimple asked.

"Quite correct," Drayton said.

"How exciting. In celebration of Halloween, I would expect." She paused and said, "What do you want me to do?"

"For now just grab a pot of tea from Drayton and refill our guests' teacups," Theodosia said.

The tea shop was buzzing when Sybil Spalding, the Heritage Society intern that Theodosia had interviewed yesterday, walked through the front door.

Theodosia recognized Sybil immediately and hurried over to greet her.

"Have you come for tea?" Theodosia asked. She was pleased to see a familiar face, a youthful face. She loved the fact that so many young people were embracing tea drinking and tea lore.

Sybil shook her head. "I'm just the designated gopher today. Here to pick up an order of scones that one of our curators phoned in."

"I have your order right here," Drayton called from behind the counter.

"And I know it's kind of last-minute, but I'm wondering if you have room for two more guests at your fancy luncheon today," Sybil said.

"Our Sherlock Holmes Tea isn't all that fancy, more like a fun event," Theodosia said. "But we surely do have a couple spots left. Will you and a guest be joining us?"

Sybil shook her head, her dark curls bouncing around

her face. "I wish. But, no, it's not for me. Claire Waltho wants to take a potential donor to lunch today, and I suggested bringing her here."

"Well . . . thank you. We appreciate the business."

"It's a woman by the name of Drucilla Heyward," Sybil said.

"I know Miss Drucilla," Drayton said. "Lovely woman with a most charitable heart. She donated a bundle to the Opera Society last year so they could stage a production of Verdi's *Rigoletto*. She also helped underwrite a jazz quartet at this year's Spoleto."

"That's good to know," Sybil said. "Because word on the grapevine is that Miss Heyward is planning to donate a chunk of money to the Heritage Society."

"That would be terrific," Theodosia said. "We'll try to help things along by giving Claire and her guest some extra special treatment."

"As we do all our guests," Drayton murmured from the counter. "And just for the record, it's either Mrs. Heyward or Miss Drucilla."

"Why is that?" Sybil asked.

"Because that's how it's done in the South," Drayton said.

Theodosia grabbed the scone order that Drayton had packaged in one of their indigo blue bags and walked Sybil to the door. "Sybil, have you ever heard of a man by the name of Henry Curtis?"

"Henry? Sure."

Sybil's breezy answer caught Theodosia by surprise. "Seriously?"

"Henry works at the Heritage Society, same as me. Only he's doing an internship downstairs in the conservation department."

"I had no idea."

"You probably even met Henry the other night. The guy with the green paint on his face and . . ." Sybil grinned as she tapped two fingers against her neck.

"The bolt in his neck," Theodosia said. "Henry Curtis was Frankenstein?"

"Still is Frankenstein," Sybil said. "Kinda cool, huh?"

Theodosia didn't think it was all that cool, but she sure wanted to know more.

"Do you know if Henry Curtis ever had a close relationship with Willow French?"

"Not that I know of," Sybil said. She turned an inquisitive gaze on Theodosia and studied her for a few moments. Then the proverbial light bulb seemed to pop on over her head. "Say, you're onto something, aren't you?"

"Just trying to piece a few things together," Theodosia said, weighing her words carefully. "Before I draw any conclusions."

But Sybil wasn't fooled. "Claire told me you were a darned good amateur detective. Now I believe it. So . . ." Her eyes fairly sparkled. "Do you want me to ask Henry about Willow?" She made an exaggerated face. "Or should I be afraid of him? Maybe . . . maybe if I was super careful I could do a little digging?"

"Please don't," Theodosia said. *Since that's exactly what I intend to do.*

When only two tables of guests lingered and the time was nearing eleven fifteen, Theodosia decided she'd better hurry up and start decorating for her Sherlock Holmes Tea. She began with pristine white tablecloths on all the tables, then added tweed table runners. From there things began to get noir and whimsical with the addition of a few old-fashioned pipes, some oversize magnifying glasses, stacks of mystery books, pairs of handcuffs, rings of keys, and several toy pistols. She'd laser printed vintage maps of London from her computer and now set those out as place mats.

"Your tables look adorable," Miss Dimple said and chuckled. "I was baffled as to what decor would work for a

Sherlock Holmes Tea, but now I can see your creativity won out. Bravo, Theodosia."

Drayton also gave his nod of approval. "Highly amusing," he said. "Very Sherlockian. And what china have you picked out?"

"I was thinking of using our Royal Crown Derby Balmoral pattern," Theodosia said. She always liked to match a china pattern to an event. It made it even more special for her guests.

"I'd say Royal Crown Derby strikes the perfect note," Drayton said.

As Theodosia and Miss Dimple put out plates, cups, saucers, and silverware, a large cardboard box arrived via messenger.

"This delivery," Drayton said, staring at a box that took up most of his counter space. "I'm guessing it somehow pertains to our tea party?"

"You didn't think you'd get away scot-free without wearing a costume, did you?" Theodosia asked.

Drayton just shook his head as he continued brewing pots of tea.

But Miss Dimple and Haley were suddenly all over the carton. Carrying it to one of the tables, opening the lid, digging right in.

"Costumes from the Big Top Costume Company," Haley declared. "Those guys always come through with the goods whenever we have a crazy idea for a themed tea."

Miss Dimple pulled out a purple velvet frock coat, squealed with delight, and promptly handed it to Theodosia. "This has a lace collar and everything, really perfect for you." She dug in again and came up with a white ruffled maid's cap and matching apron. "How very Edwardian," she said. "I do believe this outfit suits me."

But, suddenly, Haley wasn't so sure about the box full of costumes. "This stuff smells kinda funny," she said.

"That's just the dry cleaning fluid," Theodosia said.

Haley took another sniff. "I suppose that's good. At least it means the clothes have been cleaned." She hunted around inside the box and let out a whoop as she pulled out a tweed hat. "Hoo, Drayton. This has *your* name on it. You get to wear the crazy backward hat."

Drayton came over and grabbed the hat out of Haley's hands. "Bite your tongue, miss. That's not a backward hat; it's a deerstalker hat. Traditionally British and generally constructed out of houndstooth, herringbone, or twill."

"There's a matching cape for you, too," Miss Dimple said.

Drayton popped the hat onto his head and draped the cape around his shoulders. Then he struck a pose. "What's the verdict? Do I look like a serious investigator who'd prowl the back alleys of London?"

Haley studied him. "More like you belong on the BBC."

But there were still a few things that needed to be done.

Theodosia cut out black paper footprints and glued them to the floor, starting at the front door and leading into the tea shop.

"How fun," Miss Dimple said. "Like a suspect Sherlock Holmes and Watson would have to tail."

"How are the cats, Miss Dimple?" Haley asked. Miss Dimple had two cats, Samson and Delilah, that she doted on.

"Still as lively and rascally as ever," Miss Dimple said.

"I've been feeding a little stray cat who's been hanging around our back alley," Haley said.

"Bless you for being so kindhearted. The poor little thing must not have a forever home," Miss Dimple said.

"I might have seen your cat yesterday," Theodosia said. "Outside in our alley."

"Kind of a mottled orange-and-brown cat?" Haley said.

"That's the one," Theodosia said.

"I think he's wild," Haley said.

"Feral," Drayton said.

Haley nodded. "Yeah, that, too."

12

❧

Amazingly, most of their luncheon guests had taken the
Sherlock Holmes theme directly to heart. Case in point,
Theodosia had never seen so many tweed suits, ruffled
blouses, velvet hats, and jeweled stickpins in her life.

"I know I'm probably half-Edwardian and half–*Downton
Abbey*," her friend Nancy Graham confessed to her, "but I
sure had fun getting dressed this morning."

"And you look terrific," Theodosia said. "Very British
and upper-crust."

She checked off each guest's name from her list as they
arrived—Jill, Kristen, Judi, Linda, and Jessica—and led
them to seats at the various tables.

"Am I in the right place?" one white-haired lady asked
as she and her friend walked in. "Teddy Vickers at the
Featherbed House B and B made the reservation for us
so . . ." She stopped dead and gave a speculative glance
around. Then a smile lit her face. "This place is a-*dor*-

able," she purred. "Almost as if a genuine tea shop had been airlifted in from the Lake District of England."

"Thank you," Theodosia said. "Now if you'll just come this way . . ."

Both old and new friends had shown up today. Brooke Carter Crockett, from Hearts Desire Jewelers down the block, and Delaine Dish, the mercurial owner of Cotton Duck Boutique. Delaine brought along her niece Bettina, who'd recently graduated from FIT, the Fashion Institute of Technology, in New York.

And, finally, Claire Waltho from the Heritage Society arrived with her would-be donor, Drucilla Heyward. Once Claire and Miss Drucilla were seated, Drayton stepped out from behind the counter to personally pour cups of tea for them and renew old acquaintances. Needless to say, Miss Drucilla was thrilled.

"We've almost got a full house," Theodosia whispered as she brushed past Drayton.

"It's looking good," he said. "Though everyone's buzzing about the murder."

"Hard to keep something like that quiet," Theodosia said.

"The world's spinning faster," Drayton said. "Do you think that's a good thing?"

"I'm not sure."

When everyone was seated, when cups of steaming tea had been poured and lumps of sugar, milk, or lemon had been duly added to those cups, Theodosia drew a deep breath and stepped to the center of the room. This was what she lived for, but it scared her a little bit, too. Kind of like the tingle she got from investigating a murder.

"Welcome, dear friends," Theodosia said, addressing the eager, upturned faces of her guests as they gazed in her direction. "In honor of Halloween, we're saluting Sherlock Holmes, one of the literary world's experts when it comes to mystery, murder, and mayhem. For your first course we'll be serving *Hound of the Baskervilles* cream scones with clotted cream and blackberry jam. Following that, your assortment of tea sandwiches will include smoked salmon with crème fraîche, ham with mustard, and roasted red pepper with cream cheese. Your entrée will be our very own Baker Street meat pie, and for dessert we're offering a sticky date and toffee pudding that we call Moriarty's Bomb."

As peals of delighted applause rang out, a dashing-looking Drayton slipped in to take his place beside Theodosia.

"For our featured tea today, we've filled your cups with Lapsang souchong," Drayton said. "This rich, smoky tea is reminiscent of the aroma of briar pipes and fires burning in an English hearth. And for your second tea, we'll be serving our very own Sherlock Holmes blend, a flavorful black tea with hints of orange, ginger, cloves, and cardamom."

There were murmurs of "wonderful" and "how delightful."

Drayton touched a finger to his hat in a final salute and said, "As our esteemed Mr. Holmes was fond of saying, 'Life is full of whimsical happenings.'"

"And this happens to be one of them," Theodosia said. "So please . . . enjoy!"

And enjoy they did. The guests ate, drank cup after cup of tea, oohed and aahed over each course as it was brought out, and seemed to have a genuinely rousing good time.

Theodosia couldn't have been happier. She loved serving tea and she loved entertaining. And having the Indigo Tea Shop was, for her, the perfect culmination of both those passions. When she was a little girl, she'd enjoyed tea parties with her friends as well as with her stuffed animals. Now she got to live out her dream for real. What could be better?

Grabbing a fresh pot of tea, Theodosia made the rounds again. It was important to check on her guests, make sure everything was perfect, that every course was being thoroughly enjoyed. As she passed behind Claire, she overheard her telling Miss Drucilla about her stint as curator at the Norton Simon Museum in Pasadena. And how she found the pace and ambiance at the Heritage Society—and the city of Charleston itself—infinitely more appealing.

That makes two of us, Theodosia thought. She was a Charleston girl through and through. And if that meant heeding to old-fashioned manners and values, of holding family and friends dear in a world that sometimes seemed a little untethered, then so much the better.

"Excuse me."

One of her guests was asking a question.

Theodosia shook her head, bringing herself back to the here and now. "Yes?"

"I was here for the Garden Club Tea last month when you served everything on those spectacular three-tiered trays."

"Yes, we often do that," Theodosia said.

"I was wondering if there's a particular order. I mean, how do you decide what goes on which level?"

"Here's the thing," Theodosia said. "I always heed tradition and put the scones on the top tier."

"What do you mean?"

"Back in the seventeen hundreds, when tea parties first became popular, the top tier was the only tier that would accommodate a warming dome—so that's where the fresh-baked scones were placed."

The woman smiled. "And the sandwiches and desserts were arranged below them."

"Exactly."

Back at the counter, grabbing a pot of black tea, Theodosia said, "Miss Drucilla seems like a lovely person."

"Oh, she's a peach," Drayton said. "Cut from a strong

Southern mold and, even at eighty-four, is still sharp as a tack."

"And she lives all alone in that big house over on Legare?"

"Ever since her husband, Everett, died nine years ago," Drayton said.

"She has no other relatives?"

"There's a nephew somewhere, but the less said about him the better."

"Gotcha," Theodosia said. "Oh dear, now Delaine's waving at me. Duty calls."

Delaine reached out and grabbed Theodosia's arm as she approached her table.

"Theo, we absolutely must talk."

Theodosia stared into Delaine's heart-shaped face. She was a truly beautiful woman. Dark hair swept into a low chignon. Long lashes, full cupid lips, eyes that glittered. Too bad Delaine was so intense and . . . yes, she could admit it . . . a little ditzy.

"You mean, talk about Denim and Diamonds?" Theodosia asked.

Now Delaine gave a slow wink. "That and my current love life." She adjusted the handbag that sat on the floor next to her. A bag that was roughly the size of a Galápagos tortoise.

"You're still dating Tod Slawson, aren't you?" Theodosia thought he was still her boyfriend du jour.

"On again, off again, dear." Delaine cocked her head at a coquettish angle and said, "You know how it goes."

"Actually, I don't," Theodosia said. But she was well aware that Delaine was absurdly high-maintenance. Delaine demanded (and usually received) complete and constant attention from the men she dated, accompanied by lavish (and outlandish) praise and adulation. If a man was unable to fulfill Delaine's every wish, whim, desire, and demand, or if he stumbled in pursuit of her, she'd kick him to the curb without a second thought. Then she'd be back on the prowl for what she termed "a new gentleman friend."

Yes, Delaine might blush and simper and revert to old-fashioned tricks, but when it came to men she was a great white shark.

"Do you still want me to serve tea and scones at your Denim and Diamonds Fashion Show?" Theodosia asked.

"I think so," Delaine said. "If it's not too much trouble."

"No, I can manage."

"You're a doll," Delaine said, squeezing her arm again. "I'll call you later with a head count. Oh, and isn't that a sad situation with poor Willow French? I know her mother, of course. When she comes into town, she's one of my best customers."

"I didn't know that," Theodosia said. But she should have. Delaine seemed to have connections with *everybody*.

Two hours later, it was pretty much over. Miss Drucilla Heyward had been the first to murmur a genteel thank-you and take off, with half the guests following a few minutes behind her. Now, only a handful of guests remained, a few sitting around finishing their tea, others shopping for tea accoutrements.

"This was absolutely perfect," Claire said to Theodosia on her way out.

"I hope you had a good meeting with your potential donor," Theodosia said.

"I think so." Then Claire glanced around and said in a quiet voice, "After we talked yesterday, I remembered something. About Willow, that is. And I thought it might be important."

Theodosia was suddenly on high alert. "What is it, Claire?"

"I think Willow might have bought a house. Or was in the process of buying one. While she was arranging her books for the signing Sunday night, I heard her talking on the phone, and I think she was chatting with her real estate agent. It *sounded* like she was, anyway, because she was asking about assessed value."

"Do you know if her home purchase had already gone through?" Theodosia asked. A new home would definitely explain the packing boxes and general disarray they'd found at Willow's apartment.

"I don't know for sure that she *was* buying a house," Claire said. "But I'm sure her fiancé would know."

"Thank you, I'll ask him."

Theodosia said goodbye to a few more of her departing guests, rang up purchases on tins of tea and beeswax candles, and poured a final cup of tea for two women who were lingering. Then she walked up to the counter and said, "Claire Waltho thinks that Willow was in the process of buying a house."

"What's that?" Drayton looked up. He'd been busy sorting through his tea tins.

Theodosia raised her voice a notch. "I said Willow was buying a house."

This time Drayton frowned. "Are you sure? First I've heard of such thing."

"I know. It's strange that Timothy never mentioned it to us."

"Maybe Timothy didn't know," Drayton said. "Maybe Willow was in the process of buying a house and wanted to surprise him. You know, demonstrate to Timothy how well she was doing, how financially independent she'd become."

"I'm going to call and ask him."

Drayton went back to his tea tins. "Couldn't hurt."

But when Theodosia finally got Timothy on the phone, he wasn't just surprised; he was gobsmacked.

After a long, drawn-out silence, Timothy said, "House? What house?"

"Claire Waltho mentioned it when she was in for lunch

today. She said she'd overheard Willow talking to a real estate agent."

Timothy was clearly rattled, almost sputtering. "This . . . this is the first I've heard anything about a house."

"You know nothing about it?" Theodosia was caught off guard, too. Timothy had practically doted on Willow's every move. For him not to know about this was . . . strange.

"Robert Vardell never mentioned it, either. You'd think he would have said *some*thing."

"Maybe Willow wanted it to be a surprise? A wedding gift to him?" Theodosia said. She was fumbling her words, her nerves ratcheting upward as she wondered why this had been such a tightly held secret.

"A house seems like an awfully large wedding gift," Timothy said.

"Do you know . . . did Willow have money?"

"She had an inheritance, yes."

"A lot?"

"Let's just say it was sizable," Timothy said. "But Vardell supposedly has a good job as well. I don't think money was ever an issue between the two of them."

"I'm going to call my Realtor and try to . . ."

"Do that," Timothy said, in an almost pleading tone. "Please see what you can find out."

"On a related matter," Theodosia said, "do you know if Willow had a relationship with someone named Henry Curtis?"

"I've never heard of that person," Timothy said.

"Well, surprise, surprise, but Mr. Curtis supposedly works in your conservation department."

"Ah, he must be one of the new interns."

"I believe he is."

"Well, I haven't met him yet, but you're saying that Willow knew him?"

"I *think* she did," Theodosia hedged. "So there's another person I have to interview."

"When do you think you can do that?" Timothy sounded anxious and fidgety.

Theodosia thought for a minute. "Probably tonight."

"All right, thank you."

Then, because Theodosia had a few minutes to spare, and Timothy had been so upset by her mention of a house, she called Maggie Twining at Sutter Realty. Maggie was the Realtor who'd helped her buy her cottage a couple of years ago.

After they exchanged greetings, Theodosia said, "Maggie, is there some way you can check to see if a house has been recently purchased by someone?"

"Depends on who that someone is," Maggie said.

"It's Willow French. She's that poor woman who was murdered the other night at the . . ."

"Haunted house!" Maggie exclaimed. "I read about it in the newspaper." She paused, obviously curious. "You're, um, looking into *that*?"

Her unspoken question hung in the air between them. *Why are you interested?*

"If you read the article, then you know that a police detective was shot when he was sent to Willow's apartment to investigate," Theodosia said.

"Okay."

"Well, it just so happens that it was *my* police detective. My boyfriend, Pete Riley."

Maggie let out a shriek. "Theodosia, no!"

"I'm afraid so. In fact, he's still in the hospital."

"Is he okay? Is he going to recover?"

"I think so, yes."

"Thank goodness for that," Maggie said. Then she snapped back into business mode. "Okay, I can definitely check that name for you. Willow French, you said? Any idea where the property is located?"

"None at all."

"It'll probably take some digging on my part—and I've

got a showing over in Mount Pleasant at two o'clock. A high-end custom-built home with a saltwater pool and Caribbean pine floors. So I might not get back to you until later today."

"That's okay, Maggie. Thanks so much for your help."

"Talk to you later, Theo. Best wishes for your fella's quick recovery."

13

After such a lovely, successful luncheon, Bill Glass was the last person Theodosia wanted to see. But there he was, slithering into her tea room, two cameras slung around his neck, looking like the disreputable quasi-journalist-publisher that he was.

"Hey." Glass stepped up to the counter and gazed at her with a hopeful look. "That was some murder Sunday night, huh?"

"Mmn," Theodosia said. Perhaps if she was completely noncommittal Glass would go away?

No such luck.

"They shoulda called it the House of Horrors," Glass said. He slung his cameras onto the counter and favored her with a cheesy smile. Glass was mid-forties, a little stocky, dark haired, and had the sharp look of a used-car salesman. "I was all the way over in Goose Creek when I heard the call on my police scanner."

"Aren't those things illegal?" Theodosia asked. Bill

Glass was the owner and publisher of a tabloid called *Shooting Star*. He was always on the prowl for the latest juicy gossip or gritty story. For some unknown reason, he liked her. Enjoyed dropping by the tea shop.

Probably just to bug me.

"Whatever." Glass offered a shrug to indicate he was officially bored. "Anyhoo, by the time I got there the police had already cut the chick down."

"Please leave," Theodosia said.

Glass gaped at her. Theodosia had always been nice to him. Well, maybe not nice, but polite.

"What did you say?"

"If you're going to talk that way, if you're going to be disrespectful," Theodosia said, "then I don't want you in here."

"Talk what way?" Glass pretended to not understand.

"In a crude and insensitive manner."

Glass jerked his head back as he gestured wildly with his hands. "But I always talk that way."

"I realize that." Theodosia grabbed a lone cream scone that was sitting on a plate and looking a little dry. She dropped it into a bag and thrust it into Glass's hands. "Here you go."

Bill Glass frowned. "What's this?"

"Take-out order."

"Can I at least have a cup of tea to go with it?"

Drayton had overheard most of their conversation and was already on top of things, pouring tea into a paper take-out cup, briskly snapping on a lid. "Tea to go," he said. "Do enjoy."

Glass frowned. He knew he was getting the bum's rush and wasn't sure how to handle it.

"That's all I get?" he asked.

Theodosia smiled sweetly. "I'm afraid that's all we've got. Teatime's over."

"Well . . . okay."

"He's an awful pain, isn't he?" Drayton asked, once a dejected-looking Glass was out the door.

"He makes it difficult to remain civil," Theodosia agreed.

"And Glass always looks so disreputable. Like he should be moonlighting as a bouncer at the Hotsy Totsy Club."

"Drayton!" Theodosia said. Then she laughed.

Drayton's eyelids dropped a centimeter. "See? You agree."

"I suppose I do." Then, curious, "*Is* there a Hotsy Totsy Club?"

"There probably is somewhere," Drayton said, getting busy again.

Theodosia spent the next twenty minutes gathering up props from all the tables, then clearing dishes. When that was done, she went into her office and plopped down at her desk.

Theodosia's office looked like the Mad Hatter's tea party had exploded. There were teacups and saucers packed in Bubble Wrap, boxes of tea samples from a hundred different companies (oh, the choices!), books about tea, tea strainers, teapot trivets, and a towering stack of glitzy felt hats. No, she wasn't a pack rat—Christmas was just around the corner and, like a good little Girl Scout, she wanted to Be Prepared.

Shoving a stack of tea catalogs out of the way, she picked up her phone and called Riley.

"Hey there," Theodosia said when she finally had him on the line. "How about I come over for a quick visit?"

"Not today," he said.

Theodosia could barely keep the disappointment out of her voice. "Why not?"

"Ah, these hospital people have got me signed up for some kind of occupational therapy thing. I have to learn how to grip balls, stretch rubber bands, and shoot clay pigeons."

"Not clay pigeons," Theodosia said, laughing. She could tell that Riley was feeling a whole lot better. What a difference a day makes.

"Okay, not that," Riley said. "But this therapy thing is supposed to take a while. I'm told the hospital therapists aren't going to let me rest on my laurels. Or anything else."

"That's a good thing, right?"

"If you say so."

"What if I stop by tonight?" Theodosia said. "You know, bring flowers, scones, a six pack of beer?"

"Already got that covered. Some of the guys are planning to drop by."

Theodosia felt a flash of disappointment. She wouldn't be seeing him then. On the other hand, she'd have a free evening to continue her investigation.

"So you don't want me to interrupt your guy thing with your brothers in blue?" she asked.

"Well . . ."

"No problem, I'm sure I can figure out something else to do."

"Okay, talk to you later. Kisses," he said.

"Kisses," she said back.

Theodosia was packing up the costumes when Maggie Twining called.

"Your young lady Willow French did in fact buy a house," Maggie said.

"Interesting," Theodosia said. "Can you give me the address?"

"Sure. It's located at 17 Lamboll Street."

"That's a pretty fancy address."

"It's a pretty fancy house," Maggie said. "Four bedrooms, three baths, with a sizable backyard and gardens. It didn't even hit the MLS; it was a pocket listing."

"Were you able to look at financing details as well?"

"Yes, and I'm rather impressed. Your Ms. French paid cash for her property."

"She paid . . . Wait, seriously?"

"In fact, her cash offer trumped two other offers. Of course, those had contingencies. One had a ninety-day close; the other was an FHA."

"I'm stunned," Theodosia said. "So now Willow owns a house? Or her estate does?"

"In the eyes of the law," Maggie said, "a young man by the name of Robert Vardell technically owns that house."

"Oh my gosh," Theodosia said. "Her fiancé. So you're saying he owns it free and clear? Why is that?"

"Because his name is on the title."

"It doesn't have to go through probate?" Theodosia asked.

"Not if his name is on the title."

"This tale keeps getting stranger and stranger."

"Let me know how it all turns out," Maggie said.

Theodosia wasted no time in telling Drayton about this unusual new development.

Drayton was shocked. "Willow paid cash? For a *home*?"

"An expensive home in the Historic District. I had Maggie Twining check the records."

"Maggie should know; she's the expert." Drayton paused. "Well, that certainly explains all the moving and packing that was going on at Willow's apartment."

"Yes, but the really big news is that Willow put Robert Vardell's name on the property title."

Drayton gave a slow, reptilian blink. "You mean with Willow dead . . . Vardell is the owner?"

Theodosia nodded. "Sole owner."

Drayton looked stricken. "Dear Lord, you don't think Vardell might have . . . ? No, he couldn't, could he? They were supposed to be . . . married."

"I don't know what to think, Drayton."

"We have to tell Timothy about this."

"And probably the police," Theodosia said.

As the front door creaked open, they both turned to find Detective Tidwell ambling in. He glanced about nonchalantly, then walked to a table as if he didn't have a care in the world.

"Speak of the devil," Drayton said in a low voice. "Here's your chance."

"Do you think Tidwell is psychic or does he just have the ability to materialize out of thin air?"

"You ask me," Drayton whispered, "I think he likes you."

"Oh no," Theodosia said. "He's my nemesis." She wasn't in the mood for jokes, and she certainly didn't feel like having a verbal joust with Detective Tidwell. She was still digesting the news about the newly purchased, paid-in-full house.

Tidwell had just settled his bulk into a captain's chair when Theodosia arrived at his table.

"Tea?" she asked.

"Tea would be lovely," Tidwell said. "And perhaps a sweet to go along?"

"That goes without saying," Theodosia said.

She went into the kitchen, rummaged around, finally found the absolute last scone, then placed it on a plate along with a small container of strawberry jam and one of Devonshire cream. When she returned, Drayton was pouring Tidwell a cup of tea.

"This is Rose White from Elmwood Inn," Drayton said. "It's a white tea with a rather refreshing floral flavor. I daresay you don't need to add any extra sweetener."

"I can't imagine a lump or two of sugar would hurt," Tidwell said.

Drayton's brows arched as he retreated.

Theodosia placed Tidwell's scone in front of him.

"So," she said.

Tidwell stirred in a single lump of sugar, then a second one, tasted the tea, and declared, "Perfect."

"I'm glad it's to your liking."

"I understand Robert Vardell told you about the missing diamonds," Tidwell said.

"The Hibiscus Diamonds, yes."

"He and Timothy seem to think they were the primary motive for the murder and subsequent theft."

"You see it differently?" Theodosia asked.

"Not necessarily," Tidwell said. He picked up his butter knife, cut his scone in half with surgical precision, then applied generous dollops of jam and Devonshire cream.

Theodosia knew they were playing cat and mouse and it tired her. So she decided to cut to the chase.

"I've come across some information that might interest you," she said.

Tidwell glowered at her from beneath his bushy beetle brows as he chewed his scone. "You promised me you weren't going to snoop."

"I made no such promise. Besides, I didn't snoop. I had my real estate agent do the legwork for me."

Tidwell sighed. "A mere technicality."

"Do you want to know what I found out?"

"Only if it pertains to the investigation."

"It might."

Tidwell continued to nibble his scone.

"Here's the thing," Theodosia said. "It turns out that Willow French bought and paid for a rather fancy home at 17 Lamboll Street and put Robert Vardell's name on the deed."

Tidwell stared at her. He didn't seem all that shocked.

"So that begs the question . . ."

"Yes?" Tidwell said.

"Could Vardell have murdered his own fiancée?" Those words were so distasteful that Theodosia cringed as she spoke them.

"I suppose it's not out of the realm of possibility."

"But what do *you* think?" Theodosia asked.

"At this time we're pursuing several leads while we investigate a number of possibilities."

"That's a stock-in-trade police answer, and you haven't even come close to addressing my question. In fact, you haven't told me *any*thing at all," said a frustrated Theodosia.

"Which is as it should be," Tidwell said.

"You have to tell me *something*. Like . . . what did your crime scene investigators find? Did they determine how Willow was hanged?"

"With rope," Tidwell said.

"What kind?"

"Nylon. The sort you'd use on a boat. I suppose you'd call it marine line."

"Did you find any fingerprints?" Theodosia asked.

"None so far."

"What about tracks in the attic? There might have been dusty floorboards . . ."

Tidwell shook his head. "Nothing."

"There's something else you should know," Theodosia said.

"Pray tell what is that, Miss Browning?"

"Ellis Bouchard, the man who's been trying to wrest control of the Bouchard Mansion back from the Heritage Society, is going broke. His apartment buildings are apparently all in receivership."

"And this is my problem—why?" Tidwell asked.

"Because Ellis Bouchard has a motive. He's desperate for money."

"And you think this elderly gentleman is a cold-blooded killer?"

"He could be," Theodosia said.

"At this point anyone could be."

Theodosia stared at Tidwell, wishing he wasn't so obstinate, wondering if she should tell him about the sort-of love note from Frankenstein that she'd discovered in Willow's apartment. And decided not to. It was something she wanted to look into herself. Without police interference. Without Tidwell questioning her ability and making her feel silly and incompetent.

Instead Theodosia said, "Is it true that most murder cases are solved within twenty-four hours? That if the investigations run longer, then the odds of solving them are practically nil?"

"Where did you hear that?" Tidwell asked.

"From you?"

Tidwell shook his head.

"Okay then," Theodosia said. "Maybe on TV? An episode of *Law & Order*?"

"Television," Tidwell snorted.

Once the very maddening Detective Tidwell had left the tea shop, Theodosia got on the phone with Timothy Neville. She quickly told him about her conversation with Maggie Twining and then broke the rather surprising news that Robert Vardell was now the proud owner of a fancy and rather expensive new home in the Historic District.

Timothy digested her words for a few moments, then said, "I hear the doubt and worry in your voice. And I can understand why. But I have to tell you that Robert is absolutely heartbroken. I just spoke with him no more than an hour ago and he was utterly bereft. Willow meant the world to him."

"And he told you about the house?"

"Yes, he did."

Theodosia didn't think she was going to change Timothy's mind armed with just one single fact. She needed a lot more. She needed concrete evidence of wrongdoing. And if it was there, she vowed to get it.

"Okay then. I just wanted you to know the situation," Theodosia said.

"I sincerely appreciate your efforts. I really do," Timothy said.

"Well, I'm not done yet. I still plan to interview Henry Curtis the intern. Tonight, over at the haunted house."

"Good luck with that. Oh, and one more thing," Timothy said. "Willow's visitation will be held tomorrow night at Doake and Wilson Funeral Home, with a graveside service to be held at Magnolia Cemetery the following morning."

"Okay. I . . . okay." Theodosia hung up as a wave of overwhelming sadness washed across her.

14

❦

The haunted house was going gangbusters tonight. Edgar Allan Poe was glad-handing guests on the front lawn; Count Dracula was taking tickets. There was also a new feature—a chorus of moaning pirates. Theodosia wasn't sure how the pirates tied in except that they were passing out flyers for the Ghosts and Goblins Parade that was to be held Friday night. Just a little bit of cross-promotion, she surmised.

Claire Waltho was there, too. When she saw Theodosia hovering at the front door, she whispered something to Dracula and—presto—Theodosia was whisked inside. She mouthed a thank-you to Claire as she was suddenly pulled into the fray and found herself rubbing shoulders with at least a hundred eager guests.

Theodosia wandered through the ground floor of the old mansion. A magician who was all duded up in tie and tails was performing sleight-of-hand tricks. A woman wearing a purple paisley turban and shawl was reading palms. There was no guest author signing books in the parlor tonight, but there was a young sketch artist doing quick cartoon portraits of anyone who wanted to pose for a few minutes.

Going from room to room, studying the people as well as her surroundings, Theodosia kept an eye out for Henry Curtis as Frankenstein.

At the rear of the old house, a space had been transformed into a dusty sitting room where Miss Havisham from *Great Expectations* was holding court. As Theodosia ducked through a doorway that was dripping with cobwebs (all fake, but looking convincingly real), she ran smack-dab into Ellis Bouchard.

He gave a tentative smile, as if he recognized her, then the smile slipped from his face. Yes, he'd definitely placed her. From yesterday morning when he stormed into her tea shop, made a scene, and then was asked to leave.

"Hello, Mr. Bouchard," Theodosia said, buttonholing him before he had a chance to get away.

Bouchard stopped and nodded at her. Maybe he was embarrassed? Or maybe something else was going on?

"How interesting to find you here," Theodosia said.

"Not really," Bouchard said. "I still haven't given up hope of recovering this property."

"You seem to have serious issues with your properties," Theodosia said.

Bouchard's face darkened. "Excuse me?"

"I understand you've had some financial problems."

"Not really. Besides, even if I did, what business is it of yours?" Bouchard said.

"None at all. Except when it intersects with the welfare of people I care about."

"I have no idea what you're talking about." And this time Bouchard really did push his way past her and disappear into the crowd.

Theodosia stood there for a moment, feeling unsettled. Bouchard was rude and abrasive, that's for sure. But was he a killer? A cold-blooded murderer? She didn't have any evidence to that effect, just the knowledge that he was financially desperate. But that alone was enough to keep him on her suspect list.

Turning, heading back through the house, Theodosia walked past a darkened solarium where actors in plant costumes—she thought they might represent hemlock and deadly nightshade—waved their spiny leaves as they tried to caress the guests.

Kind of cute. I guess.

Still, that wasn't the reason Theodosia had come here tonight. Her real mission was to confront Henry Curtis and ask him about his relationship with Willow. She hadn't seen Frankenstein walking around tonight, so maybe Henry was wearing a different costume?

Theodosia found a stairway that was decorated with skulls and bats and headed up to the second floor. Here she found Bill Sikes from *Oliver Twist* as well as Captain Ahab from *Moby-Dick*.

Interesting. But what about the third floor? The floor where Willow met her untimely death?

Theodosia tried to look nonchalant as she hunted around for a way up to the third floor. She peeked in closets and around corners until, finally, she found it. A narrow flight of stairs that was tucked behind a carved coromandel screen.

She grabbed the railing and, feeling some serious trepidation, headed upstairs.

Ten, eleven, twelve . . .

Theodosia counted each step, wondering if poor Willow had counted steps as she was being forced up this staircase at gunpoint.

Steeling herself, Theodosia reached the third floor. And was it ever awful. A large, mostly open room with dirty wallpaper peeling off plaster lath boards. Dust motes twirled in the dim light, and the scents of mold and rodents rose up in a punishing stink. Trying to stifle her gag reflex, Theodosia would have turned around right then and there, except for the faint glow from a row of small overhead lights. Those beckoning beams prompted her to continue moving forward.

And then she saw it directly in front of her. The tower room. An architectural blip that hung out from the third-floor footprint. It was a small octagonal-shaped room with a single window boarded over with plywood. What a terrible visual reminder of the tragedy that had taken place here just two nights ago!

Theodosia forced herself to think. To try to imagine herself having the mindset of a killer. So . . . what had been his play? The killer had lured Willow all the way up here, probably holding a gun to her head. He'd grabbed the diamonds, draped a noose around Willow's neck, and then—crash!—shoved her out the window.

A key question blipped deep inside Theodosia's brain.

How did the killer escape?

Had he gone back downstairs and mingled with the crowd? Just blended in like one of the locals? Had he pretended to be shocked and outraged at the sight of her poor body dangling there? Or had he found another way out?

Theodosia tiptoed around, nervous but determined to explore this terrible place that reeked of death. There were other windows, yes. But they were small and dirt streaked, and looked as if they'd been stuck shut for decades. The house was so old and decrepit that there didn't seem to be any outside fire escape.

Maybe some kind of exit on the second floor?

Theodosia walked back downstairs and looked around, opened doors, snuck around corners. But for all her careful and methodical searching she found no secret back staircase. Tired, feeling a little out of sorts, Theodosia threaded her way down the center hallway.

Which is when she ran smack-dab into Frankenstein.

"Henry!" Theodosia cried. He'd popped up so unexpectedly, he'd startled her. "Henry Curtis."

Henry stared at her, a questioning look on his green painted face. "You can tell who I am behind all this makeup?"

"I know who you are *because* of your makeup," Theodosia said.

"Whuh?"

"You work as an intern at the Heritage Society. And you were a friend of Willow French."

Henry continued to stare at her.

"What I want to know is—how good of a friend were you?" Theodosia asked.

"Who . . . who are you?" Henry asked. "Why are you asking me questions?"

"I'm looking into Willow French's death. As a favor to Timothy Neville. You remember Timothy, your boss?"

A kind of recognition dawned on Henry's face. "Okay, I *have* heard about you. You're that tea lady who was skulking around the Heritage Society yesterday, interviewing everybody."

"I was also here Sunday night when Willow was tossed out an upstairs window and murdered."

"Well, I didn't do it!" Henry sputtered.

"But you had a relationship with Willow," Theodosia pressed. "You two were friends, maybe more than friends."

"Why would you think that?"

"Because I found the note you sent her. 'My dear Willow,'" Theodosia quoted. "'I will never forget you.'"

Henry's eyes bulged, and his face seemed to turn hot pink even under all his green makeup. "That note was between me and her. It was supposed to be *private*."

"I think you loved Willow. Which meant you were deeply upset when she got engaged to another man. So upset that maybe you did something you now regret horribly?" Theodosia threw the full force of her anger at him, biting off each word. She didn't know if anything she said was true, but she was taking a shot, seeing how Henry would react.

"No, never! I cared for Willow."

"You were in *love* with her."

Henry shook his head. "It wasn't like that. I was more like . . . infatuated with her. Willow was nice to me, encouraged me to not be afraid, to develop my talents and spread my wings at the Heritage Society. We used to joke around with each other, do pretend flirting." Now Henry's face took on a sorrowful, almost pleading expression. "You have to believe me, I would never hurt Willow! I wish I knew who did! It's been tearing me up!"

"Listen to me," Theodosia said. "I am going to turn your note over to the Charleston Police Department. To their chief investigator. They are going to contact you, and if you were involved in Willow's death, in any way, they will come after you hammer and tongs."

"But I didn't . . . I couldn't," Henry said. "Really, we were just good friends!"

He was still protesting as Theodosia spun on her heel and walked away from him.

Back downstairs, Theodosia ran into Elisha Summers, one of the curators she'd interviewed yesterday.

"Elisha, what did this place look like when it was empty, before you guys started decorating?" Theodosia asked.

Elisha made a face. "It was awful. Plasterboard walls with half the plaster falling off. No lights. Broken floorboards. Like the place should have been condemned."

"But it seems almost habitable now," Theodosia said, looking around. "At least the first and second floors do."

"That's because we made a ton of repairs," Elisha said.

"You and the other people from the Heritage Society did the work?"

"No way," Elisha said. "Most of us can barely handle a nail gun. No, we hired outside help. There's a local guy named Jack Schindler who did a lot of the carpentry and plastering. I think he's kind of a painter, too. But not just plain old house painting, restoration-type work."

"You know where I can find him?"

"Sure. For one thing Schindler's got a website. Oh, and I know for a fact that he's working at a local church doing some mural restoration. Maybe you could find him there."

"Do you know which church?"

"I think it's St. Mary's," Elisha said.

"Over on Hassell Street."

Elisha nodded. "That's the one."

When Theodosia returned home, Earl Grey was waiting for her.

"You're all geared up for a run, aren't you?" she said to her dog. Earl Grey had a dog walker and doggy day care person, a lovely woman named Mrs. Barry, who stopped by afternoons. She was a retired schoolteacher who was good for a couple of spins around the block. But she was no match for a long-legged, raring-to-go guy like Earl Grey.

Theodosia hurriedly changed into yoga pants, sweatshirt, and running shoes. Then they were out the door and bounding down the alley.

It was another cool night with a scatter of stars glimmering in a blue-black sky, a moon peeking out from behind a few wispy clouds. As they jogged down Ladson Street, Theodosia saw that many of the homes were already decorated for Halloween. Witches peeked out of windows, fat orange pumpkins squatted on porches and front stoops, and a few ghosts fluttered from bare tree branches.

Theodosia and Earl Grey breezed along for a few blocks, turned onto Meeting Street, and then slowed down as they approached St. Michael's Alley. This was one of Charleston's many hidden lanes and one of Theodosia's favorites. Most of these hidden alleys weren't found on any tourist map and were so narrow and twisty you'd hardly think twice about venturing in and exploring them.

But you'd be remiss. Because down Longitude Lane, Philadelphia Alley, and this one, St. Michael's Alley, was where history pulsed like the beating heart of old Charles Towne.

Theodosia loved the hush and quiet grandeur of St. Michael's Alley. From the slate cobblestones to the tall red-brick walls and swirls and curlicues on wrought-iron gates and fences.

Now, as she walked quietly down the alley, Theodosia paused to admire a few of the homes that were neatly tucked wall to wall and shoulder to shoulder. One ginormous home featured a striking salmon pink entry with a black enameled door. Another large home was shrouded with topiary trees that practically obscured a pristine white door flanked by a pair of brass sconces.

So beautiful, Theodosia breathed. And so old. Charleston had just celebrated its 350th anniversary, and so much was still standing!

As Earl Grey tugged at his leash, the better to inspect a puckish stone frog that kept guard at one of the gates, Theodosia unsnapped him. No danger of him wandering off here.

They continued along, Theodosia wondering about the people who'd originally built these remarkable homes and town houses, Earl Grey sniffing happily. But as they reached a yard, dark and sheltered with sprawling magnolia trees, Earl Grey suddenly lifted his head. He'd either seen something or heard something. Then he padded toward a half-open wrought-iron gate, slipped through it, and disappeared into the darkness like a wayward shadow.

Oh no.

"Earl Grey," Theodosia called after him in a low but

insistent voice. "Come back here." She stood perfectly still, listening for his returning footsteps, the jingle of his collar. And heard . . . nothing.

That's strange.

Theodosia approached the half-open gate, still hesitant to enter a private yard. She could see that, even cloaked in shadows, the house was massive. A full three stories high with a balcony that projected out over the alley. Probably the owners had security? Maybe a yard light or an inside alarm that her dog could have tripped?

But not a single light had flashed on inside the house.

Nobody home? Maybe she got lucky.

"Earl Grey," Theodosia called again, then let out a loud whistle.

Still nothing.

This isn't like him.

"Earl Grey? C'mere, boy." Theodosia was really starting to get worried. Maybe she should walk in there and . . .

A high-pitched yelp pierced the air, as if her dog was in pain!

What?

Like Usain Bolt crashing out of the starting blocks, Theodosia flew through the gate and down a narrow cobblestone walkway that led along the side of the house. Branches ripped at her face and hair as she ran, but she ignored them.

Reaching the backyard, she pulled up short and found herself in what was essentially a walled garden. She saw clay pots filled with tumbles of bougainvillea and twisted metal sculptures resting on massive cement stands. Beyond that were still-blooming hydrangeas, tall pampas grass, and a dense nest of trees.

Is he back there? Is he hurt?

Slowly, carefully, Theodosia picked her way through the garden. There were no formal stepping-stones, just winding paths. To her right she saw a tall birdbath with a stone crow attached. To her left was a stone sculpture of a grinning satyr with pointed ears.

It's a midnight garden, dark and a little strange.

Theodosia whistled again and heard a rustle back among the trees.

"Earl Grey? Is that you?" She took a tentative step forward

There was a low SQUEAK, like a rusty gate swinging open or closed.

Oh no!

Theodosia darted in the direction of the back wall. Three steps in, she slid to a halt as Earl Grey came bounding toward her. Then he leaped up and landed with his front paws planted firmly at her waist.

"Where were you?" Theodosia cried. "I was so worried." She pushed him down gently and knelt beside him, stroking his muzzle as she gazed into his eyes. "You can't just run off like that and scare me half to death," she told him as she reached for his collar so she could reattach the leash.

That's when Theodosia noticed a tiny bit of clear plastic stuck to the buckle of his leather collar.

"What's this?"

Earl Grey stared at her with earnest brown eyes.

"Did somebody try to grab you?" Theodosia asked. Her heart was suddenly pounding like a timpani drum, jolts of hot anger surging through her. "Did someone try to hurt you?" Theodosia looked around. She didn't *see* anybody. She hadn't *heard* anyone—just that strange squeak. Still, this whole incident struck her as strange and awfully sinister.

Snapping the leash back on Earl Grey, Theodosia stood up and said, "If anybody ever—*ever*—tries to hurt you, I promise they'll pay dearly."

15

❧

"*I'm back,*" *Miss* Dimple sang out as she sailed through the front door of the Indigo Tea Shop. "Did you miss me?"

"*Bonjour,*" Drayton called out to her. "And how are you this fine Wednesday morning?" He was in a cheery mood, while Theodosia had woken up feeling like she'd spent the night spinning in a hadron collider. Now, as she made little tweaks to her tea shop decor, she continued to ruminate over all the strange goings-on.

"I couldn't be better," Miss Dimple said with a smile as she shrugged out of her coat.

"Thanks for coming in early," Theodosia said to her from where she was standing at the window, adjusting one of her new blue toile curtains to let in the faint morning sunlight. "Having you for another day is a real help to us."

"Happy to do it," Miss Dimple said.

"If you don't mind, I'd like you to set up service today," Theodosia said as she came over to join Miss Dimple at the counter.

"I will if you trust me," Miss Dimple said. She looked eager but a little fluttery.

Theodosia put an arm around Miss Dimple's shoulders and squeezed gently. "I can't think of anyone I'd trust more."

"Oh my. In that case . . . where do you want me to start?"

"I have to run out in a few minutes, so I'd like you to handle the whole shebang. Select tablecloths and tea lights, put out the cream and sugars, teacups and saucers, and . . . um, probably check to make sure the floral arrangements will pass muster for another day."

"I promise to pluck out any dipsy droopy blooms."

"Perfect."

"Do you know which dishes you want to use?" Miss Dimple asked.

Theodosia looked over at Drayton. "Drayton? Any thoughts?"

"Far be it from me to exert any outside influence," Drayton said.

"Gotcha," Theodosia said with a knowing grin. She knew that Drayton adored being the arbiter of good taste and decor. It was one of his missions in life. In fact, much like his tea shelves, Drayton also art directed his bookshelves, arranging sizes, spines, and colors in pleasing patterns.

"On the other hand," Drayton said, "today is our informal pumpkin and spice luncheon, so that should probably factor in."

"Then maybe the pale-yellow tablecloths with your lovely Old Imari china?" Miss Dimple suggested. "The orange-and-gold pattern ties in, and they're a trifle exotic."

Drayton looked pleased. "I couldn't have chosen better."

While Miss Dimple readied the tea room, Theodosia was at work in her office. First, she looked up Jack Schindler on the Internet. When she found his website, a pretty cool one at that, she noted the phone number and placed a call.

Schindler answered on the second ring.

"Hello."

"Mr. Schindler? My name is Theodosia Browning. I got your name from Elisha Summers at the Heritage Society. I wonder if I could drop by and ask you a few questions."

"Questions about what?" Schindler asked. He had a pleasing baritone and sounded vaguely amused.

"Oh. Well, it would be about some of the restoration you did on the Bouchard Mansion," Theodosia said. "The one they turned into a haunted house."

"You can drop by, but I'm not at my studio right now," Schindler said. "This is my cell number."

"Elisha said you might be working at a church?"

"St. Mary's," he said. "You know where it is?"

"I do. And would this be a good time for us to talk?"

"Come on over," Schindler said.

St. Mary's was a very old church, established in the early eighteen hundreds and built in the Greek Revival style. Fronted by four massive Doric columns, it gave the appearance of an ancient temple.

When Theodosia walked into the nave of the church, she could see a man standing on a wood and metal scaffolding that had been set up at the front of the church near the altar.

"Mr. Schindler?" she called out, aware of an echo as she walked down the center aisle.

"Jack," he called back.

"Theodosia," she said as she continued in his direction. The church was cool and slightly dim with glowing stained glass windows that depicted traditional Bible scenes. Additionally, there were more than twenty stunning ceiling and wall paintings that were fine copies of Roman masterpieces.

"Thanks for letting me interrupt your work," Theodosia said.

"Not a problem."

Jack Schindler climbed down the side of the scaffold to meet her. A lanky thirty-something with long hair pulled back into a man bun, he was dressed in faded blue jeans, T-shirt, and a hoodie that said: SOME DAYS I REALLY DO WATCH PAINT DRY.

"You're painting," Theodosia said, gazing at the brush in his hand and the mural he'd been working on. "I was under the impression you did mostly carpentry and plastering."

"Plastering, painting, I do a little bit of everything." Schindler wiped his brush against a rag. "So what did you want to ask me? What's so important that you came all the way over here?"

"I'm curious as to what you did in the way of sprucing up the old Bouchard Mansion," Theodosia said.

"Oh, that. Well, first off, I shored up the floorboards on the second floor. They were in awfully tough shape, and I was pretty sure the Heritage Society didn't want people falling through the cracks."

"That might have been . . . problematic."

"From there it was mostly patch, patch, patch. Fix the walls, slap on some paint, hang some wallpaper if it wasn't patchable. You know . . . make the place look decent, make it all work." Schindler peered at her. "But I'm guessing you've probably been there and seen the place for yourself."

"I have."

"So what's your interest in that old rattrap?"

"I'm investigating the murder of Willow French."

"I see," Schindler said.

"Nothing full-fledged or authorized, mind you. Just amateur stuff," Theodosia said.

"Like Jessica Fletcher in *Murder, She Wrote*."

"Something like that."

"That sounds like a fairly interesting pastime," Schindler said. "Are you getting anywhere?"

"I think I might be."

"Cool. You mind if I work while we talk?"

"Not at all."

Theodosia followed him over to one of the walls where she watched him take a small piece of gold leaf, lay it against a mural, and then burnish and rub the gold leaf until it became part of the stucco wall.

"You do beautiful work."

"Thank you, but these repairs are kind of a labor of love. My parents were married in this church. I was baptized here." Schindler continued to work. Then, almost as an aside, he said, "You know, I think there might be another entrance somewhere."

"Excuse me?" Theodosia said. This little nugget of information seemed to come hurtling out of left field. "What do you mean? What are you talking about?"

Schindler squinted as he dabbed on more gold leaf. "Yeah, the old house. I was working there one night—oh, it must have been two weeks ago. And I thought I was all alone and that the place was locked up tighter than a drum. But then I felt this—I know it's going to sound kind of wacky and woo-woo—I had this feeling that I wasn't alone. Reminded me of that old proverb about somebody walking across your grave . . ."

"Yes?" Theodosia nodded for him to continue.

Schindler wiped his brush on a rag and looked thoughtful. "Anyway, as I was saying, I felt this *presence*. As if there were some sort of disturbance in the ozone. And suddenly I knew I wasn't alone in that house."

"Did you think it was a ghost?" Theodosia asked.

He shook his head. "I don't believe in ghosts."

"So a real person, then."

"I'm fairly sure it was," Schindler said. "Only when I called out, nobody answered."

"That's all you did was call out? Ask if someone was there?"

"Mmn, when nobody answered, I decided to look around. There was this one girl I'd been flirting with . . .

Anne something. I thought maybe she'd snuck in and was being coy. You know, fooling around."

"But no Anne?" Theodosia said.

"No nobody. I went downstairs and couldn't find a living soul."

"Interesting."

"More like strange," Schindler said. "And a little un-nerving. It was one of those deals where the hairs stand up on the back of your neck, you know?"

"I do know."

Theodosia thanked Schindler for his time and left. But as she drove back to the Indigo Tea Shop, she wondered if that mysterious person might have been Ellis Bouchard? Did the man possess a long-lost key? Maybe one of those handy-dandy all-purpose skeleton keys? One of those puppies could probably get you into half the mansions in Charleston, since most of the doors and locks were so antiquated.

Or could it have been one of the curators? Just popping in and out quickly, not wanting to disturb Schindler? Maybe they'd been so hurried, so focused on the task at hand, that they hadn't heard Schindler call out.

Or maybe, just maybe, there was a different explanation. Something a little more menacing.

Miss Dimple had done herself proud. Not only did the tea shop look perfectly charming when Theodosia returned, but it was half-filled with customers.

Theodosia peeked in, saw that everything was running like clockwork, then ducked into the kitchen to talk to Haley.

"Oh good, you're back," Haley said. "I was beginning to wonder." She sprinkled turbinado sugar on top of a pan of fresh-baked cinnamon scones, then said, "How goes the investigation?"

"Basically, it's been like slogging through molasses, but I'm now happy to report there's been some forward progress."

"That's all we can hope for," Haley said.

"You know that Willow's visitation is tonight?"

Haley gave a grim nod. "I know. It's going to be a tough one."

"I'm not looking forward to it, either. But on a more upbeat note, it looks as if you've got lunch well in hand," Theodosia said.

"Yeah, it's shaping up to be pretty cool. I gave Miss Dimple the menu if you want to take a look-see."

"How are you doing with the scones and tea sandwiches for the Edgar Allan Poe Symposium?" Theodosia asked.

"I'm working on those right now. I know Drayton's going over to the Heritage Society early, but if I pack everything up in two wicker baskets, can you schlep them over when you go?"

"I was planning on it."

"Okeydoke," Haley said.

Theodosia walked out into the tea shop where Drayton immediately held up an index finger to signal her.

"What's up?" Theodosia asked as she approached the counter.

"I'm going to head over to the Heritage Society in precisely two minutes," Drayton said. "Hopefully, the three of you can carry on without me."

"We'll be fine," Miss Dimple said. She set a Brown Betty teapot on the counter and said, "You were right about that Earl Grey green tea. The ladies at table four adored it."

"Light in flavor with a lovely hint of bergamot," Drayton said. "Always pleasing to the palette."

"Now, what can I do to help?" Theodosia asked.

Drayton whipped off his apron and handed it to Theodosia. "Trade places with me?"

Just before lunch, Theodosia took a phone call from Riley.

"Good news," he said. His voice sounded stronger and

much more upbeat. "They're springing me this afternoon. Just as soon as the lab kicks out my test results and my blood, sweat, and tears pass muster with the doctors."

"You're being discharged so soon? Do you think that's wise?"

"Are you kidding? It's the best news I've had in days."

Theodosia tried to reboot her thinking into more positive territory. "Of course it is. But to be extra safe, I think you should move in with me for a while. You know, just as a precautionary measure."

"Hey, I got shot. I didn't exactly have open-heart surgery. And while I appreciate your offer, I don't want to play the role of sick boyfriend who's also a housebound bother."

"You wouldn't be a bother."

"And, honestly, I don't mind chilling out at my own place. In fact, I think I'd feel better being around my own stuff. Besides, they're sending a whole cadre of medical personnel to visit me. You know, techs to monitor my pulse and blood pressure, some more of those occupational therapists to beat me on the head, that sort of thing. It's one of the bennies of our health insurance and disability package."

"Then I could drop by to fluff your pillows or put cucumbers on your eyes."

"Or better yet, use the cucumbers to spin me a salad. But, no, I'll be fine."

"Are you sure? It worries me to think you'll be alone."

"That's exactly my point—I *won't* be alone. Besides, there are a few things I want to work on."

"You're talking about the case."

"Of course I'm talking about the case. I need to review all the DD5s, the detective division reports."

"I'll come and pick you up then, give you a ride home," Theodosia said.

"Already got one."

16

❧

The informal pumpkin and spice luncheon at the Indigo Tea Shop proved to be hugely popular. Instead of their usual posters and e-mail, Haley had basically just carried flyers around to the B and Bs in the neighborhood. That, and word of mouth, had been enough to bring in at least two dozen guests plus several of their regulars.

"The tables look great," Theodosia said to Miss Dimple as they seated guests and poured Drayton's special cinnamon spice tea.

Miss Dimple had put yesterday's flowers into ceramic pots, added yellow candles in brass candlesticks, and punched up the arrangement with an assortment of miniature orange and white gourds.

"Where did you find the cute little gourds?" Theodosia asked.

"Haley brought them in," Miss Dimple said. "She found them at the Marion Square farmers market this morning when she was shopping for veggies."

"She's just full of surprises, isn't she? Including her menu?"

"Oh, I guess you want to know what we're serving?"

"It might help," Theodosia laughed.

"For starters we've got cinnamon scones and pumpkin bisque soup with crème fraîche and slivered almonds. Then tea sandwiches with chicken salad on pumpkin bread and turkey and cranberries on potato bread. Oh, and there's also thin-sliced radishes with herbed chèvre butter on crostini. But not the spicy sharp radishes; these are tender and buttery."

"And for dessert?" Theodosia said.

"Cinnamon ice cream and Haley's special pecan tassies."

"Goodness."

"Exactly my thoughts!" Miss Dimple said.

For some reason, the phone kept ringing with requests for take-out orders, so Theodosia was behind the counter for most of the luncheon, brewing tea, jotting down orders, and then packaging everything to go.

At one thirty she was finally able to take a breath and look around. And discovered that the tea shop had practically emptied out. Only two tables were still occupied.

"Where'd everyone go?" Theodosia asked Miss Dimple.

Miss Dimple waggled her fingers. "Off to do whatever," she said. "But the luncheon went well, don't you think? I mean in terms of customers enjoying all the cinnamon and spice goodies?"

"It was a hit," Theodosia said as she glanced at her watch. "Good heavens, I've got to grab those baskets of scones and tea sandwiches and take them over to Drayton at the Heritage Society."

"Then go. *Go*," Miss Dimple urged. "Haley and I can take care of things for the rest of the afternoon. We're happy to."

"Okay then. I'm outa here!"

Theodosia parked in the small back lot of the Heritage Society, trundled her baskets through a storage room that was jam-packed with cartons and boxes, and finally found Drayton bustling about in the small service kitchen that was adjacent to the large meeting hall.

"You're here. Good," Drayton proclaimed when he saw her. Grabbing one of the wicker baskets from Theodosia's hand, he flipped open the top, peered in, and said, "Love it."

"When's the afternoon tea break scheduled?" Theodosia asked.

"Not for another half hour. But I prefer to set everything up early."

"Sure. Were you able to sit in on any of the panel discussions?" Theodosia asked.

"Yes, and it was fascinating. One was a discussion on Poe's addiction to alcohol and drugs."

"It sounds . . . enthralling."

"Go ahead and laugh, but there are dozens of people out there who'd kill to hear a serious treatise on what drove Poe's mania," Drayton said as he opened the other basket. "Mm, and what do we have here? Scones?"

"All in all Haley packed six dozen sea salt caramel scones and another twelve dozen assorted tea sandwiches."

Drayton glanced up at her. "Assorted meaning . . . ?"

"Ham and cheddar, chicken salad with chutney, and crab salad with Bibb lettuce."

"Tasty. So let's carry the food across the hallway and lay it out on the tables in the Palmetto Gallery. The cups and saucers are already there along with my tea urn. One of the interns helped me set everything up."

"What tea are you serving?" Theodosia asked as they walked across the hall, past a lovely display of old leather-bound books that sat in an antique case with wavy glass panels.

"I'm brewing a red oolong. As you know, the large twisted leaves from this partially oxidized tea yield a nectar that's naturally sweet and has a toasty aftertaste."

"Can I help you with that?" a voice asked.

Drayton whirled around to find Sybil Spalding standing there, looking more than eager to lend a hand.

"There's my helper," Drayton said with a smile. "Theo, you're well acquainted with Sybil, right?"

"I certainly am," Theodosia said. "And it's wonderful to see you again, Sybil. Thanks so much for giving Drayton a hand."

"No problem," Sybil said. "Happy to help out."

"You're not attending the symposium?" Theodosia asked.

"I caught a couple of the talks this morning, but now I'm supposed to, like, assist with the guests and refreshments." She glanced at Drayton again. "So I should put out these scones and stuff?"

"Yes, but let's arrange the food as artfully as possible."

"Natch," said Sybil.

Twenty minutes later, the doors to the great hall opened and the seminar guests spilled out. Sybil ushered them across the hallway, and afternoon teatime, such as it was, was quickly underway.

Theodosia decided it was more expedient (and sanitary) for her to use a pair of tongs to serve the guests their scones and tea sandwiches while, at the far end of the table, Drayton and Sybil poured cups of tea.

There was an initial rush, of course, and then some ten minutes later, things started to settle down. That's when Timothy, Claire Waltho, Elisha Summers, and another dozen or so curators came through the line.

"The seminar is going well?" Drayton asked Timothy, who was looking a trifle frazzled.

"Yes, yes, seems to be," Timothy said as he picked up a plate. He held up a hand to Theodosia and said, "No scone, just a sandwich for me please."

"Here you go," Theodosia said, placing a single chicken

salad sandwich on Timothy's plate, worrying that he probably wasn't eating enough. He was elderly and awfully thin. Her worry was cut short, however, as a few more guests wandered by for refreshments and then, surprise, surprise, Ellis Bouchard was standing there looking at her with sharp, appraising eyes.

"We meet again," Bouchard said to Theodosia.

"Hello," she said cautiously. Then, because she was polite to a fault, raised to be a true Southern lady, she said, "Would you care for a sea salt caramel scone?"

"That sounds delicious," Bouchard said.

"With a dab of Devonshire cream?"

"Thank you." Bouchard glanced at her again and said, "Timothy tells me you're investigating the recent murder at my ancestor's home."

Actually, it belongs to the Heritage Society now.

But Theodosia didn't voice her opinion. Instead, she decided a noncommittal answer might be in order. "Looking into it anyway."

"So that's why all the questions?"

"That's why," she said.

Bouchard dropped his voice. "Did you know that old mansion was once a funeral home?"

Theodosia studied Bouchard carefully to see if he was serious or not. Maybe he was trying to jerk her chain? Or trying to spook her? But when he maintained his somber, earnest look, she said, "I did not know that. When was this?"

"A long time ago, at the turn of the century. And I'm referring to the century before this one when undertakers still transported caskets to the cemetery in horse-drawn carriages."

"And you're telling me about this—why?" Theodosia asked.

"Mostly as a historical anecdote. And because you seem so fascinated by the mansion. You know, I even believe the architect donated his original plans to the Heritage Society's library."

"Interesting," Theodosia said. She studied Bouchard. "Mr. Bouchard, do you actually live here in Charleston?"

"Temporarily, yes. But only until the affairs concerning my mansion are straightened out."

But the surprises didn't end there. Allan Barnaby also stopped by to sample their scones and tea sandwiches. And then, two minutes later, practically licking his chops, he was back for more.

"I'm impressed," Barnaby said to Theodosia. "The food you're serving is first-rate. Is the food this good at your tea shop?"

"Of course."

"Have you ever considered doing an Indigo Tea Shop cookbook?"

"I've been asked that before," Theodosia told him.

"And what was your answer?" Barnaby nibbled at his scone.

"That I never seem to find time to sit down and give it serious consideration."

"Well, you should definitely think about a cookbook. You know, I'm always trolling for new authors with a fresh voice."

"I'm not sure my voice is all that fresh," Theodosia said. "And, truth be told, so many of the recipes are Haley's. She's . . ."

"Excuse me," Drayton said, suddenly moving in to interrupt them. He stared pointedly at Barnaby and said, "Did I hear a rumor that you might be publishing a history of the Heritage Society?"

"It was just something I batted around with a few of the curators," Barnaby said with a wave of his hand, as though it were unimportant.

"But it's not an actual project?" Drayton's voice remained crisp and inquisitive. "Nothing's been written?"

"Not a word," Barnaby assured him. "It exists only as a concept."

Barnaby grabbed another scone and sped away as Drayton glowered after him.

"Doesn't the man realize that a project such as a documented history would have to be approved by the board of directors?" Drayton asked.

"I don't know that he meant to step on any toes," Theodosia said. "I think he's just a little . . . eager."

"Indeed he is."

"But listen," Theodosia said. "Did you hear the tale Ellis Bouchard was trying to spin?"

"What was that?"

Theodosia hastily told Drayton about Bouchard's funeral home story.

Drayton lifted a single eyebrow. "How quaint."

"Bouchard even told me the plans might have been donated to the Heritage Society library," Theodosia said. "Although he could have concocted this fantasy just to make the mansion less appealing. Or to scare me off."

"I wouldn't put it past him," Drayton said. "Of course there's only one way to know for certain."

"What's that?"

Drayton poured himself a cup of tea and took a sip. "Research. Especially if the answer you seek is right here in this building."

Twenty minutes later, with Sybil offering to clear the table and pack up the leftover scones and sandwiches, Theodosia and Drayton were seated in the Heritage Society library.

"This really is one of my favorite places," Drayton said. He gazed happily about at the enormous wooden library tables, the lamps with green glass shades, the floor-to-ceiling bookshelves, the sliding ladder, and the faded Oriental carpets that helped dampen any sound.

"Like you, I think I could curl up in a comfy chair and spend a lifetime in this place," Theodosia said.

"It would take you a lifetime to read all these books. Do you know this library contains something like ten thousand volumes? They've even squirreled away some of the battle plans from the Revolutionary War!"

"But do they have the plans for the Bouchard Mansion?"

Drayton held up a finger. "That's what I intend to find out."

Turned out, they did. The librarian had to do some serious digging, but ten minutes later, Theodosia and Drayton were seated at a table poring over several faded sketches that had been drawn on thick, crinkly paper.

"It's hard to figure these out," Theodosia said. She wore the thin cotton gloves that the librarian had given them so they could handle the valuable old paper. "There seem to be two sets of plans."

"Perhaps revisions were made to the old house?" Drayton wondered.

They passed the plans back and forth, studying them and commenting on them. Then both looked up as Timothy strode into the room carrying a stack of folders under one arm. He was rubbing his eyes, looking tired.

"What's that you're doing?" he asked.

"Looking at the architectural renderings for the Bouchard Mansion," Theodosia said.

"Looking for clues?" Timothy wore a half smile on his lined face.

"Something like that."

"Besides looking at plans, is there anything new in your investigation?" Timothy asked Theodosia.

"I'm still pursuing a few different angles," Theodosia said. Her heart ached for Timothy. He was a dear soul who clearly felt responsible for his grandniece's death.

"I know you've interviewed many of our staff members already, but I brought along our personnel files." Timothy dumped a series of folders on the table in front of Theodosia. "Have a look if you think they might help."

"It couldn't hurt," Theodosia said.

"Thank you," Timothy said. "I'll probably see you tonight at the visitation. Let me know if . . ." His voice faded to nothing as he turned and walked away.

Theodosia knew she had to come up with something fairly quick. Timothy was getting so dispirited, and the police didn't seem to be making any headway at all.

"Do you see anything at all in these plans?" Theodosia asked Drayton.

"Not really," Drayton said. "I could probably manage a more contemporary blueprint, one of those large blue sheets with white lines that indicate foundations, boundaries, electrical, and various rooms. But old plans such as these are awfully tricky. I mean, look at the various sheets, like something Thomas Jefferson might have drawn. All sketchy pencil lines and cryptic notations written in . . . what is this . . . French?"

"Can you read it?"

"I haven't studied French since my university days. I can manage *hello* and *goodbye* in French, and I can order a bottle of decent wine, but that's about it," Drayton said. "My *parlez-vous*ing is severely limited." He set one of the sheets down and pursed his lips. "These must have been drawn by a French architect."

"I'm not surprised. There were so many French aristocrats who settled in Charleston back in the seventeen and eighteen hundreds," Theodosia said.

"And their descendants still reside here."

Theodosia squinted at one of the documents, then pointed to a signature at the bottom of the page. "You see this? I think you're right. The architect was someone named Anton Géroux."

"Which explains why all the notations are in French."

Theodosia turned the drawing around and studied it.

"Now take a look right here." She tapped her finger against faint ink that indicated a small rectangle. "Tell me what you see."

Drayton cocked his head. "Could that indicate a fire-place?" Then he answered his own question. "No, that couldn't be right. A fireplace would've been situated in the main salon with another one in the kitchen or dining room." He pushed his glasses up on his nose and stared at Theodosia. "I'm afraid I don't know what that's supposed to represent. Perhaps it was a service entrance at one time? From when there were various tradespeople who came to call. You know, the butcher, the baker . . ." He smiled. "The candlestick maker."

"What does this sheet say at the top? *Sous-sol*. What does that mean?" Theodosia asked.

"Not sure. Best we consult a French-English dictionary."

Drayton walked down a row of books, ran his finger along several spines, and pulled out a volume.

"You found one?" Theodosia asked.

"I did," Drayton said as he paged through it. "And . . ." He turned a few more pages. "According to this, *sous-sol* means basement."

Theodosia frowned. "Basement? I never even thought about the house having a basement."

Drayton returned the book to its shelf and came back to study the plans some more. "From the looks of things, there is." Then, with more certainty, "There had to be one. To accommodate storage, a fruit cellar, maybe even a fur-nace."

"Then do you think that mark I showed you indicates some sort of door?" Theodosia asked.

"No idea."

Theodosia's finger tapped the sheet again. "But what if there *is*?" She was thinking about the killer and what an easy getaway he'd been able to make. "What if there's a hidden exit? One we don't know about?"

17

⌘

Doake and Wilson Funeral Home was located in a redbrick building on Montagu Street. It was your basic nineteen twenties' mansion that had been gussied up with white pillars, a circular drive, and improved landscaping. A large white stucco building with frosted windows had been tacked onto the back part of the old residence—basically the mortuary where bodies were prepared for viewing.

Theodosia had picked up Drayton, and now they sat in the funeral home's small parking lot, listening to the engine tick down. Neither of them wanted to get out of her Jeep and go in, but they knew they had to.

"We're delaying the inevitable," Drayton sighed.

"Come on then," Theodosia said, opening her door and climbing out. "Maybe we'll learn something tonight, maybe we'll pick up some bit of information."

"Maybe," Drayton said, but he didn't sound convinced. They walked up the sidewalk, where a scatter of low-

level outdoor lights shone from behind stands of bougainvillea, and pulled open one of the stately entrance doors.

"Agh," Drayton said as they stepped inside. He'd caught
a whiff of chilled air, the scent of flowers mingled with
chemicals that permeated most funeral homes. It was
hardly pleasant.

Theodosia, on the other hand, hated absolutely everything about this funeral home. The smell, sad gray carpet,
dusty potted plants, solemn funereal music that groaned
from the speakers, the overstuffed, over-upholstered chairs
in the reception area, and, most of all, the ugly, knobby
cocktail table that held a single box of Kleenex.

"We're here for the Willow French visitation," Drayton
said in a decorous tone to the gray-haired receptionist who
sat at the front desk.

The receptionist gave a practiced sad smile and lifted a
hand. "It's the room to your left," she said. "The Slumber
Suite."

Drayton turned to Theodosia. "The Slumber Suite," he
echoed.

"Of course," she said, wrinkling her nose.

They drifted through a doorway that was swagged with
plum-colored velvet draperies and into a fairly large room.
It had ghastly floral wallpaper, a few pieces of clunky up-
holstered furniture, two dozen folding chairs, and more
potted plants. At the front of the room Willow's coffin
rested on a wooden bier.

"Oh no," Theodosia whispered as she put a hand to her
mouth.

Willow had been laid to rest in a pure white coffin,
wearing a high-necked white dress with her blond hair
spread out around her on a white silk pillow. A bountiful
bower of pink and white flowers and tall, flickering candles
surrounded her. The setting was peaceful yet surreal. To
Theodosia, Willow looked just like Snow White, waiting

for her Prince Charming to come and deliver a kiss that would wake her from this terrible slumber.

Wasn't going to happen.

Instead, there was a sad procession of mourners filing past Willow's coffin. Haley was among them, as were Delaine and Timothy Neville. And everyone seemed to be either sobbing openly or wiping at their eyes.

"This is so awful," Theodosia said as they approached the coffin.

"Tragic," Drayton agreed.

Theodosia said a whispered prayer as she gazed at Willow, then joined the line to offer condolences to Willow's parents and her fiancé, Robert Vardell. Timothy Neville stood behind them, wringing his hands, his face a mixture of anguish and grief.

The room continued to fill with mourners. Allan Barnaby, Willow's publisher, arrived. So did Claire Waltho, Sybil Spalding, Elisha Summers, and dozens more from the Heritage Society. They'd all come to show the flag and honor Timothy Neville.

Strangely enough, Ellis Bouchard was also present.

Theodosia jabbed an elbow into Drayton's ribs and whispered, "Ellis Bouchard, homing in at three o'clock."

"Strange that he would show up here," Drayton murmured as he threw a quick glance at him.

"Isn't it?" Theodosia turned and studied the room. "But no Henry Curtis."

"Who?"

"You know, Frankenstein. The young man who sent Willow the note."

"Perhaps he'll put in an appearance later."

"Maybe," Theodosia said slowly. But something else was bothering her. "Drayton, when we filed past Willow's coffin, did you notice her hands?"

Drayton looked puzzled. "Um, her hands were clasped together, were they not?"

"And she was wearing that pretty moonstone ring we saw her wearing last Sunday night. Right before . . . you know."

"What are you getting at?" Drayton asked.

"If Willow was engaged, why wasn't she wearing her engagement ring last Sunday night?"

"I don't know. Perhaps the moonstone ring was part of her costume? Of her author persona?"

"There could be another explanation. One I hadn't thought of before."

Drayton frowned and leaned closer to Theodosia. "Explain, please."

"What if . . . what if Willow was no longer engaged?" Theodosia whispered.

Drayton shook his head. "I'm not sure I'm following you."

"What if Willow had broken off her engagement with Vardell?"

Simultaneously, their eyes darted to Robert Vardell, who was slumped in a chair, his hands clasped over his stomach. His expression was unreadable.

"I suppose that's possible," Drayton said slowly. "That Willow might have given the engagement ring back to him." He thought for a moment. "But she bought the house."

"Maybe that was *before*. Maybe Willow had a change of heart somewhere along the line. Or Vardell did."

Drayton looked stunned. "You think he killed her?"

"It's horrible to imagine, but maybe once Vardell knew he could have the house free and clear, he wanted the diamonds, too," Theodosia said. "Now we're probably talking a grand total of at least two to three million dollars. People have been known to commit murder for far less."

Drayton looked thoughtful. "I suppose you're right."

"The other thing is, Vardell could have gotten severely cold feet and was terrified of going through with the wedding—the bachelor parties, the rehearsal dinner, the wedding itself, the honeymoon, the whole shebang. Maybe he just wanted *out*."

Drayton frowned. "Dear Lord, it could be like those poor couples who get married, go on a fantastic honeymoon cruise, and then one of them ends up dead! Takes a header over a railing into the ocean."

"Or they get pushed," Theodosia said.

"So you're implying that Vardell . . ." Again, the word *murdered* hovered on the tip of Drayton's tongue.

But he stopped short as they both turned to inspect Vardell once again. The man's pose and expression hadn't changed.

"He does appear *somewhat* brokenhearted," Drayton said.

"Yes, but he still could have killed her," Theodosia said. Then, "*Would* he have killed her?"

"I don't know," Drayton said. "You're veering into extremely dangerous territory here."

"But something strange is going on. The police don't have any real suspects, the Hibiscus Diamonds are missing, and Vardell is the proud owner of a fancy new house."

"It's all so circumstantial," Drayton said. "I don't know what to think."

"We *have* to figure this out," Theodosia said. "For Timothy's sake, for our own peace of mind, we have to keep pushing on this."

"Then we need to buttonhole Vardell. Talk to him. Question him carefully but thoroughly."

"Maybe I should . . ." Theodosia began, just as Allan Barnaby walked up to them and interrupted.

"A sad night," Barnaby intoned.

Drayton nodded. "It certainly is."

Barnaby didn't have much to say; he just stood there looking mopey and staring at them. That is until Delaine suddenly rushed over to join them. She was wearing an adorable peach-colored skirt suit with a stand-up collar and carrying a purse that was covered with crystals and shaped like a bird. Maybe a parrot, possibly a macaw. In any case, she looked like she was ready to hop a plane to Bermuda.

"Theo," Delaine said in her hurried, breezy fashion. "I need to bounce out of here and . . ." She stopped suddenly, took notice of Allan Barnaby, and broke into a slow smile. "Why hello there," she said. "I don't believe we've been introduced."

Theodosia made hasty introductions, then pretty much stood back as Delaine took over.

"A publisher," Delaine cooed. "Isn't that absolutely *amazing.* I simply *adore* reading books." (Insert eye flutter here.) "Tell me, Mr. Barnaby . . . or may I call you Allan? What types of books do you publish? No, wait, let me guess." And Delaine was off and running, monopolizing the conversation, giggling, asking and answering her own questions, and flirting outrageously with Allan Barnaby.

Barnaby, who'd always struck Theodosia as being rather bookish and timid, was suddenly finding himself basking in the reflected glow of the giddy and exotic-looking Delaine Dish. She was clinging to his arm and hanging on his every word (but only when he was able to get a faint word in).

Theodosia threw Drayton her best *Let's get out of here* look, but their escape was foiled when Haley and Timothy Neville came up to join their circle.

That slowed things down as they all exchanged somber greetings as well as a few fond remembrances about Willow.

Then Timothy rocked back on his heels and said in a sad voice, "We can only wonder about Willow's next book. What it would have been."

"Willow's book?" Haley said. "Oh, I have it."

You could have heard a pin drop as everyone stared at her.

Theodosia was the first one to find her voice. "*You* have it?" Her words seemed to echo loudly in the room. "Why is that?"

Haley shrugged. "No big reason. Just that Willow asked me to read it. To, you know, see if it all hung together."

"Does it?" Barnaby asked. He looked like a wolverine ready to move in for the kill.

"Well, I only got a chance to read the first chapter, like, an hour ago," Haley said.

"Excuse me, are you talking about the history of the Heritage Society that Willow was thinking of writing?" Drayton asked.

Haley shook her head. "No way, this is a novel. A really good one, too. It's about this Russian . . ."

"Tereshchenko," Theodosia said.

Haley grinned. "The diamond guy you told us about, yeah. How did you know that's what Willow's novel was about?"

"Just a lucky guess," Theodosia said.

Once Theodosia and Drayton pulled themselves away from the group, Theodosia said, "What if Allan Barnaby is the guilty party?"

"You don't like him, do you?" Drayton said.

"It's not a matter of liking or not liking him. The fact is, I'm fairly sure Barnaby was at the haunted house Sunday night. So he had the perfect opportunity."

"I suppose it's possible," Drayton said. "Also, Barnaby seemed ravenously eager to get his hands on Willow's next book, if that counts for anything."

"What if Willow was going to take her book to a different publisher, a more prestigious publisher, and Barnaby got wind of it?"

"Interesting thought. So maybe, in a fit of rage, Barnaby murdered Willow, stole the diamonds, and then stole her computer?" Drayton said.

"Let's assume for the time being," Theodosia said, "that whoever stole Willow's laptop might have thought they were getting their hands on her second manuscript. And now, seeing as how Haley has it, she could be in serious danger!"

Drayton touched his bow tie nervously. "What do we do now?"

"I'm not sure. But first things first, we need to get into that haunted house again. Check out the basement and see if there's a hidden exit."

"How are we going to do that?"

"You brought along Xerox copies of the house plans, right?"

"Yes, but . . ."

Theodosia looked around the room, trying to figure out her next move. Her eyes skittered across the crowd and landed on Claire Waltho.

"I know what I'll do. I'll ask Claire for a key. That way we can go into the haunted house tonight, take our own sweet time looking around, and then lock up afterward."

"Gulp," Drayton said.

18

❧

"*I have to* make a stop," Theodosia told Drayton as they drove down Queen Street.

"What's that?"

"I want to drop off a basket for Riley. Just some food and stuff I put together for him."

"Beer and chips?" Drayton asked. He sounded amused.

"Nope, healthy stuff," Theodosia said. "More like chicken soup, zucchini bread, and a couple of sandwiches."

"Organic?"

"Well, health conscious anyway."

"Perhaps you should drop me at home before you run your little errand. You might change your mind and decide to stay awhile."

"No way, we're going to explore that haunted house, and you're coming with me."

Drayton gave a faint smile. "Aren't I the lucky one."

It really did take Theodosia all of two minutes—well, maybe three minutes—to stop at Riley's apartment, deliver her care package, and bestow a few meaningful hugs and kisses. Then she was back in her Jeep with Drayton, driving down Tradd Street, headed for the haunted house.

"It doesn't look as busy tonight," Drayton remarked as they hurried up the front walk. Where there had been fifty people waiting to get in Sunday night, now there were only a dozen or so.

"Maybe the novelty has worn off. Or maybe Willow's unsolved murder has put a damper on the fun," Theodosia said.

At any rate, they walked right into the haunted house—again without any problems—thanks to Julia, one of the Heritage Society's admin assistants who was minding the front door.

"Is Henry Curtis here tonight?" Theodosia asked her.

Julia shook her head. "Henry was supposed to be here, but he never showed up." She rolled her eyes to show her obvious displeasure. "We had to fill in for him. People are upset."

"Okay, thanks."

"Uh, you do know we're closing this place in ten minutes, right?" Julia said.

"No problem," Theodosia said. "Claire Waltho was good enough to give us a key and told us we could lock up once we're finished here. Drayton and I are just going to do a quick walk-through. Check out a few things."

Julia shrugged. "Okay then. But be sure to turn off all the lights."

Theodosia grabbed Drayton's elbow and steered him down the center hallway. They walked past a Sherlock Holmes look-alike who had a cluster of visitors around him, and a woman who was reading tarot cards.

"So how exactly do we find the entrance to this mysterious basement?" Drayton asked.

"We poke around, cross our fingers, and hope for the best."

But they didn't have to search all that hard.

In a stripped-out kitchen that was clogged with cardboard boxes and basically being used as a storage room, they found a narrow door leading to the basement.

"Spooky," Drayton said as he peered down into the darkness.

Theodosia wasn't looking forward to a creepy-crawl through a dingy basement, either, but she tried to keep a stiff upper lip. They were investigating, after all. This was what investigators did. They took risks.

"Are there lights?" Drayton asked. "Please tell me there are lights. The last thing I want to do is fall and break a hip."

As if to answer his question, Theodosia flipped a switch that turned on a single bare bulb dangling at the foot of the stairs.

"And I brought along a small Maglite," she said as she started down the flight of narrow steps that creaked and groaned beneath her. "Come on. Just be a little careful. Use the handrail."

"I feel like Schliemann searching for the lost city of Troy," Drayton said.

"Drayton, your analogies are always so academic."

Drayton smiled as they descended the narrow basement stairs. "Do you know the story?"

"About Schliemann?" Theodosia shook her head. "No. What is it?"

"Holding a copy of *The Iliad* in one hand, Schliemann stood in the prow of a small boat and navigated according to all the landmarks that were mentioned in the text."

"You're kidding."

"And that's precisely how he discovered the lost city of Troy."

"True story?"

"Cross my heart."

"That's amazing," Theodosia said as they arrived at the bottom of the steps. "Sounds like he was an archaeologist and an investigator." She turned to face Drayton. "Okay, now we've got to buckle down and do that same kind of thing here. Use our blueprint to . . ."

"Try and figure out if there's a hidden entrance," Drayton said.

"More like an exit, an escape door."

Drayton pulled his copy of the floor plan out of his jacket pocket and unfolded it. "Here, shine your light on what we surmise is the basement plan."

Theodosia complied.

"So if this is the bottom of the staircase, then what we're looking for should be on the opposite wall," Drayton said.

"Works for me."

But nothing ever comes easy. The floor was packed earth, and the ceiling was low and confining. Cobwebs swept their heads. And when they took a few tentative steps, they were confronted by piles of junk.

"What is all this stuff?" Drayton wondered. "And are there more lights?"

"The answer to both questions is I don't know," Theodosia said.

"Shine your light over to where we think that wall is," Drayton said, gesturing nervously.

Theodosia's flashlight barely pierced the basement's darkness, but what it did reveal were several old wooden trunks, an antique birdcage, some stone statuary that might have come from a garden, and a rack of clothing that had to be many decades old.

Drayton put a hand out, brushed against a piece of clothing, and immediately sneezed.

"Dusty down here," he said.

"It's awful."

Slowly, a step at a time, they eased their way through the maze of boxes and cartons that were stacked head high and greatly impeded their movement. Picking a path forward was slow going.

"Shine your light over this way, will you?" Drayton asked. "I think I see something."

Theodosia flicked her small beam of light to the right to suddenly reveal a set of eyes peering at them out of the darkness.

"Dear Lord!" Drayton cried. "Is that a child sitting down here in the dark?" He sounded like he was ready to jump out of his socks.

"Take it easy, Drayton, it's just a doll." Theodosia studied it carefully. "And by the look of its clothing and porcelain face, an antique doll at that."

Drayton shuddered. "Ugh, its face is cracked, and it's got weird eyes. Frightening eyes. They follow me when I move."

"Then don't look at it and don't talk yourself into a state of blind panic," Theodosia cautioned. She wasn't having a jolly time down here, either. The basement was dark and scary, with a terrible musty odor.

They kept moving forward, bumping into things, then cautiously easing their way around them.

"We should be getting close to that far wall," Theodosia said, even though she felt as if she was whistling in the dark. *Hoping* they were almost there.

A loud CLANK rang out followed by a scuffling sound. Scurrying rats? No, it was Drayton.

"Ouch! What did I just run into? What on earth is this old metal table?" Drayton asked, obviously perturbed. "Or perhaps it's not a table at all but some other strange apparatus."

"Let me see."

Drayton was flailing around with his hands. "It's got holes in it."

As Theodosia flashed her light toward him, her throat went dry as the Gobi Desert. "Drayton, it's an old-fashioned embalming table!"

Drayton jumped back as if it were writhing with poisonous snakes.

"Sweet Fanny Adams, this really *was* a funeral parlor!" Drayton turned toward Theodosia, and his shoulders jerked convulsively, as if he were about to make a run for it. "That's the last straw. We're out of here. I don't like this snooping business one bit."

"But we're making progress, don't you see?"

"By poking around in a place that used to be a mortuary? No, I don't see any sense in it at all."

"Wait a minute. Here, give me the floor plan and you take the flashlight. Hold it steady now," Theodosia said. "I want to check . . ."

"What?" Drayton asked. He was both frightened and impatient.

Theodosia bent over the plan, studying it. "This notation here, Drayton. Do you know what *porte du cercueil* means?"

"No, and at this point I don't think I want to know."

"It could be something important."

Theodosia pulled out her iPhone, hoping it would work down here—it did—and hastily typed in *porte du cercueil*.

"Drayton!" Theodosia was almost incredulous. Though it wasn't easy to read the screen in the dim light, she could read it well enough. "It means casket door!"

Drayton's face was a pale oval in the glow of the flashlight. "Seriously?" His voice trembled. "Where is it?" He was nervous but also a tiny bit curious.

"It has to be . . ." Theodosia moved forward cautiously. "Over this way." As she reached out, her fingertips brushed against a damp stone wall. She recoiled immediately. "Ugh. I think I found something."

"Found what?"

Now her fingers tentatively touched the wall again, then moved along the cool, bumpy stones until she felt a large piece of metal set flush against the wall. "I think I found the casket door."

Feeling bolder now, Theodosia continued to explore.

"And I think there might be a latch." Her fingers moved expectantly across the metal. "Holy Christmas, Drayton, there *is* a secret exit. Like, right here!"

"Does it open?"

"Aim the light over."

Drayton pointed the light, revealing a rusted hunk of metal that was hinged at the bottom and had a strange-looking latch at the top.

"We've got to try and see if it opens," Theodosia said.

She jerked and fiddled with the latch, but it seemed to be stuck tight.

"Here, let me try," Drayton said.

But after a few minutes of fussing and jiggling, they still weren't making any headway.

Theodosia wasn't to be deterred. "Maybe if we . . ." She balled up her fist and gave the hunk of metal a hard smack.

There was a sudden loud CREAK, like rusted hinges that hadn't been oiled in decades. Then . . .

"Watch out!" Theodosia cried as they both jumped back.

A loud, ominous CLANK rang out as a large metal flap dropped open. It was like a giant mailbox opening in the side of the wall.

They both stared into the dark, gaping hole. It was a perfect rectangle, about five feet wide and four feet high.

"Look at that! The opening is just wide enough and high enough to slide a casket in and out," Theodosia cried. She was breathless with excitement.

Drayton peered into the dark hole. "It's like gazing into the pit of hell."

They both let that remark percolate in their brains for a moment. Then Theodosia said, "No, Drayton, I think this is how our killer escaped!"

19

❧

Back upstairs, the place was totally deserted. The guests had left, so had all the fortune-tellers, literary characters, and Heritage Society folks who'd been minding the store.

Good, Theodosia thought as they quickly flipped off all the lights. After a quick check and a callout of "Anybody here?" they stepped outside and locked the front door behind them.

Then it was a mad scramble around to the back of the old mansion to locate the outside exit for that coffin door.

Of course nothing ever comes easy.

"It's a mess back here. Overgrown shrubbery, brambles, and some kind of thorn bush," Drayton complained. "And the fact that it's dark as a coal mine makes our task even more difficult. I can't imagine where that coffin door is."

"We have to try," Theodosia said. "Here, you hold the Maglite, and I'll scrunch in between these bushes."

"Easier said than done," Drayton declared as he watched

Theodosia wedge herself into the shrubbery and try her darndest to get closer to the foundation.

"I think I'm . . . No, maybe I need a push," Theodosia said. She was huffing and puffing now, caught tight in what was a giant, gnarly hedge. "I've got to . . ."

SNAP. POP.

". . . break some of these branches. Then I think I can squeeze through."

"Better you than me," Drayton mumbled.

"I'm almost in," Theodosia said. "I just need to . . ." She inhaled sharply, bulldozing forward with all her might, and finally popped on through. "Okay, I'm in."

"What do you see?"

"Nothing. It's like being lost in an English maze back here. Pass the flashlight over, will you?"

"Here you go," Drayton said as he stuck his arm through the brambles and passed her the light. "Ouch."

"You okay?"

"Only that I was practically punctured by a bramble," he said. "Now do you see anything?"

"Hang on a minute. Okay, yes. It's muddy back here, and the ground is all churned up. Like someone was back here recently."

"Maybe Sunday night? While everyone was staring at the ghastly figure of poor Willow, the perpetrator was getting away?" Drayton said.

"That's exactly what I'm thinking," Theodosia said.

"But do you see where the casket door opens out?" Drayton asked.

Theodosia crouched down and ran the light up and down the side of the house. "I don't see anything yet."

"Keep trying."

"I will, but I've got all of eight inches to maneuver in back here. Maybe if I . . ."

The rest of her words were lost to Drayton.

"Theo?" Drayton said. "Are you still there? Are you all right?"

When Theodosia spoke next, her voice came from ten feet away from where she'd been standing.

"It's here Drayton," she said excitedly. "I found it. The casket door. It's concealed extremely well. There's a kind of crumbly plaster caked all over the outside of it, so it looks as if it's part of the foundation. Probably done after it ceased to be used."

"But it's the door?"

"Has to be because it's pretty much the same proportions as the door in the basement."

"Very clever," Drayton said.

"Okay, I'm coming out." And then, "This is big. We have to tell Timothy."

Timothy Neville lived in baronial splendor in an Italianate mansion on Archdale Street some three blocks from the Bouchard Mansion. Theodosia and Drayton wasted no time in rushing to his house, which wasn't really a house at all, but a three-and-a-half-story riot of cupolas, dormers, balconies, eaves, tall narrow windows, and double doors. A veritable wedding cake of a house.

"Do you think Timothy is still awake?" Theodosia asked.

Drayton lifted the brass boar's head knocker to the right of the front door and let it drop against the metal plate. A booming echo sounded deep within Timothy's home.

"We'll soon find out," he said.

A minute later, Timothy Neville opened his front door. He was wearing—and this was God's honest truth—a maroon smoking jacket with his family crest embroidered on the breast pocket, and gray wool trousers.

Drayton, who favored conservative tweedy garb, wasn't

the least bit fazed by this. Theodosia, on the other hand, could barely contain the urge to ask Timothy if he'd had a recent invitation to pose for the British version of *GQ*.

No. There's no joking around tonight. I've got to stick to the business at hand.

"We have news," Drayton said.

"Then you'd better come in," Timothy said.

He led them through a large entryway where a Greek statue of some minor deity held sway, and into a side parlor. There, enormous mirrors with gilded frames, antique lamps, a crystal chandelier, pale-green silk wallpaper, and fine furniture greeted them. A fire blazed in the fireplace. Over the mantel was an oil portrait of Timothy's grandmother that had been done by George Whiting Flagg, the renowned portrait artist. The atmosphere in the room was elegant and luxurious.

When Timothy was seated in a tufted blue silk armchair and Theodosia and Drayton sat opposite him on a matching sofa, Timothy said, "Now what's your news? Or, more likely, our newest problem?"

"We just discovered that the Bouchard Mansion was once used as a funeral home," Theodosia said.

"Truly?" Timothy frowned. "I've never heard that before."

"What's even more disconcerting is the fact that we discovered a kind of exit door in the basement," Drayton said.

"The exit door Drayton is referring to is technically known as a casket door," Theodosia said. "It's noted as such on the old architectural plans."

Timothy stared at her, looking more than a little confused.

"A casket door is an opening that allowed caskets to be slid in and out," Theodosia explained. "The bodies were embalmed in the basement, then put into caskets and slid out the casket door to, um, probably the hearse. Or taken to whatever room in the old house served as a funeral parlor."

"Think of it like a coal chute," Drayton said. "Only for bodies."

Timothy's face slowly crumpled into a look of angst. "If there's a hidden door then it must have served as an escape route for Willow's killer."

"That's our theory, yes," Theodosia said, hating that their discovery was causing Timothy so much additional pain. "We think that's exactly why Willow's killer got away undetected."

"I'd no idea such a door existed. Then again, I don't think anyone was aware the old place had been used as a funeral home," Timothy said in a hoarse voice.

"Ellis Bouchard knew," Theodosia said. "He's the one who told me about it."

"Did he now?" Timothy said.

They sat for a few moments lost in thought, listening to the pop and crackle of the fireplace.

Finally, Drayton spoke. "Well, someone besides Bouchard could have figured the casket door out as well. I hate to bring this up, but it's possible the killer is someone who works at the Heritage Society. I mean, they're the folks who readied the old mansion, so they were undoubtedly in and out at all hours of the day and night."

"Someone could have stumbled upon it," Theodosia said. "That is a distinct possibility."

"You think someone from the Heritage Society could have . . . ?" Timothy touched a hand to the side of his face. "Dear Lord, no. It's . . . too horrible to even contemplate."

"Did Willow spend a lot of time at the Heritage Society?" Theodosia asked.

"Recently, she did. Almost every day. Using our reference library as she worked on her books," Timothy said.

"So everyone knew who she was," Theodosia said. "And maybe . . ." She stopped short of what she was about to say.

"And maybe what?" Timothy asked. "Maybe someone noticed her diamond earrings?"

"Could have happened that way," Theodosia said. "Did she wear the diamonds often?"

"Often enough," Timothy said.

"Of course there are any number of outsiders who also knew Willow," Drayton said. "Who also knew about the diamonds."

"It's also possible it was someone extremely close to Willow," Theodosia said.

"Don't," Drayton said to her sharply.

"I think I pretty much have to," Theodosia replied.

"What are you two dithering about?" Timothy asked.

"I hate to bring this up, but there's an outside chance that Robert Vardell might be involved," Theodosia said.

Timothy looked suddenly defiant. "No, he can't be. Please don't even plant that seed of doubt in anyone's mind."

"We have to look at the facts," Theodosia said. "Vardell was familiar with Willow's suite of diamonds. And now the diamonds are gone, and he's inherited a very expensive home."

"But they were in love!" was Timothy's vehement response.

"Then why wasn't Willow wearing her engagement ring at the book signing Sunday night?" Theodosia asked.

Timothy was caught without an answer. "I . . . I don't know. She loved that ring. It was usually on her finger."

"And where's the ring now?" Theodosia asked. "We checked Willow's apartment fairly carefully Monday night. If we didn't find the ring then, it probably wasn't there."

"I don't know," Timothy said. He seemed to grow more and more flustered as the conversation went on.

Drayton noticed Timothy's unease and decided to step in.

"What about Henry Curtis?" Drayton asked. "He sent Willow a kind of love note. He was notably absent from tonight's visitation, and he failed to show up for work at the haunted house."

"That could all be damning evidence," Timothy said.

Theodosia leaned forward. "It could be. But here's the tricky thing. We have a number of possible suspects."

Timothy gave a slow nod as he gazed at her. "Yes?"

"We know that Ellis Bouchard is in dire financial trouble," Theodosia said. "So who knows what he's capable of doing? Allan Barnaby knew nothing about the novel Willow had written, so that's highly suspicious right there. It's even indicative of a huge crack in their relationship. Henry Curtis, one of your interns, wrote Willow a love note, but now he's—I don't know—disappeared, skipped town, hiding out somewhere? And, yes, we have to throw Robert Vardell's name into the mix as well. Whenever a woman is murdered, it's generally the boyfriend or husband who comes under suspicion and, I might add, is the person the police most fixate on. And then, I hate to keep harping on this, but there's an entire cast of characters at the Heritage Society. Any one of whom could hold an angry grudge against you, be in deep financial trouble, or have coveted Willow's diamonds in the worst way possible."

Timothy tapped his fingers against the arm of his chair as he mulled over Theodosia's words. "Those files I gave you?" he said finally.

"Yes?"

"I'd appreciate it if you went through them again. As carefully as you possibly can."

And that's exactly what Theodosia did once she'd dropped Drayton off at his home and arrived back at her own place.

But first she took Earl Grey out for a short walk and then a romp in their backyard. As Theodosia savored the cool, refreshing autumn air, she wished she could linger. There seemed to be the promise of a storm somewhere out over the Atlantic, and the tossing trees, dark skies, and stirred-up ions made Theodosia feel alive. As much as she loved sunny days, she was also comfortable with the night. Loved the idea of silky darkness wrapped around her like a comforting blanket.

But, just as she'd promised Timothy, she dutifully returned to her kitchen, fixed herself a fortifying cup of Ceylonese green tea, and headed upstairs to study the files.

As Theodosia sat in her armchair and paged through the various personnel records, she thought about how much of a person's life was contained within them. Their education, background, employment history, even their skills, abilities, and ambitions. Really, here in her hot little hands, were the entire time lines of three dozen individuals who held current positions at the Heritage Society.

Trying to be as diligent as possible, Theodosia read through each of the files. When something interesting struck her, she marked a page with a yellow Post-it note. For example, Charles Dreyfus, the curator of drawings, had once worked at an auction house that specialized in fine paintings and precious jewelry. The information wasn't damning; more like a fact that should be examined more carefully.

She looked at Elisha Summers's file, then the personnel files for Harold Roman and Donovan Street, but nothing struck her as odd or unusual. She started through the final dozen files, her head beginning to swim as she parsed through page after page of information. It was getting late and she was tired. The clock was crawling toward midnight, so it was almost time to hang it up for the night.

Thank goodness Claire Waltho's file was fairly straightforward. She'd gotten her MA in art history at Northwestern, then her PhD at the University of Iowa. Her job history included a three-year stint as a curator at the Shelby Museum in South Dakota.

Hmm.

Theodosia shuffled through the various pages. For some reason, she remembered a mention of Claire working at the

Norton Simon Museum in Pasadena, not the Shelby. On the other hand, Claire could have worked at both places. It was a slight discrepancy, maybe a paper misplaced, but something Theodosia would probably want to double-check nonetheless.

Finally, Theodosia opened Henry Curtis's file. There wasn't much there. He was just a lowly intern after all.

Henry had graduated from the Palmetto Academy, a private school for grades nine through twelve, and was currently enrolled as a junior at the College of Charleston. He was working on a double major in art history and American studies. Henry's employment history was negligible. He'd worked part-time at a Books-A-Million as well as a local antiques store.

And now Henry's an intern at the Heritage Society where he rubbed shoulders—and corresponded with, I might might add—Willow French.

Theodosia decided that she needed to question Henry again. And question him fairly hard.

Then, on an impulse, Theodosia reached over and grabbed her laptop. She opened it up and clicked along to Willow's Facebook page.

What she saw was heartbreaking. Pictures of Willow smiling out at her, looking happy and expectant. As if she was beyond thrilled with her promising career as an author and was looking forward to a long and productive life.

Tears sparkled in Theodosia's eyes. "I'm sorry, Willow," she whispered. "I'm hunting for your killer, really I am. I'll try not to let you down."

20

❧

With one hundred and thirty acres of graves, tombs, chapels, and mausoleums, Magnolia Cemetery stood as a prime example of Victorian cemetery design. And today it was being doused with rain. The storm cell that Theodosia had sensed hovering out over the Atlantic had charged its way into Charleston overnight, chilling down the air a good twenty degrees and unleashing a light spatter of rain.

"It would have to rain today," Drayton said. He was hunched in the front seat of Theodosia's Jeep, fussing with the heater. Haley sat in back looking glum. Rain pattered down as they drove through the cemetery's stately gates.

"Perfect weather for a funeral," Theodosia said. She was still frustrated with herself for not being more proactive, for not being able to figure things out. All her life she'd possessed a keep-moving-forward, get-it-done attitude, but now she was starting to worry. She had suspects, strange discoveries, and multiple theories, but still no concrete answers. Nothing seemed to jell.

"Now we'll have to stand in a downpour and get soaked," Haley said. She'd been grumpy since the minute Theodosia had swung by the tea shop and picked her up.

"It's a drizzle, not a downpour. Besides, I've got umbrellas tucked in back," Theodosia said. After her discovery of the casket door last night, her mind was in too much turmoil to be bothered by a little bad weather.

"Thank goodness for that," Drayton said as he peered through the rain-spattered windshield. "Now we just have to figure out where the grave site is and which road to take."

Magnolia Cemetery was a warren of dirt and blacktopped single-lane roads that snaked through the extensive grounds. Besides all the graveyards and additions, there were two small lagoons and dozens of ornate sculptures, many dating back to the eighteen fifties. Thick stands of live oak dripping with Spanish moss, magnolia bushes, weeping willows, and cypress trees served to curtain off entire areas.

"There. Go left," Drayton said.

"You sure?" Theodosia asked as she cranked her steering wheel.

"Pretty sure. Well, at least it's a start."

"More like a commitment," Theodosia said. "Once we're on one of these one-way roads it's practically impossible to circle back to point A."

But they were in luck. Past the chapel, around bird circle, then a half mile on, near a series of mausoleums and pyramid-shaped tombs that held a who's who of former senators, governors, and Confederate generals, they came upon a scatter of cars. And beyond the cars, they saw a dark-green canopy that had been erected to shield a cluster of mourners who were milling about, hoping to claim a seat on one of a dozen black folding chairs.

"Here we are," Drayton said, as Theodosia swerved to the side of the road and rolled to a stop. "We've arrived."

After unfurling umbrellas, the three of them tromped across soggy, spongy grass to the grave site where the mourners had taken refuge from the rain and battering wind beneath the green canopy.

Sybil Spalding saw them coming and came out to greet them, hunching in the rain, handing each of them a printed program.

"Thank you," Theodosia said as she accepted her program. "By the way, is Henry Curtis here?"

Sybil shook her head. "I haven't seen him yet."

"Do you think he'll show up?"

Sybil gave a shrug. "Who knows?"

But certain other parties were there.

Allan Barnaby was there with Delaine—big surprise—though Theodosia figured Delaine was probably leading him around by the nose.

Robert Vardell, the fiancé, was seated in the first row of chairs along with Willow's parents and Timothy Neville. Behind them were people she recognized from the Heritage Society, both employees and board members.

Theodosia, Drayton, and Haley found seats in the last row of chairs. And after Sybil handed out her last program, she came and sat next to Theodosia.

"Cold," Sybil said. "Not as many people showed up as we thought."

Theodosia took a look around, then her brows pinched together.

"Claire's not here. Claire Waltho," she said.

"Oh, you didn't hear?" Sybil said. "Claire's mother is seriously ill."

"Oh no."

"Claire's been walking a kind of tightrope these last few weeks, trying to take care of her mother and still carry on her duties at the Heritage Society."

"What a shame," Theodosia said as she watched the minister step up to the podium. "About her mother, I mean. I had no idea."

The minister was a friend of Timothy Neville's, an associate pastor at the French Huguenot Church. He led the small group in a number of prayers, then gave a wonderful talk about Willow, highlighting her accomplishments for someone so young, and ruing the fact that her life, though filled with great promise, had been cut woefully short. The minister did not mention that Willow had been murdered, or that her killer was still at large.

Always a little jittery at funerals and memorial services, Theodosia glanced around the crowd. She noted that Willow's parents were huddled together in stunned silence, while, standing at the back of the pack, was Detective Burt Tidwell. He seemed to be assessing the mourners rather than following along with the service.

Must be a trick of the trade, Theodosia thought. *Hang out at the funeral, see who shows up and who doesn't.*

When the final prayer had been concluded, when the mourners had done their very best at singing an a capella rendition of "Amazing Grace," the minister thanked everyone for coming, then announced that all were invited to attend a funeral brunch at the Lady Goodwood Inn.

That seemed to be Tidwell's cue to sidle over and catch Theodosia, just as she was about to head back to her car.

"You were right about Ellis Bouchard," Tidwell said out of the corner of his mouth. "I did some checking, and the man is slowly going broke. It's no wonder he's contesting the will and trying to regain control of that mansion."

"You talked to him?" Theodosia was surprised he'd actually listened to her.

Tidwell pulled his lips into a semi-sneer. "No, but we plan to."

"Soon, I hope." Theodosia hesitated. Should she tell Tidwell about finding the casket door last night? She mulled it over for a few moments and decided she almost had to. It was a critical piece of information.

"There's something else you should know," Theodosia said.

"There usually is."

"No, this is something that figures directly into the investigation."

Tidwell lifted a single bushy eyebrow. "Yours or mine?"

She ignored Tidwell's sarcasm and quickly told him about the mansion's bizarre past as a funeral home and then recounted her and Drayton's adventure in the basement last night.

Much to Theodosia's surprise, Tidwell listened thoughtfully.

"No one's ever mentioned the funeral home angle to me," Tidwell said. "And you say there's an actual casket door? How very nineteenth-century macabre. No wonder it's been turned into a haunted house." He pursed his lips. "Tell me, does anyone else know about this strange exit door?"

"Only me, Drayton, Timothy Neville, and, I'd guess, the killer."

"Then let's keep it that way, shall we?" Tidwell said as he turned and walked away.

Timothy Neville looked frazzled beyond belief as he crossed the wet grass to bid goodbye to Theodosia, Drayton, and Haley.

"Thank you all for coming," he rasped.

"A sad day," Drayton said, clasping Timothy's hands in a solemn handshake.

"Probably the worst day of my life," Timothy said. The shoulders of his trench coat were damp, and he looked absolutely bereft. "To top it off, one of the Edgar Allan Poe books we had on display at our symposium yesterday has gone missing."

"What do you mean missing?" Drayton asked.

"As in vanished from sight, probably never to be seen again," Timothy said.

"It's a valuable book?" Theodosia asked.

"A volume of the same imprint and vintage sold for more than three thousand dollars at Christie's last year," Timothy said.

"Then it's more than just missing," Theodosia said. "That sort of theft is considered a felony offense and carries jail time. You need to report this to the police immediately, let them investigate."

Timothy's face went slack. "If I do, they might pull someone off Willow's case. And that would break my heart."

"So what are you going to do?" Drayton asked.

Timothy shook his head. "I don't know."

He looked, Theodosia thought, as sad and despondent as anyone she'd ever seen.

As the three of them walked back to her Jeep, Theodosia watched Allan Barnaby help Delaine into the passenger seat of a small brown van. And she wondered about him. Just how well was Barnaby's publishing firm doing? Theodosia knew that signing authors to contracts, publishing books, and getting good distribution was a tough, grinding, competitive business. Besides the large New York publishers, there were thousands of small, independent presses that were jockeying for position. To say nothing of self-published authors.

Could Barnaby have murdered Willow and then broken into her apartment and stolen her computer? Theodosia wondered. Maybe stealing the diamonds was just a last-second whim when what he really wanted was to get his hands on her new novel.

Maybe, but it was a long-shot maybe.

On the ride back into town, Theodosia probed Haley gently about Willow.

"I take it you two were pretty good friends?" Theodosia glanced at Haley in the rearview mirror.

"I guess," Haley said.

"Did she share much information about Robert Vardell?"

"Not really. Willow was funny that way. It was like they existed in their own little bubble. Apparently, Robert is some kind of financial hotshot. He's always frantically busy following the stock market and wooing important new clients. Taking them out for drinks, or golfing at the Country Club of Charleston."

"So Robert Vardell is quite successful?" Drayton asked. He knew that particular country club was not only private, but had a waiting list to join.

"To hear Willow talk about Vardell, he was a financial genius who'd probably end up heading his own hedge fund within the year," Haley said.

"Do you know anything about their engagement or wedding plans?" Theodosia asked.

"A little," Haley said. "I know Willow was planning to have a small wedding with family and a few close friends. And then later that night, there'd be a reception for a larger group of people at the Avalon Hotel. Kind of like a cocktail party. You know, very tasteful. Martinis and cosmopolitans, a jazz quartet, that sort of thing.

Drayton turned in his seat to gaze at Haley. "And you were invited to attend?"

Haley sniffled loudly. "That was the plan, yeah."

They had reached Broad Street when Drayton looked at his watch, an antique Patek Philippe, and said, "We have enough time to drop by the funeral brunch."

"That's what I thought," Theodosia said.

"Not me," Haley said. "I don't want to go."

"Whyever not?" Drayton asked.

"I'm not in the mood," Haley said. "I'd rather go back to the tea shop, shove some blueberry scones in the oven, and get things ready for lunch. In fact, you can drop me off right here. Pull over, Theo, will you? I'll walk the rest of the way; it'll help clear my head."

"Come have a quick bite with us," Drayton urged. "It'll cheer you up."

"You know what would cheer me up?" Haley said.

"What?" Theodosia asked as she slowed her car and pulled to the curb. She had a pretty good idea of what Haley was going to say.

Haley set her jaw in a hard line. "I'd be happy if Willow's killer was caught and put in prison to rot for all eternity."

21

❧

As Theodosia and Drayton walked into the Rose Room at the Lady Goodwood Inn, Drayton took one look at the swarm of people queuing up for the buffet and said, "There are significantly more people here than attended this morning's graveside service."

"I'm sure people were fearful about the weather," Theodosia said.

"But delighted to partake of free food," he said in a droll, disapproving voice.

"Looks that way. Care to get in line then?"

"After you," Drayton said.

"How's my hair?" Theodosia was worried the high humidity had caused it to expand to gigantic proportions. "Has it gone bouffant?"

"Maybe a little."

She patted it self-consciously. "Oh dear."

"You're fine," Drayton said.

The food that the Lady Goodwood's executive chef was

serving in large silver chafing dishes was absolutely splendid.

There was golden-brown French toast stuffed with cream cheese and strawberries. Zucchini blossoms oozing with cheese. Crab cakes with rémoulade sauce. And several more elegant dishes.

"Be still my heart," Drayton said as they moved down the line, helping themselves. "They're serving their special roast chicken perloo."

"And baked monkfish with mustard and herb crust," Theodosia said.

"Mmn, and is that dessert I see?" Drayton asked expectantly, even though his plate was practically filled to overflowing.

"Looks like raspberry tartlets and lemon cheesecake squares."

"This is my idea of a classy brunch. Now what we need"—Drayton scanned the room—"is to find ourselves a table."

"There are a couple of empty seats over there." Theodosia nodded. "Where Delaine and Allan Barnaby are sitting."

"Do we have to?"

"Play nice," Theodosia told him.

But when they sat down, Delaine only gave them a cursory howdy-do. Then she went back to bending Barnaby's ear with a monologue about the all-too-fabulous Italian knits they'd just gotten in at Cotton Duck.

"I tell you, the jackets and skirts drape the body like spun silk," Delaine enthused. "Those weavers are absolute geniuses, and the knits are the most remarkable colors. Primrose pink, honey butter yellow, patina green, golden flax, and . . ." Her eyes practically crossed. "Have you ever heard of peanut? Well, that's one of the actual colors. A *fabulous* color. Utterly divine yet *terribly* subtle . . ."

Drayton shot a look at Theodosia. As he'd once remarked, the woman dined out on adverbs.

Delaine prattled on as Barnaby's enthusiasm for his new lady friend seemed to wane. Delaine might look like a fabulous hothouse flower, someone you'd love to have on your arm, but once you got to know her, you realized the woman had an edge. An edge that could relentlessly scrape away at your sanity.

Fact was, Barnaby looked positively relieved when Robert Vardell walked up to their table. Until Vardell started screaming at him, that is.

"You!" Vardell shrilled at the top of his lungs. "Barnaby!"

Looking startled, Barnaby rose in his seat.

"Excuse me?" he said.

"It's all your fault!" Vardell shrieked.

"What'd I do?" Barnaby's face was a mixture of embarrassment and confusion.

"You're responsible for Willow's death! First you paraded the poor girl all over town, from bookseller to big-box store, then you set up a book signing at that ridiculous haunted house. There wasn't an inkling of security to protect her from those crazy costumed characters. And nothing to protect her from the hordes of people who came flocking in. It was a recipe for disaster!"

Barnaby finally found his voice. "Willow *wanted* to do the book signing!" he sputtered. "She asked for it. Saw it as a wonderful opportunity."

"More like an opportunity for you!" Vardell shouted. His face had turned beet red, and blobs of spit flew from his mouth.

"For me?" Barnaby was taken aback.

Both men were shouting at the top of their lungs now. Conversation in the room quickly came to a screeching halt. Heads turned, ears were cocked, chairs were jockeyed in order to get a better view of the bizarre fight that was unfolding.

Vardell continued to rain harsh vitriol down upon Allan Barnaby.

"My fiancée is *dead*! And now that her murder's been

splashed across every newspaper and television station, you're probably selling a *ton* of books. Don't writers and artists always become more famous once they're dead!"

Delaine fluttered her hands in front of her face in a gesture of foolish helplessness. Then she turned toward Theodosia and begged, "Theo, *do* something!"

But Theodosia didn't have to lift a finger. Or raise her voice. There was a sudden loud shuffle of heavy footsteps, then the door to the Rose Room flew open and Detective Burt Tidwell burst in. Looking highly official as well as determined, he was flanked by two uniformed officers. All of them looked as if they had serious business to attend to.

The room was suddenly quiet as a tomb.

Tidwell glanced dismissively at Vardell and Barnaby, who were still squared off like a couple of squabbling chickens. Then his beady eyes darted from table to table until they finally landed on Ellis Bouchard.

"Mr. Bouchard," Tidwell said in a loud, brook-no-nonsense tone.

Ellis Bouchard, who was two tables away from Theodosia, seemed to shrink and cower in his chair.

"If you'd come along with us," Tidwell said.

"Me?" Bouchard's voice rose in a piteous squawk. "Why me?"

"Please, just come along with the officers."

"But why? What did I do?" Bouchard's face had turned a pasty white as the two officers walked over and stared down at him.

"We're not accusing you of anything," Tidwell said. "We just want to talk with you and clarify a few points."

Every eye followed Ellis Bouchard as he was escorted from the room by the two officers. Vardell, looking as if he'd escaped a fate worse than death, slunk away. Barnaby sat down, pulled out a white hankie, and blotted his face.

"Allan," Delaine said. "You look like you're ready to faint." She sounded annoyed rather than concerned.

"Well," Drayton said, once the buzz of conversation started up again. "That was interesting."

Theodosia smiled. She figured that Tidwell had taken her words to heart and couldn't wait to pepper Bouchard with a barrage of questions about the old mansion and its secret casket door. And maybe quiz him a bit more on his failing real estate business.

Could this be it? she wondered. *Is Bouchard the killer?*

Then she thought about the case she'd made to Timothy last night. How she'd tossed Robert Vardell's name into the mix of suspects.

"Pardon me," Theodosia said. She put a hand on Drayton's shoulder as she stood up. "I need to talk to someone."

"Who?" Drayton asked.

But Theodosia was already making a beeline for Robert Vardell.

She caught him just as he stood up from his table after saying goodbye to Willow's parents.

"Excuse me," Theodosia said.

Vardell spun around to face her. "Yes?" His face was flushed as he buttoned his jacket hastily, looking as if he were in a terrific hurry.

"Why wasn't Willow wearing her engagement ring in the days before she was murdered?" Theodosia asked him. "Can you explain that?"

Vardell stared at her, a hard, distrustful look spreading across his face. Then he shook his head. "You people."

"*Excuse* me?"

"You amateur detectives. Always jumping at shadows and seeing suspects at every turn." Now his voice was both smarmy and disdainful.

"I asked you a question," Theodosia said. She wasn't about to let Vardell off the hook. Especially when he was being so nasty.

"You know what?" Vardell said, as he slipped past her.

"This is not a good time. I have important business back at my office."

"Really?" Theodosia shouted after him. "Your business can't wait? Even on the day of your fiancée's funeral?"

Theodosia stood there. Feeling angry and a little foolish. Vardell had blown her off as if she were nothing at all.

"Problem?" Drayton asked, coming up to her.

"Not only did Robert Vardell refuse to talk to me, he was incredibly rude and dismissive."

"I'm afraid that's a common malady these days."

Theodosia shrugged. She knew she had to let it go. For now, anyway. Others were watching her, and Willow's parents were still seated at the table, looking sorrowful and a little dazed.

"I suppose it's time to get back to the tea shop, yes?" Theodosia said. "We've probably worn out our welcome here."

Drayton glanced over at Willow's parents. "We haven't just worn it out, we've extinguished it."

22

❧

Theodosia and Drayton arrived at the Indigo Tea Shop a little before eleven o'clock, just in time for lunch. From the wonderful aromas that perfumed the air it was obvious Haley hadn't just baked the blueberry scones that she'd mentioned earlier. A quick stop in the kitchen revealed apple tea bread, mushroom quiche, and lentil soup. Haley had also brewed a couple pots of tea.

Now she was digging in a cardboard box that sat on one of the tables, pulling out Halloween decorations.

"If you're stringing up images of witches and goblins, you must be feeling some better," Drayton said.

Haley turned and favored him with a wan smile. "I guess so."

"Good to hear," Theodosia said.

"How was the brunch?" Haley asked.

"Delicious," Theodosia said.

"Slightly manic," Drayton said.

"Haley, why don't you let me finish decorating," Theodosia said. "I'm sure you've got lots to do yet in the kitchen."

Haley nodded. "Yeah, I think I'm also gonna do a harvest salad and throw together some curried chicken salad puffs. It'll be a slightly abbreviated menu today, but a good one."

"Sounds wonderful," Theodosia said.

"And thanks for brewing a pot of Keemun tea," Drayton said. "It's the perfect rainy day pick-me-up."

"Yeah, whatever," Haley said as she dashed off.

"She's still bummed," Theodosia said.

"She'll survive," Drayton said as he picked up a tabloid that was sitting on the counter.

"You think we'll get many customers today?" Theodosia asked. She'd just replaced the CLOSED sign on the front door with one that said OPEN FOR TEA AND LIGHT LUNCHES.

Drayton shook his head as he turned pages. "No idea."

"What's that you're reading?"

"Today's issue of *Shooting Star*. It was sitting here with the rest of the mail."

"Oh no, did Bill Glass put anything in there about Willow?"

"Only if you count a page-one story," Drayton said.

"Please tell me he didn't print a photograph."

"No, thank goodness." Drayton glanced up as the front door opened and a whoosh of wind and rain swept in along with Leigh Carroll, the woman who owned the Cabbage Patch Gift Shop down the block.

"Brrr," Leigh said, clutching a shawl around her shoulders. "It's downright chilly out there." Leigh was African-American, in her early thirties, and a former coffee drinker that Drayton had converted to tea. She was always upbeat, oozed tons of charm, and, with her almond eyes, sepia-toned hair, and skin the color of rich mahogany, was quite elegant.

"Drayton," Leigh said, "that Spode teapot—the one you were so interested in—it finally arrived."

"The Kingsley pattern?"

"That's the one."

Drayton tipped a finger at her. "I'm going to drop by later and have a look."

"Do that," Leigh said. "I think it'll be a great addition to your collection." Then she turned to Theodosia and said, "The-o-do-sia! Did I hear via the Church Street rumor mill that your handsome boyfriend was wounded in some kind of crazy shoot-out?"

"Oh, Leigh, it was awful," Theodosia said. "Riley was investigating Willow French's murder at that haunted house . . ."

"The one over on Tradd?" Leigh asked.

"Yes. And then, when he went to Willow's apartment to look around, he stumbled upon what we suspect was the killer and got shot."

Leigh's face immediately registered sympathy. "That's absolutely terrifying, Theo, you must've been horribly upset."

"I was. For a while."

"So Riley's laid up in the hospital?"

"He was just released," Theodosia said. "But with a gunshot wound to his arm. He claims he's feeling much better but . . . I don't know. I'm still worried."

Leigh touched a hand to her chest. "Of course you are. I'll be sure to say a little prayer for him tonight."

"And for Willow," Theodosia said.

"Oh, poor Willow." Leigh's face crumpled in a look of pure distress. "Such a lovely girl. And such a talented writer, too. You know she was registered with me?"

Theodosia wasn't sure what Leigh was talking about for a second. Then she said, "Oh, you mean your bridal registry?"

"Well, Willow was probably registered with a few other

shops, too." Leigh paused, as if she were thinking something over. "But if the rumor I heard was true, I'm not sure Willow's wedding would have even taken place."

Theodosia stiffened. "What are you talking about?" What did Leigh know that she didn't? Had the wedding been called off? Postponed? Did this have something to do with Willow not wearing her engagement ring? Just as she'd theorized, had a nasty rift developed between Willow and Robert? Was that why Robert Vardell wouldn't answer her questions this morning? Was he embarrassed about being dumped? Or could he be racked with guilt?

Seeing Theodosia's distress, Leigh said, "I heard from my friend Mindy McGovern—you know she's catering manager over at the Avalon Hotel—that Willow canceled her evening reception."

Theodosia stood there, her mouth practically dropping open. All she could manage was, "No way."

Leigh gave an uncertain shrug. "That's what I heard anyway. Maybe there was a last-minute change of plans and Willow was going to have her reception someplace else? But I really don't know."

"Maybe I'll give Mindy a call and see if she can confirm that," Theodosia said.

Leigh narrowed her eyes. "Girlfriend, what crazy thing are you involved in anyway?"

"Well, Riley *is* my boyfriend. And Willow was Timothy Neville's grandniece."

Leigh put a hand up to her mouth. "Timothy's . . . oh, that's right."

"You know how Timothy is. He has such a strong sense of responsibility and takes everything personally. So he's not only grieving for Willow; he feels responsible for her death."

Leigh shook her head. "He shouldn't."

"That's just Timothy. He's a pillar of stoicism . . . until he isn't."

"And let me guess, Timothy asked you to get involved?"

"I'm already involved," Theodosia said for the ump-teenth time that week, then decided she had to stop repeating it. She was getting tired of hearing herself say it.

Poised at her desk, Theodosia called the number for the Avalon Hotel. Mindy wasn't there, but Eric Reiffer, the ho-tel manager, was. And he was able to confirm to Theodosia that Willow had indeed canceled her reception.

"Wow," Theodosia said as she hung up. Things were starting to pop. But clearly not in Robert Vardell's favor. She could hear Drayton talking with customers out in the tea room and knew she should hustle out there to help. She still needed to call Henry Curtis and grill him about a few things, but she decided there was another, more important call she had to make first. Hastily googling the firm of Met-calf and Solange, she found their website and contact infor-mation, then dialed their number.

The phone was promptly answered with a friendly, "Good day, Metcalf and Solange."

"Hello, I was wondering if you could connect me with Robert Vardell," Theodosia said.

"Just a moment . . . Oh, wait, I'm afraid he's gone for the day."

"Then perhaps I could leave a message with his admin-istrative assistant?"

"Um." The receptionist paused for a long moment, then said, "I'm sorry, perhaps you've been misinformed. Robert Vardell *is* the administrative assistant."

"What!" Theodosia couldn't help herself.

"He works under Mr. Collingsworth, our senior account executive. Actually, Robert is the second assistant. Perhaps you'd like to speak with the first assistant? I could put you through."

"No, I'm . . . a little confused here. I thought Robert Vardell held a major position in your company."

The receptionist gave an embarrassed laugh. "Well, he was up for a trainee job as a junior customer service representative, but that position was given to someone else."

"I see," Theodosia said. "Thank you."

Her heart was racing a mile a minute as she hung up and rushed out into the tea room.

23

He's a flunky, Theodosia cried. "A poseur."

Drayton's hands hovered above the two pots of tea he'd just brewed as he looked up and said, "Pardon?"

"Robert Vardell." Theodosia windmilled her arms in frustration. She felt frazzled and oddly betrayed. "He's not a high-test executive at all. He *works* for one. He's an assistant. Actually, the second assistant."

"How on earth did you . . . ?"

"I just called his office where the receptionist spilled the proverbial beans to me!"

"Gracious," Drayton said. "And all along we thought Vardell was . . ."

"An investment hotshot. A financial whiz kid. Well, he's not."

Drayton stared at her. "What do you think this means?"

Theodosia lifted one shoulder. "Are you kidding? If Vardell lied about work, what else do you think he lied about?"

"Could be anything. Or everything."

"Could be his relationship with Willow?"

"You think *he* killed her?" Drayton said.

"It's not out of the realm of possibility," Theodosia said. "What if Willow found out that Vardell had been lying to her and then confronted him in a major way? What if Willow *thought* she was marrying a financial genius only to find out she was engaged to the office gopher? A guy who might have only been in the relationship for the money."

"So a nasty argument ensues, and Willow breaks off the engagement? As well as the wedding?" Drayton surmised.

"And then Vardell, who had high hopes of sitting fat and sassy with Willow's money and, I might add, a brand-new house, suddenly finds himself left out in the cold."

"So he switches out his plan, murders Willow, steals her diamonds, and keeps the house?" Drayton's words poured out rapid fire—bing, bang, boom. He seemed to have readily bought into Theodosia's theory.

"Jeepers, Drayton, it *could* have happened that way. I mean, it really could have!" Theodosia was both terrified and excited. She had to know more. No, what she really needed to do was find Robert Vardell and confront him directly! Watch his face when she hurled her accusations at him!

Drayton burst her bubble.

"You have to tell Tidwell about this," he said. "Like, right now."

"But I was planning to track Vardell down and . . ."

"And what? Confront the man in person? Throw the bitter truth in his face?"

"Something like that," Theodosia said.

"That's far too dangerous. You need to turn this information over to the authorities. Let them deal with Robert Vardell." Drayton stared at her. "Think of it as your contribution to law enforcement."

"Maybe the authorities already know."

"And maybe they don't. Go ahead, call them," Drayton said.

"Now?"

"There's no time like the present."

Theodosia went back to her office, still trying to decide if she should make the call. She plopped down in her desk chair, picked up a pen, and twiddled it between her fingers. She mulled it over, the pros and cons, changed her mind a few times. Then, finally, she called Detective Burt Tidwell's office.

She didn't reach Tidwell directly—he was harder to get hold of than the president—but she did talk to an investigator named Glen Humphries. She told him about her discovery, trying to be as calm and succinct as possible. Humphries listened carefully, thanked her, and assured her they would follow up on the information.

"You're sure you don't want me to come over there?" Theodosia asked. "Go through this in person with Detective Tidwell? Lay it all out for him?"

"No," Humphries said. "We'll take care of it."

Because it was still drizzling outside, only half of the tea room was filled for lunch today. Good thing, because Theodosia was still vibrating with outrage and excitement. Discovering that Robert Vardell was a bold-faced liar had pretty much changed everything. He'd suddenly been catapulted from a maybe directly to numero uno on her suspect list. And what Theodosia still wanted most of all was to confront him face-to-face. Before the Charleston Police Department got their hot little hands on Vardell, before he lawyered up. Easier said than done, however, because Vardell seemed to be a moving target. And if he knew he'd been exposed as a fraud, he might just go into hiding.

Theodosia's brain was in a whirl as she took orders, served lunch, and hustled back to the kitchen to pick up the food. She needed to tell Timothy about this new development, too. Although she feared it would upset him even more, maybe even tip him over the edge.

"Earth to Theo," Haley said. "Here are your two bowls of lentil soup."

Theodosia pulled herself out of her head and back into the here and now.

"Okay, thanks, Haley. You do know your chicken salad puffs are going like hotcakes out there? The guests are loving them."

"Is Drayton serving the Queen's Blend green tea from Plum Deluxe? You know that's such a nice accompaniment to chicken."

"I'm pretty sure he did brew a pot."

"Hey, remember when you were asking me about Willow? About her engagement and stuff?"

Theodosia cocked her head at Haley. "Yes?"

"Well, I remembered another thing. I don't know if it's going to help . . ."

"What is it, Haley? What did you remember?"

"I know Willow was working with some hotshot wedding planner. A guy who specialized in super elegant weddings and was taking care of all the picky little details for her."

"Do you know the wedding planner's name?"

Haley thought for a few moments, then shook her head. "Nope. She told me, but I guess I forgot."

"Okay. Still, that's an interesting sidebar."

By one fifteen, things had settled down at the tea shop. Keeping an eye on her late customers, as well as a few who were still lingering, Theodosia finally called the Heritage Society and asked for Henry Curtis.

"Henry's not here," one of the women in the conservation department told her. "He was supposed to work today, but he never showed up."

"Did he call in?"

"Not to my knowledge."

"Okay, thanks," Theodosia said. She thought about Henry Curtis and decided his no-show at the haunted house, the funeral, and now his internship at the Heritage Society was also puzzling. Did Henry have something to hide? Was she barking up the wrong tree with Robert Vardell? Maybe Vardell was just a liar and a poseur. Maybe Henry Curtis was the one she should be investigating.

Theodosia's thoughts were interrupted when Haley came out into the tea room to talk with her.

"Got something I want to run by you," Haley said.

"Sure."

"You know that Enchanted Garden Party we're catering at the Featherbed House this Saturday?" Haley said.

Theodosia nodded.

"I was thinking of making a raven cake."

Drayton peered at Haley over his half-glasses. "You're going to bake a raven? Won't the feathers gum up your oven?"

"Not a *real* one," Haley laughed. "A cake that's in the *shape* of a raven."

"In other words, you're going to make one of your fabulous fondant creations," Theodosia said. "A glitzed-up Halloween cake."

"Yeah," Haley said. "Probably sculpt my raven out of chocolate cake, make feathers out of fondant, and use colored candy for the eyes." She paused. "Do you think Angie would like that?"

"I think she'd love it," Theodosia said. Angie Congdon was the owner of the Featherbed House B and B and one of Theodosia's dear friends. Angie also loved a good theme party.

"You know what else would be cool? I mean, for Drayton to do?" Haley said.

"I await your suggestion with bated breath," Drayton said.

Haley reached out and poked a finger at Drayton's chest. "You could do one of your readings."

"Ah. You were thinking perhaps a work by Edgar Allan Poe?" Drayton asked.

"Why not? It'd be perfect for Halloween. More than perfect," Haley said.

"Interesting idea," Drayton said. He spoke in a casual, offhand manner, but Theodosia and Haley could see that he was almost gung ho to do it.

"Just noodle it around," Haley said as she disappeared back into her kitchen.

"What do you think?" Drayton asked Theodosia. "About my doing a reading?"

"I think it's a grand idea. Angie and her guests will love it. I mean, they're decorating the garden to look all spooky, so a reading will fit in perfectly. Besides, it's Halloween. People expect a few thrills and chills."

Drayton scratched his head. "I'm not sure I have a book of Poe in my library at home. Pity that special one went missing from the Heritage Society."

"Tell you what, I'm pretty sure I know where I can lay my hands on one," Theodosia said.

Lois Chamberlain, the proprietor of Antiquarian Books, looked up from the book she was reading as Theodosia walked through her front door. Lois was a compact woman in her late fifties who today wore a dark-green pullover sweater, black yoga pants, and bright-red half-glasses. Her long gray hair was plaited in a single braid that extended halfway down her back.

"Thank goodness, a customer," Lois said with her trademark crinkly smile. She was a former librarian who'd opened a used-book store when the previous occupant, a small map store, had gone belly-up and moved out owing several months' rent. Now Lois occupied the space and dealt in used, vintage, and collectible books. With her smarts and knowledge of the book world, she seemed to be making a go of the place.

"Hey, Lois," Theodosia said. "Do you have anything by Edgar Allan Poe?"

"Does a one-legged duck swim in a circle?" Lois asked. Then added, "I probably have two shelves full of Poe. Over there, Theo. The bookcase against the far wall. Look under the red sign that says P to Q." She chuckled. "Or maybe I should change it to read P's and Q's."

Lois actually had more than four dozen books on Poe, but Theodosia chose the one that she knew contained the poem "The Raven" to complement Haley's proposed cake. Theodosia carried the book to the counter and set it down.

"How much?"

"Ten dollars," Lois said. "Let me guess. Is Drayton doing a reading?"

Theodosia nodded. "A little extra entertainment for the Enchanted Garden Party at the Featherbed House."

Lois picked up the book and studied it. "Good old Edgar Allan. Ever since he spent that year or so here in Charleston, stalking our windswept beaches and writing poetry, he's been one popular fella. Especially when Halloween rolls around. Even so, I sell a lot of these books all year. Sometimes it's hard to keep them in stock."

Theodosia opened her wallet, pulled out a ten-dollar bill, and slid it across the counter.

"Lois, you're a book person. Does the name Allan Barnaby ring any bells with you?"

"Sure does," Lois said, as she put the Poe book into a small paper sack.

Theodosia didn't think she'd strike pay dirt quite so easily. But seeing that she had, she decided to ask Lois a couple of questions.

"Really? How do you know Barnaby? Or I should say, *what* do you know about him?"

"You mean Barnaby's curriculum vitae? All I know is he's a partner in a newish publishing firm."

"Barnaby and Boise."

Lois cocked a finger at her. "That's it. You know, I even stock a couple of their authors."

"How are those books doing?"

"Okay, I guess."

"Actually, I'm more interested in how the publisher is doing," Theodosia said.

"Obviously, Barnaby and Boise is new to the game, but their sales and distribution seem fairly solid," Lois said. "Though I'm not sure their consumer marketing efforts have been all that extensive. Allan Barnaby's expertise, of course, lies mainly in used books."

Had Theodosia heard her correctly? "*Used* books?"

Lois nodded. "Sure. Allan Barnaby made his chops as a rare-book dealer."

Theodosia's heart skipped a beat. Was Barnaby still dealing rare books on the side? Could he have stolen the Heritage Society's Edgar Allan Poe book?

"Do you know, was Barnaby fairly successful as a dealer of rare books?"

"Well . . ." Lois blinked. "I know that Allan Barnaby owned a bookshop down in Savannah for several years. On Whitaker Street where some of the more upscale retailers are located. So I'm guessing he did fairly well."

Back at the tea shop, Theodosia handed the Edgar Allan Poe book over to Drayton and said, "Guess what."

He gazed at her, a question on his face. "This is Timothy's missing book?"

"I wish. Guess again."

"I couldn't possibly."

"Lois just told me that Allan Barnaby used to be a rare-book dealer."

Drayton frowned. "That information strikes me as fairly . . . ominous."

"Tell me about it. Just when I'd settled on either Robert Vardell or Ellis Bouchard as the killer, good old Barnaby breaks from the back of the pack and comes racing down the homestretch," Theodosia said.

"Just because Barnaby might have filched Timothy's rare book you think that makes him a killer?"

Theodosia put both hands on the counter and leaned forward. "Drayton, I don't know. I guess what I've got to do is . . ." She stopped for a few moments and tried to focus her thoughts. Did she know what she had to do? Well, yes, she actually did. "If I want to come up with persuasive evidence that I can present to the police, evidence that points directly to one single person, then I've got to work a whole lot harder."

"No," Drayton said. "*We've* got to work a lot harder."

Theodosia saw the look of intensity on Drayton's face. "You're still willing to help? Really?"

"Haven't I been helping so far?"

"A person couldn't ask for a better amateur detective partner," Theodosia said, flashing him an appreciative smile.

"Well there you go," Drayton said. "We'll just keep sticking our noses in where they don't belong."

"I guess it's like they say in poker, Drayton. We're all in."

24

❧

Tonight was a big night for Earl Grey. For Theodosia, too. They'd shown up at Pete Riley's apartment around six thirty and immediately started cooking dinner. Well, Theodosia was doing the cooking; Earl Grey was more like hanging out and kibitzing.

"This is so great of you guys to come over," Riley said. He was walking around in jeans, a T-shirt that said BACK THE BLUE, and stocking feet. His left arm was in a sling, and he was sipping from a can of Hilton Head Crab Pilsner.

"You're not taking pain meds with that, are you?" Theodosia asked. She didn't want him to doze off before dinner. Or put himself into a stupor.

"Nope, I'm good," Riley said. "Don't even need the pain pills anymore. I didn't take any yesterday, either."

"Well, I'm glad we finally have some together time. I'm glad you found a break in your busy schedule for us," Theodosia said.

"Yeah, well, it's been weird. This whole week has been weird."

"Tell me about it."

Riley had requested Theodosia's famous chicken with cheese and prosciutto, so that's what she was busy fixing. She'd already dipped her chicken in an egg and herb mixture and was now browning it lightly in olive oil.

"You won't forget to add the garlic, will you?" Riley asked.

"No, I've got it right here." Theodosia tossed in three cloves of garlic, let them soften for a few minutes, then mashed them gently.

"Gee, this is great of you to fix dinner for me," Riley said. "I know you've been busy."

"I have been busy," Theodosia said. She diced three slices of prosciutto and chopped up some provolone cheese to add later, once the chicken had baked in the oven for twenty minutes. "I've discovered a few strange things that relate directly to Willow's murder."

Riley peered at her from across the counter. "Such as?"

"For one thing, that so-called haunted house has a secret exit. But I think you already know that. I think you've probably been on the phone with Tidwell, burning up the lines, pressing him for as many details as possible."

Riley didn't confirm or deny. Instead, he took another sip of beer and said, "And you think that's how the killer escaped." It was a statement not a question.

"Probably," Theodosia said.

"Which would point to Ellis Bouchard," Riley said. "Since he had intimate knowledge of the building."

"Yes, but there are a few other wrinkles. It turns out that Robert Vardell is a complete skunk. That he was leading Willow on."

Now Riley started to look interested.

"What do you mean? How so?"

"Vardell managed to convince everyone—especially

Willow—that he was some kind of financial genius. That he was bringing in a high six-figure salary at his investment firm. But the truth of the matter is, Vardell's a flunky. He doesn't have an assistant; he *is* the assistant."

"Vardell was making a play for Willow's money?" Riley said slowly. "So he had motive."

"Beaucoup motive."

"Somehow I doubt that Vardell willingly divulged his personal information to you. How did you find out?"

"Contrary to what you might think, I didn't break into his building in the dead of night and rifle through secret files. I simply called his office and spoke with the receptionist."

"That's it?"

"Sometimes the most direct route is the best."

"Did you tell Tidwell about this?" Riley asked.

"Yes. I didn't want to show all my cards, but Drayton sort of forced me into it. Said it was my civic duty or some such thing."

"Good for you." Riley tipped his half-empty can toward her. "You have been busy. Tell me more. Wait, is there more?"

"Yes. I discovered that Henry Curtis, an intern at the Heritage Society, sent Willow a sort of love note."

"Why would he do that?" Riley asked.

Theodosia just stared at him. "Maybe because he really, really liked her?"

"Okay, but . . . have you quizzed this guy Curtis about it? Tried to pin him down and find out what the relationship really was? I mean, what if there was a love triangle?"

Theodosia smiled. "You do have a suspicious mind, don't you?"

"Don't you?"

"I suppose."

"Hey, I'm the guy who's stuck at home and getting all this tasty information secondhand. I'm not out there on the front lines anymore," Riley said.

"Let's try and keep it that way," Theodosia said. "Until you get a lot better." She scooped her chicken breasts into a baking dish and stuck it in the oven. "That's got to bake for twenty minutes before I toss on the prosciutto and cheese."

"Want me to open a bottle of wine?" Riley asked as he chucked his empty can into the trash.

Theodosia looked carefully at Riley. "Maybe you've had enough to drink tonight."

"Keeping tabs on me, huh?"

"As you are on me."

Riley grinned at her as he reached out with his good arm and pulled her close.

"Touché," he said.

It was almost ten o'clock by the time Theodosia and Earl Grey left Riley's apartment. And because Theodosia was still vaguely curious about Willow's wedding planner, she decided to double back to Willow's apartment. This time alone.

Well, not quite alone. She did have Earl Grey along as her trusty investigative sidekick. And, luckily, she still had the key Timothy had given her.

Because she was doing this super surreptitiously, Theodosia parked her Jeep a block away from Willow's apartment. And, at the last minute, she pulled on a black hoodie that she had stashed in the car. Earl Grey went au naturel.

This time in, Willow's apartment didn't look any different. Maybe a little dustier, a little sadder and lonelier. Theodosia moved through the place fast, heading for the white desk. She sat down in the chair and clicked on a small desk lamp. Then she pulled open the file drawer and went through it again. This time a lot more carefully.

She found the wedding planner's information on the second pass through. A square-shaped business card on heavy, expensive-looking stock that was embossed with the name CARSON CROISSET. And underneath, in fancy script, CROISSET & COMPANY WEDDING PLANNERS. Very elegant, extremely tasteful. She dropped the card in her pocket, hoping that perhaps this wedding planner might know something she didn't.

Then Theodosia stood up and did a closer inspection of the apartment. It didn't look as if the police had been back. A rubber tree was slowly dying of thirst, an empty glass still sat on the kitchen counter, the bathroom had a tube of toothpaste on the sink, Willow's dry cleaning was still in a plastic bag and hung on the back door of her closet.

Nothing here. Nothing more to go on.

"C'mon, fella."

Earl Grey stood up from where he'd been resting on his haunches, patiently watching Theodosia do her silent walkthrough.

She let her dog out, then turned and locked the door behind her. Together, she and Earl Grey walked along the side of the house, heading for the street.

Just before they emerged from the shadows, Theodosia noticed a van parked across the street. And was there . . . ? Yes, it looked as if someone was sitting in the driver's seat.

Skulking in the dark and watching me? Or waiting for someone else?

Theodosia paused as she searched her memory. Who did she know who drove a van?

And then it struck her.

Allan Barnaby drove a van.

Could he be . . . ?

She strained to see the driver, but he was too far away. His face was only a pale oval, completely unrecognizable, almost lost in total darkness.

Still, Theodosia felt a blip of anxiety course through her. She stepped off the curb, feeling nervous, but ready to scurry across the street and see who it was. That's when the van's engine suddenly fired up, the lights flashed on, and it roared away from the curb.

She stood there with her dog and watched red taillights flare as the van braked slightly at the corner, then disappeared down the street.

And couldn't help wonder . . .

Barnaby, is that you?

Theodosia decided she had one more errand to do tonight. She drove the few blocks to Timothy Neville's home, parked, and walked up to his front door.

When he peeked out, Theodosia said, "I think I may have figured out a piece of the puzzle."

Timothy opened the door wider. "Come in." He squinted at Earl Grey. "Your dog may come in as well. Chairman Meow is already upstairs in bed, so he won't be bothering us." Chairman Meow was Timothy's Manx cat who didn't much care for creatures of the canine persuasion.

Theodosia and Earl Grey followed Timothy into his dimly lit side parlor. Silk chairs once again beckoned, and glowing portraits stared down at them from the walls.

"So what's this puzzle piece you claim to have found?" Timothy asked as he settled into a chair. "What's it all about?"

"I think Allan Barnaby might have stolen your fancy Edgar Allan Poe book."

Timothy stared at her, blinked in disbelief, and said, "Are you seriously talking about Willow's publisher?"

Theodosia hastened to explain, told Timothy how she'd learned from Lois at Antiquarian Books that Allan Barnaby had been a rare-book dealer in his previous life.

"He owned a fairly thriving rare-book shop in Savannah," Theodosia said. "Before he moved up here. Before he decided to go into publishing."

"Oh my," Timothy said, one hand stroking his chin. "Allan Barnaby? And here I thought he was . . ." He sighed. "Reputable. Well, that does change things, doesn't it?"

"Yes and no," Theodosia said. "Because I've got some news that might be even more disheartening."

"Concerning . . . ?"

"I did some snooping and found out a few details about Robert Vardell."

Timothy looked almost fearful. "Oh no. Now what?"

Theodosia quickly told Timothy about talking to the receptionist at Metcalf and Solange and learning that Vardell was employed there not as a financial manager, but as an assistant. The second assistant to boot.

Timothy listened to her carefully, then said, "You're absolutely positive about this? What you're telling me is that Robert Vardell is a complete and total fraud?"

Theodosia nodded. "I'm afraid so."

"And that he pulled the wool over everyone's eyes?"

"It looks that way."

Timothy's gnarled hands gripped the arms of his chair. "This is absolutely . . . excruciating."

"I know. I'm sorry to have to break it to you like this."

Timothy licked his lips, trying to recover. "So do you think he . . . ?"

"Was in it only for the money? That Vardell might have even murdered Willow? That I don't know," Theodosia said.

"Do the police know about Vardell? Does Tidwell know?"

"As soon as I found out about Vardell I called the Charleston PD and gave them the whole sad story. Needless to say, they plan to investigate him."

"But what if Vardell *didn't* do it?" Timothy said. "What if the police waste their time shaking down a garden-variety liar while the real killer goes free?"

"There's always that chance," Theodosia said.

Timothy touched a hand to his heart. "I don't know that I can take much more of this."

Theodosia gazed at him. Poor Timothy, he looked so frail and vulnerable. Her heart went out to him.

"Listen to me, Timothy, I promise you, no, I *swear* to you . . ." Words, emotions, were suddenly bubbling out of Theodosia. "I swear that I'll find out exactly who's to blame and that they'll be punished." She leaned forward in her chair to emphasize her point. "I'm going to solve this mystery and find justice for Willow if it's the last thing I do!"

25

"I stopped by Timothy Neville's house last night and broke the bad news to him about Robert Vardell's imaginary career as a financial genius," Theodosia said to Drayton.

It was Friday morning at the Indigo Tea Shop, and faint sunlight was streaming through the windows that faced busy Church Street. Horse-drawn jitneys were already clip-clopping past, ferrying tourists on sightseeing rounds throughout the Historic District.

"Good for you," Drayton said. "It was the right thing to do. How did Timothy take it?"

"Stunned surprise."

Drayton shook his head. "Still, it had to be done."

"Now it's going to be a free-for-all on Robert Vardell," Theodosia said.

Besides Timothy going after Vardell, she knew that Tidwell would be hauling him in for questioning as well. Hacking his way through the man's colossal web of lies, quizzing him mercilessly on his whereabouts last Sunday night when Willow was murdered. She figured Vardell might even lose his job, such as it was.

Serves him right. If I can't make Vardell spit out a confession, kicking and screaming all the way, then maybe Tidwell will have better luck.

While Drayton bustled around behind the counter, Theodosia worked to get the tea shop ready. The sun was back in its rightful place in the sky, and she was feeling cautiously optimistic. Information was being revealed, and, just as she'd told Timothy, a few pieces seemed to be falling into place. Now she needed to keep pushing. With a dose of good luck, Willow's killer would soon be apprehended.

Theodosia pulled open the doors of one of her highboys and scanned her multiple sets of dishes.

"I'm going to put out the Aynsley Wilton Green today," she called to Drayton.

"Feeling upbeat, are we?" he said.

"Actually, yes."

"It must be catching, because I'm thinking about brewing a pot of cranberry-orange and a pot of gunpowder green."

"The good pinhead gunpowder green from Stash Tea?"

"Please. Is there any other kind?"

Theodosia took down a stack of small plates and studied them. "I do love these bright purple, gold, and green colors."

"That particular china should go beautifully with the purple thistle mums that were delivered this morning," Drayton said.

"We got flowers? First I've heard."

"I think Haley must have ordered from Floradora. Anyway, the mums are sitting in a bucket in your office just waiting for a pair of artful hands to arrange them. And I nominate you."

"Then I guess I'd better get to it. Maybe display the mums in, um . . . ." Theodosia thought for a moment. "Ceramic crocks?"

"Definitely autumnal," Drayton said.

Theodosia covered the tables with cream-colored tablecloths, set out the breakfast plates, teacups, and saucers, and added crystal glassware. She grabbed several small tea lights in brass holders and added those to her table.

"Are we still going to the Goblins and Ghosts Parade tonight?" Drayton asked.

"I don't know why not? It goes right past here, doesn't it? Right down Church Street."

"Yes, but you've got Delaine's Denim and Diamonds Fashion Show at three."

"But I should be back here by five, five thirty at the latest. What time does the parade start?"

Drayton shrugged. "Six thirty, maybe seven?"

"No problem then."

On the way to her office to grab the mums, Theodosia stepped into the kitchen to speak with Haley.

"Haley, tell me what we're . . ." Theodosia stopped abruptly when she saw Haley's downcast face. "Haley, what's wrong?"

Haley looked up from where she was arranging nut and raisin scones on a silver tray. "Nothing really. Well, it's just that I've been reading Willow's book."

"Okay."

"And one of her stories got me thinking."

"Maybe you shouldn't be reading ghost stories right now," Theodosia said gently. She knew that Haley was young and impressionable. Ghost stories on top of a murder on top of a sad funeral probably weren't doing much to bolster her spirits.

"I was reading about the legend of Alice Flagg. And the wedding ring that her secret fiancé gave to her."

"I've read the story, yes," Theodosia said. "What about it?"

"The legend says that if you walk around Alice Flagg's grave twelve times, her wedding ring will magically appear. Do you think that will work with Willow's grave?"

"I'm sorry, but no."

"This is reality, huh?" Haley said.

"Haley, I know everything seems awfully unsettled right now. But I promise you things will get better."

"I hope so. You're still investigating, right?"

"Of course I am."

"Then I'm going to pin all my hopes on you," Haley said.

"Oh, Haley." Theodosia put her arms around her young chef. "I know you're feeling sad, but that's going to change. And pretty fast if I have my way. I promise we'll find Willow's killer."

Haley sniffled. "And if you don't?"

Theodosia squeezed Haley again. "Failure is not an option," she said.

Back out in the tea room, Theodosia arranged the mums while Drayton ruminated about the stolen Edgar Allan Poe book.

"I've been racking my brain," Drayton said. "And I can't for the life of me figure out if that book pertains to Willow or any of our other recent disasters."

Theodosia placed a bouquet on one of the tables and gave a shrug. "Maybe the book doesn't relate to anything at all. Maybe it's just a one-off. An odd circumstance. A piece of bad luck for the Heritage Society."

"So you're saying Allan Barnaby could be innocent?"

"Of Willow's death, possibly. Of stealing the book, perhaps not."

"But we really don't know, do we?" Drayton said.

"It's all up in the air at this point," Theodosia said. She fluffed her last bouquet of mums, then walked to the front door and hung out her open for business sign.

Ten minutes later, like a self-fulfilling prophecy, the tea shop was busy. Guests showed up, and shopkeepers from up and down Church Street popped in for their morning cuppa. Theodosia served strawberry scones, banana nut bread, and pear and brown sugar muffins. Drayton brewed pots of English breakfast tea, vanilla-flavored tea, and, to honor a special request, toasted coconut oolong tea. Midmorning brought UPS and a new shipment of Theodosia's special T-Bath products. She'd had to reorder her Green Tea Lotion and Green Tea Feet Treat, as well as her Ginger and Chamomile Facial Mist and White Tea Bath Oil.

Theodosia did her tea shop ballet, filling teacups, bobbing to clear tables, rushing back to the front door to greet new guests.

"Do you think you can handle things by yourself for twenty minutes or so?" Theodosia finally asked Drayton. It was almost eleven o'clock, and they were in that leisurely period (others might call it a slump, but not Theodosia) between serving breakfast cream teas and a full-fledged lunch.

"Probably," Drayton said. "Where are you dashing off to?"

"I want to talk to Willow's wedding planner, see if he has any information or insight."

"That sounds like a stretch," Drayton said. "What information is he going to offer that you don't already have?"

"Maybe nothing," Theodosia said. "But, hey, I have to at least give it a shot."

Croisset & Company Wedding Planners was located on Broad Street, the offices situated directly above the Dusty Hen Antique Shop. Theodosia climbed a narrow stairway, walked down a sleek, carpeted hallway, passed a white lacquered door that belonged to Julian Wolf-Knapp Fine Art Consultants (By Appointment Only), and eventually found herself at Croisset & Company.

Theodosia knocked on pebbled French double doors that

had the words CROISSET & COMPANY WEDDING PLANNERS
stenciled on them in fancy gold script.

"Come in," a voice called out.

Theodosia walked into an office that could best be described as a riot of alabaster silk fabrics, displays of
almond-colored china, dozens of cream-colored pillar candles, and stacks of ecru table linens. Or as Pete Riley probably would describe it in a police report, beige.

"Mr. Croisset?" Theodosia said.

A thirty-something man with bright-blue eyes, a sunlamp-
tan complexion, and a swirl of gelled blond hair suddenly
looked up expectantly from an enormous desk that was
covered with save-the-date postcards, wedding invitations,
fabric swatches, and three cartons of champagne flutes. He
wore a yellow-and-black Versace shirt, neatly pressed
jeans, and bright-white Nike sneakers.

"Come in," Croisset said. "And welcome. I presume
you're Ms. Newbury, my new bride-to-be?" He half rose in
his chair to greet her.

Theodosia shook her head. "Sorry, no. I'm Theodosia
Browning."

Croisset sat back down and reached for a pen and paper.
"That's a lovely name. Very British-sounding." He favored
her with a puckish grin. "Should look good on the invitations. So you're recently engaged then? Planning to be married?"

"Not right now, Mr. Croisset."

"Call me Carson," Croisset said as he studied her. "And
what a pity you're not, because I've just sourced the most
amazing shade of golden lilies that would complement your
auburn hair perfectly. Have to jet them in from Peru, of
course. Not cheap, but what's a few extra dollars when
you're fashioning the most memorable day of your life!" He
tilted his head back, and his eyes took on a faraway look. "I
can see it now. Billows of gold-and-russet-colored silk chiffon draped on the church pews, you in a Vera Wang fit and

flare with a sage-green sash, and carrying a bouquet of those jaw-dropping golden lilies with perhaps a few white tuberoses thrown in for fun."

Theodosia was tickled by his vision.

"What about the altar?" she asked.

"Riots of delphiniums," Croisset said. "Most definitely. And hanging white votive candles as well as pillar candles in glass holders." Then he shook his head, as if to snap himself back to the here and now. "If you're not getting married, then how may I help you?"

"You've been working with Willow French," Theodosia said.

Croisset's face didn't just fall; it crashed. "Dear sweet Willow," he said in a mournful tone. "Such a tragedy. Practically Shakespearian." He touched the tip of an index finger to the side of his face and said, "She was a friend of yours?"

"I have close connections with Willow's family," Theodosia said. "And because of that, I've been investigating her murder."

Now Croisset fluttered his hands. "That sounds very mysterious."

"Not really. It's more about asking a few questions. Talking to people that Willow had been in contact with lately."

"Interesting," Croisset said.

"I was wondering if I could ask you a few questions," Theodosia said.

"Certainly. Have a seat, ask away."

Theodosia sat down in a white faux fur–covered club chair that faced his desk. It was comfy but tickly.

"There's a distinct possibility that Willow might have been changing her plans," Theodosia said.

"You mean her wedding plans?" Croisset's eyebrows shot up. "I don't believe so. I mean, not that I was aware of."

"You two hadn't talked for a while?"

"We hadn't. I know Willow was busy with her book launch, so I didn't want to bug her too much. I left a couple messages on her answering machine, but she never got back to me. Now you're telling me the wedding might have been off?"

"It's possible."

Croisset slumped in his chair. "Gracious."

"Did Willow ever say anything to you—or did you pick up any subtle hints that Willow wasn't completely happy with her fiancé?"

"With Robert?" Croisset shook his head. "She never said a peep about him."

"Did you ever meet him?"

"No. Which I thought was a trifle strange. But, then again, all brides are different. Some are more, shall we say, hands on and singular in their focus."

"Self-absorbed," Theodosia said.

"There is that."

"So you never detected anything in Willow's demeanor that might have hinted at her being upset in any way?" Theodosia asked.

"No, but I hadn't spoken to her in the week before she . . ." Croisset looked pained.

"The week before she died," Theodosia said.

"Right. But from my experience, all brides are nervous as cats," Croisset said. "That's the nature of planning your own wedding, of putting yourself front and center and being the star."

"So Willow had been nervous?"

"Just the usual prewedding jitters, but I certainly wouldn't characterize her as having cold feet." Croisset sat forward and grabbed a crisp white folder from a stack of crisp white folders. "Look at this. Look what I've had to do." He pulled out a sheaf of papers and tossed them in the air. "Canceled. All canceled," he cried. "The church, the minister, the six-tier wedding cake, the reception dinner, the string quartet, the flowers and bridal bouquet, the DJ for the after-party, even the snow-white Bentley that was supposed to carry Willow and her beloved off on their honeymoon."

Croisset looked so upset that Theodosia said, "You realize, Willow didn't do this to you on purpose."

"I understand that," Croisset said. "And I don't mean to bemoan the point. It's just that Willow's wedding was on track to be flawless . . . to be absolute perfection."

"I'm sure."

"Willow was a dream bride, as clever and detail oriented as any I've ever seen. She stood in my florist's cooler for over an hour, deciding on the exact flowers for her archway. She actually hand selected every single beeswax candle for her reception tables."

"That's really . . . wonderful," Theodosia said.

"You know," Croisset said. "I've dealt with nervous brides, angry brides, demanding brides, and brides so hungover I've had to shove a bouquet in their hot little hands and practically push them down the aisle. But I've never had a murdered bride."

"There you go," Theodosia said. "It's definitely a first."

26

"Well?" Drayton smiled at Theodosia from his post behind the front counter. "Did you talk to the wedding planner? Did you learn anything new?"

"Yes to your first question and no to your second," Theodosia said.

"Pity."

"Tell me about it."

Drayton snuck a glance at his watch and said, "FYI, we're about to get busy. Or, in Haley's vernacular, slammed. Besides our regular reservations, we have a rather large party coming in at twelve fifteen. A group of ten guests from the Dove Cote Bed and Breakfast."

"Hmm, that is new."

"They only called fifteen minutes ago."

Theodosia reached for one of the black aprons that hung on a nearby hook. "Then I guess I'd better get cracking."

"And I'd better get brewing," Drayton said.

As Theodosia stepped into the kitchen to check on lunch, Haley looked up from a steaming pot of soup and said, "Did Drayton tell you the news?"

"That we've got a party of ten coming in?"

"Yup, a late addition. So what I'm going to do is add carrot and ginger soup to our menu. Today's offerings will also include chicken salad on sweet Hawaiian rolls, cream cheese and crushed pineapple on nut bread, Monterey Jack cheese and zucchini quiche, and smoked trout on pumpernickel. Along with what's left of our scones and muffins, I have some peach crisp baking in the oven."

"Sounds like a great menu," Theodosia said. "The full monty. You're sure this won't interfere with your making tea sandwiches for Delaine's shindig today? I can certainly pitch in and help if you want."

"Naw, I'm just going to whip up some Brie and sliced apple sandwiches and some tarragon chicken salad sandwiches. It's not a problem."

Theodosia studied Haley as she spun about her kitchen and wondered if her state of mind had improved. "Are you feeling some better?"

"Actually, I am," Haley said. "I started thinking about how you and Drayton have been asking all the right questions—and then I thought about how you guys went creeping through the basement of that haunted house, looking for answers—and it gave me hope. You know what Maya Angelou said about hope?"

Theodosia thought she might have an inkling about what the wise woman had said, but instead she said to Haley, "No, tell me."

"She said, 'Hope and fear cannot occupy the same space. Invite one to stay.'"

"Sage words. And you invited hope?"

Haley nodded. "Sure did."

"Bless you, Haley."

* * *

When the clock struck twelve, the lunch rush was on. Guests with reservations made their way in, visitors who'd wandered in off Church Street looking for a tasty lunch showed up, and eventually so did the Dove Cote's gang of ten.

Theodosia seated guests, poured tea, took orders, and served lunch. Because they were so busy, Drayton was also at the ready to grab entrées from the kitchen and hustle them out to their guests.

Until, that is, one of the Dove Cote guests ordered a pot of Margaret's Hope Estate Darjeeling. Drayton, always delighted to brew one of his highly prized teas, readily complied. And then, when he presented the tea in a glazed yellow teapot from India, he immediately offered to do one of his infamous recitations.

"Yes!" they agreed en masse. "We'd love to hear it."

Drayton cleared his throat and began:

> At four o'clock the day becomes liquid
> casting a Darjeeling shadow on itself.
> This is the time between,
> an hour without destiny.
> I must be careful
> not to disturb the scent of oranges
> that rests on the mist,
> not to veer off the steamy path
> as I raise the china lip
> to meet my own.

Applause rose from the Dove Cote table, then the other guests joined in.

"Goodness," Drayton said, looking a little embarrassed at all the fuss, "I guess I went off in a poetic reverie."

But the guests thought otherwise and there were cries of . . .

"We loved it."

"You were wonderful."

"Highly entertaining."

Theodosia just smiled and maintained her calm demeanor. If her tea sommelier sometimes quoted snatches of poetry or recited Japanese haiku, it was just part and parcel of the ambiance of the Indigo Tea Shop. And more likely than not, guests would be back for more. She knew there was a dearth of charm and whimsy in today's world, so in her eyes, Drayton was simply doing his small part to help restore it.

At one o'clock, with the guests enjoying banana nut bread and peach crisp with their tea, Angie Congdon walked in.

"Bet you know why I'm here, don't you?" Angie said to Theodosia, who was grabbing a couple of take-out bags from behind the counter.

"To firm up plans for the Enchanted Garden Party tomorrow?" Theodosia said.

"Yes. Teddy and I love the menu you sent over . . ."

"Actually, Haley put it together," Theodosia said.

Angie grinned. "Well, whoever is responsible, it's wonderful."

"So no last-minute changes or additions?"

"I wouldn't touch a thing. It's perfect as is," Angie said. "But I did want to give you a heads-up about this fun showbiz thing we've got planned. It's an old-fashioned magician's trick that was popular during the late eighteen hundreds called Pepper's Ghost."

"Sounds like fun. Do I have to do anything?"

"Maybe agree to disappear?"

"That sounds . . . a little weird," Theodosia said.

Angie shook a finger at her. "Wait and see how well the illusion works. You'll be surprised!"

"You think I'll want to jump in and go poof?" Theodosia snapped her fingers as an accompaniment.

"I hope so," Angie said.

* * *

Just when Theodosia thought they were finished for the day, that the coast was finally clear and she could start bracing herself for Delaine's event, Detective Burt Tidwell sauntered (as much as a fat man could saunter) into her tea shop. And he was accompanied by, surprise, surprise, Pete Riley.

"What are you doing here?" Theodosia asked Tidwell. And then, practically shouting at Riley, "And you're supposed to be on medical leave, which means you should be home in bed recuperating!"

"Recuperating is boring," Riley said. He managed an offhand grin, but Theodosia thought it looked forced. That his face still looked drawn and tight.

"Recuperating is absolutely necessary," Theodosia shot back. Then she turned to glower at Tidwell and said, "Why on earth did you drag him along when you know he needs his rest?"

Tidwell took a delicate step backward, a look of feigned innocence lighting his broad face.

"Don't blame me," Tidwell said. "Detective Riley called and asked, rather, he practically demanded, to be let back into the investigation."

"That's so not a good idea," Theodosia said.

"You know what's not a good idea?" Tidwell said. "You shoehorning yourself into my investigation."

Theodosia wasn't about to back down. It simply wasn't in her nature.

"Why are you two even here?" she asked.

"We actually have an update," Riley said.

"Then you may as well come sit down," Theodosia said. She glanced over at Drayton and said, "Do you have any of that fancy Darjeeling left?"

"Should be enough for two or three cups," Drayton said. He started grabbing for teacups and his teapot.

"Okay then, let's do it," Theodosia said.

They all sat down at a table while Drayton poured cups of tea.

"You mentioned you had an update," Theodosia said. "What is it?"

"We're now able to eliminate one of our key suspects," Tidwell said. He curled his hands around his teacup, lifted it, and took a sip.

"Which one?" Theodosia asked. Here was the kind of news she'd been hoping for. That they'd all been praying for.

"Allan Barnaby has now been cleared of any possible wrongdoing," Tidwell said. "He has an ironclad alibi concerning his whereabouts on the night of Willow French's murder."

"What?" This was startling news to Theodosia. "I thought Barnaby was pussyfooting around the haunted house that night."

"No," Tidwell said. "He was not."

Theodosia looked from Tidwell to Riley. "Are you sure?" Her gut instinct told her to be cautious.

Riley nodded. "We're sure."

"So what's Barnaby's alibi? Where was he that night?" Theodosia asked. *This better be good.*

"Barnaby was delivering a lecture at Charleston Southern University on the state of publishing today," Tidwell said.

"You're one hundred percent sure about this?" Theodosia asked. "You checked this out carefully."

"I personally spoke to Professor Donneley, who invited Mr. Barnaby to address his Media Today class. The good professor, along with two dozen students, attended Barnaby's lecture," Tidwell said. The detective seemed to relish his assuredness.

"Okay," Theodosia said. "If you say so." She knew she had to seriously adjust her perspective on Barnaby, so her brain zonked into overtime. She raised a finger in an *aha* gesture and said, "But Barnaby could still be the one who stole the book."

Tidwell and Riley exchanged puzzled glances.

"Book?" Riley stuttered out. "What book?"

"From the Heritage Society," Theodosia said with an insistent tone. "Didn't Timothy call you people about the stolen Edgar Allan Poe book? It's been missing since they had the symposium this past Wednesday? The book's a very rare edition of Poe's work and worth a small fortune."

Tidwell pursed his lips. "We don't know anything about a stolen book."

"Well, you should," Theodosia said. Then, "Do you *want* to know?"

"Not particularly," Tidwell said.

Theodosia wanted to grind her teeth together but didn't. Instead she said, "Okay then, what happened when you questioned Ellis Bouchard yesterday?"

Tidwell managed a small grin. "Once I started questioning Bouchard, he folded like a cheap card table. Bouchard is under the impression he can reclaim the mansion and flip it to some fool who'll turn it into a fancy bed and breakfast. He told me a suite at the nearby Montrose Inn goes for upwards of six hundred dollars a night."

"Hmph." This from Drayton behind the counter.

"I doubt Bouchard's ever going to get his hands on that mansion," Theodosia said. "Timothy's lawyers will have him wrapped up in court for years."

Tidwell shrugged. "Maybe so. But Bouchard is still a person of interest."

"I would think you'd be more interested in Robert Vardell," Theodosia said. "Now that he's been exposed as a world-class liar."

"We interviewed Vardell this morning," Tidwell said. "Myself and Detective Humphries."

"And?" Theodosia said. She was growing increasingly frustrated. Extracting a meaningful answer from Tidwell was like doing the backstroke in a vat of molasses.

"And we released him," Tidwell said with a slight flourish.

Theodosia sat back in her chair, surprised. "You let Vardell go free? Just like that? After he told all those outrageous lies?" She couldn't quite believe it. He had to be guilty of something, right?

"In dealing with criminals we consistently see this pattern of behavior," Riley said. "But lying doesn't necessarily equate to committing a capital crime. Vardell may not be the killer at all."

"But you don't know that," Theodosia said.

"Not yet we don't," Tidwell said. "But we're still pursuing several angles. Pulling threads together, coming up with what we feel is actionable information."

"If you guys are so smart, if you've already amassed so much information, then what are you doing here?" Theodosia asked.

Tidwell ducked his head, looking a trifle sheepish. "Actually, we came by to pick up a dozen scones."

Theodosia gave him a stony look. "Scones?"

"For our late-afternoon meeting," Riley said. "With members of our task force."

"You've got a task force working on Willow's murder?" Theodosia asked. She suddenly felt heartened by this news. "That's great. In fact it's wonderful. Tell you what, why don't I deliver the scones in person? That way I can sit in on the meeting." Theodosia was making fast mental calculations. She'd have Haley or Drayton drop the tea sandwiches at Cotton Duck so she could attend the task force meeting. Delaine wouldn't mind; she'd be frazzled anyway and just relieved that her refreshments had shown up.

"Thank you, but no," Tidwell said. "We really only need the scones."

27

❧

Champagne glasses clinked, loud music blasted from the DJ's mixer and oversize speakers, and Delaine Dish was dripping in ice. The sparkling diamond kind, that is.

It was the afternoon of Delaine's Denim and Diamonds Fashion Show, and at least a hundred women were crammed into Cotton Duck Boutique. They helped themselves to glass after glass of champagne, snatched up pieces of designer denim, and gaped at the amazing displays of diamonds.

Theodosia had arranged her tea sandwiches on three-tiered stands and placed them on a table. Then, realizing it was a serve-yourself situation, she decided to do a little shopping and mingling of her own.

"The shop looks fabulous today," Theodosia said to Janine, Delaine's perpetually overworked assistant.

"Thank you," Janine said. She was mid-forties and slightly stooped, as if she spent her days lifting heavy boxes. Today her face glowed red from exertion and her blouse was already untucked from her skirt. "We were working here until midnight last night."

"You and Delaine?"

Janine shook her head. "No, Bettina and I did all this. The unpacking and the merchandising. Delaine was . . . I don't know where Delaine was. Maybe making last-minute calls to clients, getting final RSVPs."

"Sure," Theodosia said. Knowing Delaine, she figured the woman had probably relaxed with a glass of wine, slapped on a beauty mask, and then turned in early.

Still, last night's efforts had certainly paid off. The shop, always glamorous and stuffed with glitzy clothing and accessories, was now a total fantasy.

Racks of denim jackets, skirts, and slacks were jammed next to soft sea island cotton dresses and diaphanous beach cover-ups. A circular rack held long ball gowns and filmy silk wraps to match. Antique highboys spilled out offerings of jeweled belts, strappy sandals, hand-painted silk scarves, bangle bracelets, and beaded handbags.

"Do you love it?" Bettina asked.

Theodosia turned to find Bettina dressed adorably in a tight white T-shirt and a pair of hip-hugging blue jeans. There was a three-inch strip of bare skin between the hem of the T-shirt and the waist of the jeans, but on Bettina it looked cute.

"I do love it," Theodosia said. "Janine was just telling me how hard you guys worked to get all the clothes steamed and onto the racks."

"Like rented mules!" Bettina practically screamed. "But we got it done. Cool, huh?"

"Very cool."

Bettina gave Theodosia a quick hug and then she was off. Probably to make a few women jealous with that fabulous little twenty-something figure of hers.

"Theodosia!" Delaine Dish called out loudly and with authority. Then she came careening over on five-inch-high

Manolos, a manic grin pasted on her face. "Many thanks for bringing those delightful little noshes. My guests are *loving* them."

"You're welcome," Theodosia said. She gazed at Delaine, who wore a full-length denim evening gown ruffled at the hem and about a hundred carats' worth of diamonds. Diamonds glittered from Delaine's ears, from almost every finger, and from deep in the soft cleft of her cleavage.

"Let me show you something *fabulous*!" Delaine trilled. She grabbed a denim blouse and dangled it in front of Theodosia. "You see this? It's *shredded* denim, the very latest."

Theodosia thought it looked as if Dominic and Domino, Delaine's Siamese cats, had clawed it. "Nice," she said.

"Strategically shredded, of course," Delaine said as she grabbed a pair of super skinny jeans. "And I'm positively gaga over this new ombre denim."

Theodosia peered at the faded and mottled blue jeans. "Ombre denim kind of reminds me of stonewashed denim."

Delaine put a finger up to her mouth to shush her. "Essentially, yes. But *stonewashed* sounds so horribly downmarket and old-fashioned, while *ombre* is trendy and fun. Far more appealing to my millennial customers."

"Of course it is," Theodosia said. She studied the racks of denim jeans, jackets, skirts, short shorts, and long gowns and decided they were for the woman who had everything. After all, who wanted to slip into an old-fashioned chiffon ball gown when you could wear *ombre* denim?

"Have you had a chance to check out our various diamond displays?" Delaine asked. "I invited Brooke from Hearts Desire and Lynnette from Troubadour Diamonds to bring along their bestest, sparkliest baubles today."

"I'm going to do that right now," Theodosia said.

She glanced Brooke's way and saw she was busy with three women all vying for her attention. So she turned to Lynnette, who was busy laying out a half dozen diamond tennis bracelets on a blue velvet pillow.

"See something you like?" Lynnette asked. She was tall, dark haired, and slender in a black skirt suit. Her shop, Troubadour Diamonds over on King Street, specialized in super high-end pieces. In other words, diamonds to drool over.

"I love it all," Theodosia said.

Lynnette smiled. "Of course you do. All women do."

"I was wondering, do you ever carry colored diamonds?" Theodosia asked.

"I have maybe three or four pieces in stock right now," Lynnette said. "But they're getting hard to find. And prices keep climbing."

"I can imagine," Theodosia said.

"The real rarities, of course, are the blue and red diamonds, with red being extremely rare. The blue diamonds we see are mostly from the old Cullinan Mine in South Africa, now owned by Petra Diamonds."

"And what about yellow diamonds?" Theodosia asked. She was thinking about Willow's Hibiscus Diamonds. Who carried them, what might they be worth.

"Yellow diamonds are also somewhat rare," Lynnette said. "You know, that yellow color is caused by small amounts of nitrogen contained within the diamond's crystal structure. So they're only found in certain parts of the world."

"Interesting," Theodosia said.

She glanced at the price tag attached to one of Lynnette's tennis bracelets—nine thousand dollars—and decided it was a little out of her price range. Actually, more than a little.

"Just out of curiosity, a pair of flawless yellow diamond earrings, five carats total . . . what would they normally sell for?" Theodosia asked.

"Retail?" Lynette said. "Probably around seventy or eighty thousand dollars."

"And if there was a matching pendant?"

"Oh, you're talking about an entire suite? Then the price

would be considerably higher. Well over a hundred thousand dollars."

"Wow," Theodosia breathed as a jingle inside her purse suddenly interrupted their conversation. Her phone. "Excuse me," Theodosia said. She wandered off and stood beside a rack of denim skinny jeans. "Hello?"

"Miss Theodosia?" It was a man's voice. Whispery and young.

"Yes?" Theodosia noticed that a few pairs of jeans had feathers sewn around the cuffs.

"This is Henry Curtis," the voice whispered in her ear.

"Henry," Theodosia said, suddenly jolted to full alert. "Where have you been? I've been trying to get hold of you."

"Good, because I need to talk to you!" Henry sounded harried. Maybe even a little bit scared.

"Henry, are you okay?"

"I've put some pieces together . . ."

"Wait, you mean concerning Willow?" Theodosia asked.

"Yes, and I have a pretty fair idea . . ."

"An idea about what? About who killed her?" Theodosia asked.

From across the room, Delaine looked over at Theodosia and frowned.

"Henry, what are you saying? Talk to me," Theodosia urged. "Tell me what's going on."

"Not over the phone. We need to meet in person."

"When?"

"Tonight."

"I'm supposed to go to the Ghosts and Goblins Parade tonight," Theodosia said.

"Afterward, then?" Now Henry sounded even more jittery.

"You're being awfully mysterious," Theodosia said.

Then she wondered . . . if Henry was the killer, meeting him could be some sort of setup or trap. Still, he sounded awfully anxious, as if he'd made some kind of connection or stumbled onto some important information.

"Okay, Henry," Theodosia said. "Give me your address. I'll see what I can do."

Theodosia hung up her phone just as Delaine walked over and handed her a flute of champagne.

"A toast," Delaine said. She pushed back a hunk of dark hair to reveal a shimmer of diamonds at her ears.

"To your very successful Denim and Diamonds," Theodosia said, clinking glasses with her.

"Hopefully," Delaine said as she took a quick sip. "They may be buying like crazy now, but will this good luck carry over into my Christmas season?"

"Christmas," Theodosia said. She was already planning her Victorian Christmas Tea Party. So many guests had expressed interest that she'd had to move it from the Indigo Tea Shop to a much larger venue.

"My sister might come for Christmas," Delaine said suddenly, her eyes glittering. "So it should be an exciting time. I haven't seen Nadine in almost two years."

"How's she doing?" Theodosia asked.

"Oh, pretty good."

The last time Nadine had been in town, she'd shoplifted her merry way down Church Street. The result—yes, she'd been caught—had not been pretty. Delaine had shed hot tears of embarrassment, and Nadine had been arrested and barely escaped going to jail. There was no telling what Nadine was up to now. For all Theodosia knew, Nadine could be heading up a ring of international art thieves. For Delaine's sake, she hoped not.

"There you are," Drayton said when Theodosia strolled into the Indigo Tea Shop. "It's almost six and we've barely enough time to gulp down a few bites of dinner before the parade starts."

"We're having dinner?" Theodosia asked. First she'd heard.

"Well, not technically dinner. I brewed a spot of Nilgiri tea and set out some tea sandwiches and the last of the scones that I pretty much had to hide from Detective Tidwell's prying eyes." Drayton gestured toward a table that he'd set up for them. "I figured we'd want to eat light so we could enjoy a goody from one of the various food trucks."

Theodosia sat down at the table.

"This is nice."

"Isn't it?" Drayton said. "I probably shouldn't admit this, but I kind of like the tea shop when the workday is finished and it's just us two."

Only a few lights shone in the dimly lit tea shop, and Drayton had placed three cream-colored candles in the center of the table. The dancing flames gave the tea shop a warm, golden glow.

Drayton set a steaming teapot down on a trivet, then seated himself across from Theodosia.

"We haven't had a chance to hash over Tidwell's announcement," he said. "You had to flutter off to Delaine's soiree."

"You mean about Allan Barnaby having such an ironclad alibi?" Theodosia asked.

Drayton nodded. "I'm guessing that by now you've thought about this and pared down your suspect list accordingly."

Theodosia spread currant jam on her scone and said, "I do have my favorites."

"Vardell still being the front-runner?" Drayton asked.

"Has to be. Just because he's such a bold-faced liar and because I'm fairly certain Willow broke off her wedding with him."

Drayton nibbled a bite of scone. "You think he killed Willow for the diamonds? And because he'd inherit the house she purchased?"

"It's possible."

"But not a one hundred percent probability."

"Not yet," Theodosia said. "I also suspect Ellis Bouchard because he's in such dire financial straits."

Drayton picked up a chicken salad tea sandwich and chewed thoughtfully. "Plus he's a prickly character."

Theodosia sighed. "Still . . . nothing's for certain." She felt bad that she wasn't making the progress she'd hoped for. Yes, she had two good suspects, but still no verified absolute-concrete evidence. Nothing she could slap down hard on Tidwell's desk and say, *Here, you go. Here's your proof!*

Drayton saw Theodosia's uncertainty and hastened to change the subject.

"How was Delaine's event?" he asked. "She pull a good crowd? Café society and all that?"

"It was typical Delaine. Hectic and a little crazed, with women snatching denim jeans and jackets out of one another's hands like they were spun gold. But I'm guessing when all the receipts are counted it was a huge success."

"How about the diamond part?" Drayton asked.

"I saw several well-heeled women handing over American Express Black cards," Theodosia said.

Drayton nodded. "Like I always say, plenty of money in this town. *Old* money, the very best kind."

"But that's not the really big news."

"Pray tell what is?"

"Henry Curtis called me."

Drayton looked surprised. "Ah, the missing Mr. Curtis with the green-painted face. The one who's also earned a spot on your suspect list. And he called you . . . why?"

"He says he has something to tell me. Something important."

"Do you think it is? Important, I mean?"

"I don't know," Theodosia said. "I couldn't quite get a feel for what was buzzing in Henry's mind. Though I have to admit, he sounded nervous."

28

❧

Pint-size trick-or-treaters raced down Church Street, their ghost and witch costumes flapping in the breeze, plastic treat bags rattling at their sides. Adults ghosted by in costumes as well, anxious to see the parade then head off to the various zombie crawls and haunted pub crawls that were taking place directly afterward.

And right on cue, a full moon emerged from behind mauve-colored clouds to shine its ghostly glimmer on the Ghosts and Goblins Parade.

Theodosia and Drayton strolled down Church Street to Elliott and took up their post on the corner. A covey of five food trucks was already parked nearby, their heavenly aromas tantalizing the crowd that ebbed and flowed around them.

"What do you think?" Drayton asked. He was practically sniffing the air. "What should we sample first?"

Theodosia gazed at the brightly painted food trucks. Their offerings included gourmet burgers, Carolina barbecue, fried shrimp po'boys, fried sweet plantains, bulgogi beef tacos, and lobster rolls.

"I think maybe . . . a lobster roll," Theodosia said.

"That makes two of us," Drayton said. "Hold my spot and I'll be back in a jiffy."

As Theodosia stood on the curb, an amazing parade of costumed revelers streamed past her. There was a Medusa woman with plastic snakes writhing in her hair, a cadre of witches, some Venetian lords and ladies, even a French cancan girl in a va-va-voom ruffled skirt.

"Here you go," Drayton said, handing Theodosia a giant lobster roll. "Some nice knuckle and claw meat dripping with butter and served on grilled brioche."

Theodosia took a bite. "Yum." It was delicious. Sweet and definitely buttery.

"Did I miss anything?" Drayton asked.

"Just a bunch of people in crazy costumes. The actual parade hasn't started yet."

"Maybe we should have brought Earl Grey and Honey Bee along," Drayton said. "They might have enjoyed this." Honey Bee was Drayton's sweet little Cavalier King Charles Spaniel.

Theodosia shook her head. "Halloween is one of those holidays, like Fourth of July, that dogs pretty much hate. Too many masks, flapping costumes, and ringing doorbells. They usually just want to hide until it all goes away." She took another bite of her lobster roll. "Although there is a dog costume contest tomorrow night. Not that Earl Grey wants any part of it."

There was a thunderous pounding of drums off in the distance, and then a loud cry rose up from down the block.

"I think something's happening," Drayton said.

"The parade's starting!" Theodosia was excited. Although the Ghosts and Goblins Parade had been going on for several years, this was the first time she'd attended. She stood on tiptoes now and watched as the first contingent rolled down the street. There were flickering dots of light—maybe torches?—and patches of lavender and blue. The marchers looked like a moving pointillist painting as they moved toward them.

"A torchlight parade," Drayton said, sounding pleased as the marchers swept past them.

Those marchers were followed by giant puppets, an entire ensemble of zombie drummers, and a dozen people all gently wafting giant butterfly wings.

"Look at those gossamer wings," Theodosia said. The ten-foot-long wings flowed and billowed in the night breeze almost in slow motion, the bright colors looking lovely and shimmery.

Drayton smiled. "Maybe we should hold a butterfly tea sometime. Do it outdoors and hire these costumed folks to waft about."

"It sounds crazy but I love it," Theodosia said.

They watched as parade floats, marching bands, and giant skeleton puppets passed by them.

Twenty minutes later, it was all over. Except for the crush of people and two more food trucks that had just pulled in. The evening was still young, after all.

"That one's selling wine," Drayton said, indicating the new truck. It was painted purple with images of tipsy wineglasses stenciled across it. "Care for a glass?"

"You don't have to twist my arm," Theodosia said.

Together they strolled over to the truck and got in line. And ended up running into Elisha Summers from the Heritage Society.

After exchanging greetings, Drayton said, "How's Claire doing? We understand her mother is ill."

"Yeah, Claire's decided to take some time off from work," Elisha said.

"Really," Drayton said. "It must be serious."

"I think Claire's taking things day by day," Elisha said.

Theodosia suddenly remembered glancing through Claire's personnel file. And finding that slight discrepancy.

"Elisha, Claire's been here for about three months, right?" Theodosia asked.

Elisha looked thoughtful. "Something like that, I guess."

"Do you remember where Claire worked before she came to the Heritage Society?"

"Mmn, I'm not really sure. Though I'm pretty sure she mentioned it once," Elisha said.

"Try to remember, will you?" Theodosia said. "It's kind of important."

Elisha squeezed her eyes half-shut, as if in deep concentration. Then they popped open. "Okay, don't quote me on this, but I think it might have been someplace in the Midwest."

"Not the Norton Simon Museum in Pasadena?" Theodosia said.

Elisha shook her head. "Not that I know of."

"For some reason I thought Claire worked at the Norton Simon," Theodosia said.

"That sticks in my mind, too," Drayton said.

"Well, maybe she did at one time," Elisha said. "I don't really know. I just wish Claire didn't have to take her furlough without pay. Because I know she really needs the money."

Theodosia was caught off guard. "Needs the . . . ?"

As Elisha stepped up to the window to order her wine, Theodosia and Drayton hung back and exchanged glances.

"Claire needs the money," Theodosia whispered. She said it with a *tone*.

Drayton raised an eyebrow. "You're thinking . . ."

"What if it's Claire?" Theodosia said, her suspicion bubbling up, even though the idea of Claire as Willow's killer produced a sick feeling in the pit of her stomach.

Theodosia and Drayton got plastic glasses filled with

chardonnay and walked slowly down Church Street. Festivities were happening all around them—face painting, costume contests, craft beer tasting—but they were suddenly laser focused on Claire Waltho.

"If Claire needed money badly enough . . ." Theodosia said.

"And Claire figured out exactly how to get her hands on some money," Drayton said.

"Just to be clear, you're talking about Willow's diamond earrings?"

"I hate to think the worst, but it is possible."

"Horrible but possible," Theodosia said.

Drayton sipped his wine, looking worried, then said, "The thing that worries me is, if Claire lied about working at the Norton Simon . . ."

"Then she could have lied about a lot of things."

"On the other hand, maybe it's just a misunderstanding on Elisha's part. She just *thought* Claire had worked somewhere in the Midwest."

"Maybe," Theodosia said. "But it still bothers me. A lot."

They walked along, thinking, worrying. The discrepancy was clearly bugging both of them.

"You know what? We should just call the Norton Simon and ask them," Theodosia said.

"It's late. I'm sure they're closed by now," Drayton said.

Theodosia glanced at her watch. "It may be seven o'clock here in Charleston, but it's only four in the afternoon in California. What do you think?"

"Well . . ."

Theodosia could see Drayton starting to dither. So she made an executive decision, pulled out her phone, and googled the Norton Simon Museum in Pasadena. As soon as she found the website and phone number she called them.

"May I speak with someone in the registrar's office?"

Theodosia asked when the phone was answered. She said it fast so she wouldn't lose her nerve.

"Hold, please." There was a click, a low hum, and then another person came on the line.

"Carol Corcoran here."

"Miss Corcoran?" Theodosia said.

"It's Mrs. Corcoran, but that's okay. How may I help you?"

"I'm doing a quick check on a potential employee," Theodosia said, making up an excuse on the spot. "Ah, for the Heritage Society here in Charleston, South Carolina?"

"Yes?"

"I'm checking personal references," Theodosia said. "And I wanted to verify that a Ms. Claire Waltho was employed as one of your curators for, let's see . . ." She looked at Drayton and shrugged. "Approximately three years?"

There was silence at the other end of the line.

"Mrs. Corcoran?" Theodosia said. "The employee's name is Waltho. Claire Waltho."

"I'm sorry, but I . . . have no knowledge of that person."

"Claire Waltho *wasn't* employed at the Norton Simon Museum?"

"Not that I can recall, and I've worked here almost thirteen years."

"How interesting," Theodosia said. "Okay, I'm sorry for interrupting your day, and I do thank you for your time."

Theodosia hung up the phone and said, "Claire never worked at the Norton Simon Museum. The registrar never *heard* of her!"

"How bizarre," Drayton said. Then, "What does that mean to us?"

"Well, it's not good. If Claire falsified her employment records, it means she could have graduated to more serious crime."

"By serious crime you mean . . ." Drayton stared at her.

"That she might have murdered Willow French? I don't

know what to believe anymore. The Claire we know is a sweet, demure, capable woman. However, when people are under great stress, when they find themselves unable to handle a crushing financial burden, they can be pushed to terrible lengths."

"What do we do now? What's our next step?" Drayton asked.

"I think we have to confront Claire."

"We do? When?"

Theodosia sighed. "Right now?"

Claire Waltho lived in North Charleston in a neighborhood of working-class homes. They were by no means seedy, but neither were they the real gems—the cute cottages, Queen Annes, Italianate mansions, and Victorian mansions—that were located in that sweet spot of Charleston real estate known as South of Broad.

They walked up a cracked sidewalk and onto a sagging front porch.

"I think there's a light on inside," Theodosia said as she rang the doorbell.

They stood there and waited. And waited some more. Nothing happened. Nobody came to the door.

"Perhaps Claire's not home," Drayton said.

"Or maybe she skipped the country. Or maybe she doesn't really have a sick mother she's tending to," Theodosia said as she pushed the doorbell again. She was anxious, her heart was racing, and she was bouncing on the balls of her feet. She wasn't looking forward to a major confrontation, but she knew it couldn't be helped.

Finally, they heard faint footsteps approaching the front door.

"I think maybe . . ." Theodosia started to say.

Then the front door was swept open and Claire gazed at them through the screen. Her features seemed to tighten as her eyes flicked from Theodosia to Drayton and then back to Theodosia.

No escaping this, Claire, Theodosia thought to herself.

Then Claire surprised them. She pushed open the screen door and, with a resigned look on her face, said, "I suppose I've been expecting you."

"Good," Drayton said. "Because we know what you did."

Claire's face turned chalk white as she let out a small gasp. "What?"

"I think you heard Drayton correctly," Theodosia said. "We know. We know everything." They didn't really. It was all an enormous bluff. But Theodosia was hoping that Claire might panic and start talking. Start confessing and help fill in some of the blanks.

"How did you find out?" Claire asked in a small, defeated voice.

"A lot of footwork and some good guesswork," Theodosia said. "We also checked your employment record. You never worked at the Norton Simon."

"Ah," Claire said. "My little white lie." She swallowed hard. "You must have overheard me tell Drucilla Heyward that I'd worked there."

"Why did you lie to her?" Theodosia asked.

"I don't know. Maybe I thought the Norton Simon sounded better than the Shelby Museum in South Dakota," Claire said. "More upscale."

"You were inflating your résumé," Theodosia said. "Giving it a big fat pouf."

"And you were trying to tip the odds in favor of Mrs. Heyward donating to the Heritage Society," Drayton said.

"It seemed like a good idea at the time," Claire said.

"But that's beside the point," Theodosia said. Her heart felt heavy in her chest, but she was determined to forge ahead. To confront Claire with the truth and try to wring a confession from her.

"Are the police involved?" Claire asked suddenly.

"You know they are," Drayton said.

Claire shook her head. "No, I don't know that at all."

Drayton frowned as he shot Theodosia a puzzled look.

How could she not know? Theodosia wondered.

"Then I suppose I'd better hand it over," Claire said. "I had an offer, a really good offer from a serious party, but then I hesitated. I couldn't go through with it." Her chin quivered, her eyes reddened, and she looked like she was about to cry. "I guess my conscience got the best of me."

"Wait a minute," Theodosia said. She was confused. What was Claire talking about? The diamond earrings? Or something else?

"Claire," Theodosia said. "You need to be perfectly up-front about this. It's the only way."

"I know," Claire said. "And I am being up-front. Really."

"So tell us about the diamonds," Theodosia said.

A look of utter confusion appeared on Claire's face. "Diamonds?" She frowned, not understanding, as she shook her head. "I don't know . . ."

Uh-oh, Theodosia thought. *There's something weird going on here. We don't seem to be on the same page.*

"The diamond earrings?" Drayton prompted.

"Earrings?" Claire said. Now she looked completely lost. As if Theodosia and Drayton had suddenly started speaking ancient Greek. "No. I thought you came for . . ."

Claire stepped away from them, quickly grabbed something off her fireplace mantel, and came back.

"Here," she said. "Isn't this what you're looking for?"

Claire handed Drayton a small black leather-bound book. It looked old and incredibly fragile. As he turned the antique volume in his hands, he saw it was the missing Edgar Allan Poe book.

Drayton's eyes practically popped out of his head. "*You* stole the book?"

"That's it?" Theodosia said. "*That's* what you had to confess?"

"Please let me explain," Claire said.

"Please do," Drayton said. His voice was as smooth and cold as glare ice.

"It's because of my mother," Claire said. "I was going to sell it to pay for her cancer treatments. They're . . . experimental."

Theodosia put a hand on a nearby chair to steady herself. She was completely flummoxed. What she thought was going to be a confession of murder had turned into a terribly sad melodrama about a book and a sick mother.

"You had nothing to do with Willow's death?" Theodosia managed to choke out.

Claire stared back at her. Her face registered absolute shock for a few moments. And then, finally, a dawning comprehension.

"Wait," Claire said. "You think *I* killed Willow?" Now her expression was even more shocked than Theodosia's. "Oh, dear Lord, no. No, no. I would never have harmed Willow. Not in a million years."

29

❧

"Well, that didn't go exactly as planned," Drayton said. He was sitting in the passenger seat, clutching the Edgar Allan Poe book, as they drove down Meeting Street.

"It really puts us in a pickle, doesn't it?" Theodosia said.

"You think Claire will sue us for libel? For making false accusations?"

"No."

"What do you think we should do with the book?"

"Nothing to do but return it to its rightful place at the Heritage Society," Theodosia said.

"Are you going to tell Timothy how we found it?"

Theodosia stared straight ahead at the road. "I haven't decided yet."

"If you tell him the truth Claire will lose her job."

"I'm aware of that."

"But if we don't tell him . . ."

Theodosia slowed her Jeep as she approached a stop

sign. She reached a hand up and rubbed the back of her neck where a knot of tension had gathered.

"You know what, Drayton? We have a more pressing problem on our hands."

Drayton gave her a quizzical look. "What do you mean?"

"Henry Curtis."

"Oh, him." Drayton relaxed back in his seat. To him Henry Curtis was obviously small potatoes.

But Theodosia was worried. She thought about how she'd tried to get in touch with Henry for the past couple of days. He hadn't turned up at Willow's funeral and he'd been absent from both the haunted house and his job at the Heritage Society. Then, today, out of the blue, he'd called asking to talk. Said it was urgent.

Is it urgent? Maybe so.

"We have to make a detour," Theodosia said.

"For what? Oh, good gravy. You mean for Henry?" Drayton didn't look happy.

"That's right."

"You think we're going to hear another faux confession?" Drayton asked. Then he reconsidered his words. "Maybe not faux, because Claire really did take the book. But some sort of gibberish that will send us spinning in the wrong direction?"

"Maybe, maybe not. I'm getting a sneaking suspicion that Henry might have figured a few things out."

"Concerning Willow's murder?" Drayton asked.

"Why else would he have called me?" Theodosia drove along for another few blocks, thinking. "We know it wasn't about the book."

Drayton opened the book, gazed at it for a few moments, then closed it carefully. "Do you know where Henry lives?"

There was a grim smile on Theodosia's face. "We're headed there now."

* * *

"This is it?" Drayton asked. They pulled up outside a shabby-looking duplex some two blocks south of the University of Charleston. All around them filmy white ghosts fluttered from trees; orange pumpkins leered from front porches. Even though Halloween was technically tomorrow night, Charleston was already in full celebratory mode.

Theodosia checked the address she'd tippy-typed into her phone. From when Henry Curtis had called her earlier.

"This is it," she said.

"Looks awful."

"He's a student. And an unpaid intern," Theodosia said. "What do you expect?"

"Better than this," Drayton mumbled.

"No, this is how kids live. Or at least get by."

"You think Henry's even home? Don't students go to beer dabblers or keggers or some such thing on weekends?" Drayton asked.

"We'll soon find out," Theodosia said. "Besides, I expect that he's expecting me. So come on. Let's get this over with."

Drayton remained rooted in his seat. "You want me to go in, too?"

"You can be my bodyguard," Theodosia said.

That gave Drayton pause. "Do you think you need one?"

Theodosia's throat felt a little dry as she said, "I sincerely hope not."

They walked up a crumbing sidewalk, climbed two cement steps, and stood on the rickety porch of a two-story duplex. The place had been painted gray at one time, but now the paint was peeling away from the silvered wood in long strips. Rain, hurricanes, and industrial-strength humidity had that effect on wooden houses in Charleston.

"Here we are," Theodosia said.

There were two front doors with black metal mailboxes mounted beside each one.

"Which one is Henry's?" Drayton asked. "Where's his apartment?"

Theodosia leaned forward and peered at the mailbox that hung next to the left-hand door. There was a faded white sticker with the typed name HARRIGAN. Under it was another sticker with the name CURTIS.

"This one," Theodosia said. "He's got the left-hand side of the duplex." Drawing a deep breath for courage, she knocked on the door.

"He's not home," Drayton said almost immediately.

"Let's wait and see." Theodosia waited a few moments, then knocked again.

"Henry's sitting in a coffee shop somewhere, drinking a flavored macchiato and playing games on his phone."

Still no answer. Theodosia frowned. "Hmm."

"Mark my words," Drayton said.

"Maybe we should check around back," Theodosia said.

Drayton shrugged. "Personally, I think it's a wild-goose chase, but . . . okay, I guess we can try the back door."

The side of the duplex was lost in shadows, but a faint bit of light from a streetlamp halfway down the block shed a small puddle of yellow on a cracked back patio. There was a broken metal picnic table with a bike chained to one of its rusted legs.

Theodosia climbed the three steps up to the back door and knocked. Harder this time because now she had a partial view into a back window and could see that a small light was on inside. So maybe Henry Curtis was home after all. Maybe there was a back bedroom or a back office and he hadn't heard her knock? Could be.

Drayton shifted behind her. He was tired and getting antsy, ready to head home.

"I'm afraid this just isn't our night," he said.

Theodosia put a hand on the doorknob.

Drayton saw the movement of her hand and said, "Do you really think that's a good . . ."

Theodosia turned the knob, and the door, almost as if it had a mind of its own, creaked open an inch.

". . . idea?" Drayton finished.

"I think he's in there," Theodosia said. Maybe Henry Curtis was scared or upset or maybe he'd been threatened by someone. Whatever. Theodosia decided she was going in and would hopefully find some kind of answer if she could just talk to him.

"Okay," Drayton said. "But promise me. That's as far as you're going to go."

"Right," Theodosia said as she pushed the door open and stepped inside.

Theodosia took a few moments to get her bearings. She was standing in a warm, dark kitchen that smelled like someone had either made popcorn or heated up chicken soup in the last couple of hours. There was a tiny light on over the stove, but it shone down on the four burners rather than penetrating the darkness of the rest of the space.

"Henry?" Theodosia called out. "Are you here? It's Theodosia Browning. You wanted to talk with me, remember?"

There was no answer.

Theodosia blinked, her eyes straining to see the rest of the room. To figure out how to navigate this dark space.

"Theo?" Drayton said. He was standing close behind her now. And he definitely sounded nervous.

Theodosia took another step forward and stopped. Someone was sitting at the kitchen table. Quiet as a mouse, not moving an inch.

"Henry?" she said, allowing a few moments to go by, letting her eyes adjust.

Henry Curtis was there all right. He was sitting in a kitchen chair, slumped forward, with a plastic bag over his head.

Theodosia's breath caught in her throat as she registered the plastic bag. And knew instantly that Henry was dead. Panic fizzed through her, and she backtracked so hastily she stumbled into Drayton, who was directly behind her.

"Ouch," Drayton said. She'd stepped on one of his feet. Then, "What? What's wrong?"

Theodosia whirled around to face him. "We've got to get out of here. Like right now."

Drayton tried his best to peer around Theodosia. "Something happened?"

"Don't look!" Theodosia cried.

"But I . . ."

"Henry's dead. I'm pretty sure he's been murdered!"

"What?"

"We have to call the police!"

Those words finally sent Drayton scurrying out the back door with Theodosia right on his heels.

30

❦

They heard police car sirens before they saw flashing red and blue lights, a loud, brazen WHOOP WHOOP that probably caught the attention of the entire neighborhood. Then two black-and-white patrol cars swooped in, one a slick top without a light bar, the other a regular cruiser. They rolled to a stop out front where Theodosia and Drayton were waiting, tires squealing as they connected hard with the curb. Those two cruisers were followed by an older-model Crown Victoria that plowed right up over the curb and onto the grassy median. Theodosia knew that all the detectives on the force had gone to Ford Escape except for one.

"Tidwell," Theodosia said. "And he didn't waste any time." She wondered if Tidwell came out on every emergency call. Was he that driven? Did the man not have a private life?

Four uniformed officers formed a flying wedge as they

ran toward Theodosia and Drayton. Then Tidwell shouted, "Everyone, stop right there."

The officers were nobody's fools. They stopped dead in their tracks. They knew darned well who was in charge.

Tidwell came huffing up. He was wearing baggy khaki slacks and an oversize blue sweatshirt with yellow FBI letters stenciled on the front. He may have retired from the Bureau but his clothes were still on duty.

"No," he said at seeing Theodosia. "No, no, no."

"He called me," Theodosia said by way of a hasty explanation. "Henry Curtis did. I'd been trying to get hold of him for the last few days, and he finally called me today. Said he needed to talk." Her words came tumbling out. "And then we—Drayton and I, that is—came over here and found him . . ." Theodosia suddenly ran out of steam and breath. Her shoulders sagged, she threw up her hands, and she said, in a choked voice, "He's dead."

"You found him dead. How convenient," Tidwell said.

"Convenient for who?" Theodosia asked.

"Certainly not for me," Tidwell said.

"You don't think *we* killed him, do you?" Drayton said, stepping forward to assert himself.

"If I'm to believe the call that came in via my dispatcher, Henry Curtis, an intern at the Heritage Society, is stone-cold dead inside that house," Tidwell said. "Do I have that right?"

"Yes," Theodosia said.

Tidwell rocked back on his heels. "This is the second murder connected to the Heritage Society."

"I'm afraid so," Drayton said. "But the thing is . . ."

Tidwell held up a hand cowing Drayton into silence.

"And I understand he was asphyxiated?" Tidwell said. "The caller—I presume it was you, Miss Browning—said there was a plastic bag pulled over his head?"

"Yes, but I didn't . . ." Theodosia began.

This time Drayton cut in to interrupt her. "It might possibly be a suicide. Henry Curtis could have murdered Willow French and was then unable to live with the consequences. With his own guilt."

Theodosia turned to face him. "But what if Henry *didn't* kill Willow?" she argued. "What if the person who killed Willow also murdered Henry?"

"Two wildly divergent theories wrought by amateurs," Tidwell said. "How absolutely fascinating."

Tidwell gazed out toward the street where a shiny black van emblazoned with the words CPD CRIME SCENE had suddenly pulled up.

"Good," he said. "They're here. Now we can get down to business and determine what really happened."

Once the uniformed officers had cleared the house—making sure no one else was inside—the two crime scene techs went in. Dressed in white Tyvek suits and blue booties, they studied the scene, set up two bright lights on stanchions, then came back out to grab their gear.

"We're going to do photos first, but you're welcome to come in," the one whose name tag read BERGER said to Tidwell. He was short and wiry, with dark hair and an earnest expression.

The other tech was an African-American woman with dreadlocks and a lovely oval face. Her name tag read JONES.

Theodosia stood on tiptoes and peered in through the open back door as Drayton pressed up right behind her. She watched the two techs do their work, but mostly she watched Tidwell. She tried to read his face, tried to determine what critical information he might be picking up.

"What?" Theodosia asked when she saw Tidwell flinch.

"There's tape around the victim's neck, and his hands were pulled behind him and tied with plastic flex strips," Tidwell said. "Someone thought this out. They came prepared."

"Oh no," Theodosia murmured. "How awful." She wanted to cry great gluts of tears for Henry Curtis. To rage for a young life cut short. But mostly she wanted to know what monster had committed this terrible deed. So, with feelings veering wildly between anger and bewilderment, Theodosia watched as Berger shot about a million photos of the scene. And forced herself to stand quietly, poised to listen and learn and hope for a sliver of a clue.

When the photos were done, Berger took a video camera and carefully recorded the scene. When he was finished, he looked at Jones and said, "Ready?"

Jones nodded. "Let's go ahead and hit the lights."

The lights were turned out as Jones crept into the kitchen holding a spray bottle and an apparatus that looked like a chunky flashlight but wasn't.

"What is that?" Drayton whispered in Theodosia's ear.

Theodosia shook her head. "Not sure."

"Ultraviolet light," Tidwell mumbled. "She's going to fluoresce the area, then scan for prints."

Everyone watched and held their breath as Jones sprayed the kitchen table, the chairs, the floor, and the deceased with the plastic bag still over his head. Then she pulled on a pair of protective orange goggles and turned on her UV light.

She was thorough, running the light up and down the table, all around it, then carefully over the plastic bag. It was awful, but fascinating.

"I got prints," Jones called out.

Tidwell moved forward as Berger handed him a pair of protective goggles.

"Show me," he said.

"Right here," Jones said, moving a gloved hand. "A partial friction ridge print. And then over here, one that's a little better."

"And they're different from the deceased?" Tidwell asked.

"Yeah, that's a positive," Jones said.

"What does that mean?" Theodosia muttered. Then answered her own question. "Oh, it means Henry was definitely murdered, doesn't it? That someone tied his hands and put a bag over that poor boy's head."

"Looks that way," Berger said.

"Okay," Jones said. "You can turn the lights back on."

The lights came back on and everybody blinked. With the extra wattage, the kitchen looked garish and stark, like an old black-and-white newspaper crime photo.

"You see here," Jones said in a soft voice to Tidwell. "The victim was incapacitated first. There's a gash on the back of his head. A fairly deep one at that. Definitely premortem."

"You mean someone hit Henry on the head and knocked him out?" Theodosia asked, a note of horror in her voice. "Then, while he was unconscious, they choked and strangled him?"

Jones looked over at her. With an almost sympathetic tone, she said, "Probably, yes."

Theodosia stared at poor Henry Curtis. His eyes were mere slits; part of the plastic bag had been sucked into his mouth. Even unconscious, Henry Curtis had fought to live.

"When did it happen?" Tidwell asked.

"Hour. Two at the most," Berger said. "There's no obvious decomp yet."

At hearing that, Theodosia's stomach lurched. Then she willed herself to stay strong. To stay in the moment. Maybe there was something to be learned here.

"Bod Squad's here," Berger said.

Theodosia and Drayton stepped back as a collapsible gurney with a body bag on it was wheeled in by two men.

"Why would someone kill that poor boy?" Drayton wondered.

"I think Henry must have known something," Theodosia said. "Maybe he really did figure out who murdered Willow."

Berger had a clipboard and was writing something, making quick scratches with his pen. "Death by asphyxiation," he murmured.

"Ghastly," Drayton said.

"First Willow, now Henry," Theodosia said. "Who could do this?"

Detective Tidwell turned to stare at her. "Good question," he said. "But whoever it is, they're getting good at it."

31

"I've got some bad news," Theodosia said.

It was Saturday morning, and she'd just invited Haley to sit down with her at the table by the fireplace. The tea shop wasn't open yet, but there were important matters to discuss.

"You've got a scary look on your face," Haley said, fidgeting in her chair. "Did something happen? Something really awful?"

"I'm afraid so," Theodosia said.

Haley squirmed in her chair. "Am I being fired?"

"Haley, no. Of course not!" Theodosia cried.

"Then what is it?" Haley asked.

"Henry Curtis is dead."

Haley did a classic double take. Her mouth dropped open, her body twitched as if she'd been touched with a hot wire, and she almost leaped from her chair. Her hands flew out, smacked the edge of the table, and gripped hard, every knuckle going white.

"He's that kid you told me about, right? The one who dressed up like Frankenstein? Who sent the love note to Willow? Oh man oh man." Haley's words poured out in one long agonized stream.

"He's the one," Theodosia said.

"What happened?" Haley asked. "I mean how . . . ?"

"He was asphyxiated," Drayton said as he carried a teapot over to the table and set it down. Dressed in a tweed jacket and trademark bow tie, he seemed unnaturally calm.

"How do you know all this?" Haley asked as Drayton sat down and poured each of them a cup of tea. "Were you guys there?"

"Unfortunately, Drayton and I were the ones who discovered Henry's body," Theodosia said. "At his apartment over by the university."

Haley grabbed her teacup and took a fast sip, as if to calm herself. "So what happened? I mean *really* what happened?"

"We found Henry Curtis sitting in his kitchen with a plastic bag over his head," Drayton said.

Haley winced, then her eyes went round as saucers. "That's how he died? He was suffocated? That's awful."

"It is awful," Theodosia said.

Haley was digesting their words, trying to recover from her shock, hoping to make the pieces fit. They didn't, of course.

"Do you think Henry was the one who killed Willow?" Haley asked. "And then he committed suicide because he felt so terrible?"

"We thought that might be the case, but that's since been proven false," Theodosia said. "Our theory—and Detective Tidwell pretty much goes along with this—is that whoever killed Willow also murdered Henry."

"To keep him quiet," Drayton said.

Haley shrank back in her chair, her fear palpable. "You're telling me the killer's still *out* there?"

"That does seem to be the problem," Theodosia said.

"But who . . . who is it?" Haley asked. "You guys have been looking into things like crazy so you must have some inkling."

"We looked hard at Allan Barnaby, Willow's publisher, but he has an ironclad alibi and was officially cleared by the police," Theodosia said. "And Claire Waltho, one of the curators at the Heritage Society, was a suspect for about two minutes, but that didn't pan out, either."

Drayton was slowly shaking his head. "We honestly don't know who the killer is. We have a few theories, but that's all they are."

"Jeepers," Haley said. "This is so spooky. Today's Halloween and now, with Henry getting killed . . . it feels like a really bad omen."

"More like a killer trying to cover his tracks," Theodosia said. She was more pragmatic. She didn't believe in omens and portents. She believed in reality. In this case, moving doggedly ahead in the pursuit of justice.

"It's still awful scary," Haley said.

"Of course it is," Drayton said.

Haley stared at them. "Do you think, um . . . that we're in danger?"

"Highly doubtful," Drayton said.

"Well," Theodosia said, drawing the word out slowly.

Haley sat back and tapped a finger against the table. "Come on, guys, which is it?"

"I think we should all stick close together for the time being," Theodosia said.

"You mean like the buddy system?" Haley asked.

"Yes," Drayton said. "That might be a smart idea after all. Let's definitely do that."

Once Haley was back in her kitchen and Drayton was brewing tea, Theodosia got to work readying the tea room.

They'd advertised a noontime Halloween tea and had a book full of reservations. So that's what she focused on right now. Snazzying up the tables with orange tablecloths, adding sprigs of bittersweet in white ceramic skull vases, putting out black linen napkins, then setting the tables with a patchwork of plates, teacups, and saucers—a fun mix of different patterns.

When her phone rang, Theodosia glanced at the caller ID and felt a pang of worry. It was Riley. His morning check-in call.

For the first time this week she was reluctant to answer because of what she knew he'd say. But she picked up anyway with a bright, "Hey. How are you?"

Riley's voice boomed in her ear. "You've been busy. You snooped around and got *involved* again. In another murder!"

"I didn't set out to," Theodosia said, trying to keep her voice light, hoping she didn't sound too intimidated.

"Do you *realize* what you're doing? That you're putting yourself in terrible danger?"

"No, because things are finally happening. It feels like this investigation could come to a logical conclusion at any moment."

Riley snorted. "More like an explosion. Or an *im*plosion."

"I suppose there's always that chance," Theodosia said. She wasn't nearly as pessimistic as Riley was. Ellis Bouchard and Robert Vardell were still hot and heavy on her suspect list, and neither she nor the police had cleared either of them. So Bouchard or Vardell could easily be the guilty party. She just had to figure out who.

"What's on your calendar for today? Besides investigating?" Riley asked. Some of the worry and tension seemed to have ebbed from his voice.

"We've got our Halloween luncheon and then tonight's the Enchanted Garden Party at the Featherbed House."

"Good. That should keep you occupied and out of trouble."

"You're welcome to come tonight."

"Maybe I will," Riley said. "I'll have to let you know."

"How are you feeling?" Theodosia asked.

"Truthfully? Worried about you and a little tired."

"Take a nap, why don't you."

"Okay, I will. Kisses, talk to you later."

"Kisses back. Later," Theodosia said.

"We didn't draw a bad crowd at all," Drayton observed. Thirty-two guests were already seated for their Halloween tea, sipping cups of Drayton's special autumn spice tea and slathering Devonshire cream on Haley's Indian chai scones.

"It's especially good since most people are in a panic over Halloween tonight, and it's the start of a busy weekend," Theodosia said.

"So lots of events as well as trick-or-treating."

"And tons of parties," Theodosia said. She personally had three friends who were throwing masked balls. She'd been invited to all of them but had to beg off since she'd already committed to catering the party at the Featherbed House.

"What's next on Haley's menu?" Drayton asked.

"We're serving crostini with sliced ham and white cheddar, and then wedges of crab quiche with an Amontillado sherry drizzle."

Drayton chuckled. "Amontillado as in . . . ?"

"Poe's 'Cask of Amontillado.'"

"Who doesn't love a literary reference."

"And for dessert Haley is serving ginger cake," Theodosia said. She glanced at her watch. "But I may not stick around for that. I still want to deliver the recovered Edgar Allan Poe book to Timothy."

"He's working at the Heritage Society today?" Drayton asked.

Theodosia shook her head. "He's at home. I called earlier to check."

"Then you'd better get cracking. This is a busy day."

Timothy Neville was not only thrilled to have his book returned, he also knew about the murder of Henry Curtis.

"The police called me," Timothy said. "First thing this morning." His sharp eyes probed at Theodosia as she sat across from him in a leather club chair. "They also told me that you and Drayton were the ones who found him."

They'd settled in Timothy's home library, a place of grace and elegance, filled with a trove of leather-bound books. But Theodosia still felt a trifle uneasy.

"We . . . yes," she said, fumbling her words a little. "We thought Henry had figured out who Willow's killer was. And that he was going to tell us, which is why we went over there." She frowned, thinking about the horrific surprise they'd found. "Turns out we were too late, that we missed the mark entirely."

Mentioning Willow's name seemed to bring sadness back to Timothy's lined face.

"Ah well," he said. "But the police are working hard to solve these crimes. And, if I could look on the bright side for a moment, you did manage to recover a very valuable book."

"Sure," Theodosia said. In the scheme of things, the book seemed like a minor victory.

"Dare I ask where you found it?"

"I really wish you wouldn't."

Timothy looked as if he was going to push for an explanation, then thought better of it. Instead he said, "I have something to tell you."

"What's that?"

"Robert Vardell was just here. In fact, you missed him by all of five minutes."

Theodosia eyebrows shot up. "What was on *his* mind?"

"This may come as a shock to you—it surely did to me—but he handed over the paperwork for the house," Timothy said.

"The house," Theodosia responded, not fully comprehending his words.

"The one Willow purchased for them. Robert told me he didn't feel it was rightfully his."

"You mean now that he's been 'outed' as a gold digger?" Theodosia said.

"He talked about that, too. Begged my forgiveness for his transgressions. Swore to me that he loved Willow very much."

"And you believed him?"

Timothy nodded. "I did. If you could have seen the poor man . . . the pain he was in, the sincerity etched across his face . . ."

Theodosia didn't want to hear about Vardell's sincerity. She figured it was an act. Like everything else.

"I believe you misjudged him," Timothy said. "Because he gave me the engagement ring, too."

"Willow's ring?"

"Robert said she threw it at him. Right after she broke off the engagement."

"Because . . . she found out about him?" Theodosia asked.

"Because they had a fight," Timothy said. "About her buying a house without talking to him."

"Still, Vardell never mentioned the broken engagement when we talked to him in your office," Theodosia said. "When he gave us the story of the Tereshchenko diamonds."

"Robert said he was too embarrassed. And frightened of being a suspect."

"And you believed him?"

Timothy's head bobbed. "Yes."

"So what's Vardell's plan now?" Theodosia asked.

"For one thing he's leaving town."

This was news. "And going where?"

Timothy shrugged. "Robert wasn't entirely clear about his plans. But his car was packed to the gills, and I'd guess that he intends to spend some time with his folks in Myrtle Beach. A few days anyway."

"You mean until he gets his act together," Theodosia said. "Until he adopts a new charade."

"You're being awfully harsh," Timothy said.

Theodosia shrugged. "Maybe." Then she considered her words. "I suppose you're right; I am being harsh. So you say Vardell is on his way out of town?"

"Yes, but first he's going to stop at the cemetery."

"Magnolia Cemetery?" Theodosia blinked. "So Vardell can . . . ?"

Timothy looked profoundly sad. "He wanted to visit Willow's grave."

Robert Vardell was still a huge sticking point for Theodosia. In her estimation, he was a snake in the grass bunco artist. Long story short, she didn't trust him as far as she could throw him.

That might be why Theodosia was speeding down Morrison Drive on her way to Magnolia Cemetery at this very moment. She wasn't sure why she was tailing Vardell; she just was. She had no intention of following him to the ends of the earth. Just to the cemetery.

And what do I do once we get there? Theodosia asked herself. *Confront Vardell? Yell at him? Beat a heartfelt confession out of him?*

All good questions. Probably there was an answer lurking there somewhere.

The low-hanging sun was strafing the trees as she drove through the gates of Magnolia Cemetery. And this time

Theodosia knew exactly where to go. Hang a left, pass the chapel, drive up the hill, and continue past the pyramid tomb.

When Theodosia finally saw Vardell's black VW Jetta parked up ahead, she slowed to a crawl. Poking along, she saw a spot where the spreading branches of a live oak tree dipped to meet the road and would offer a perfect hiding spot. She pulled her Jeep to the side of the road and turned off the engine. Her eyes followed Vardell as he walked slowly across the grass, headed for the granite stone that marked Willow French's grave.

Slowly, quietly, Theodosia opened the driver's side door and slipped out.

From there it was a piece of cake to jump from tree to tree, hiding behind each one as she crept up on Robert Vardell.

Theodosia watched with rapt attention as Vardell approached Willow's grave. He stood there for a moment gazing at the headstone, then knelt down in front of it. He was doing something with the flowers that were there—rearranging them? She wasn't sure.

Theodosia slipped around a small willow and crouched down behind a crepe myrtle.

There. Now she had a good sight line on Vardell.

He was talking to himself out loud, but she couldn't quite make out what he was saying. She caught every third word or so as it floated back to her on a cool breeze. It was like listening to a faulty AM radio station that faded in and out.

Theodosia still wasn't sure why she was hunkered down here, spying on Robert Vardell. Did she still suspect him? Maybe. And if she suspected him of orchestrating Willow's death, did that mean he'd murdered Henry Curtis, too?

Maybe.

Did Vardell do it or not? Was he a stone-cold killer or just a misguided soul? Maybe Vardell existed in his own universe. Maybe he wasn't a bad guy; he was just brimming with visions of grandeur. Maybe he really had loved Willow.

Now what's he doing?

Theodosia watched as Vardell pulled something from his jacket pocket and placed it carefully on Willow's headstone. She wondered what it could be.

Then Vardell knelt down, and his right hand began moving to and fro in the dirt.

How strange.

Finally, after two or three minutes, Vardell got back on his feet, brushed off his slacks, and walked slowly back to his car.

Theodosia waited until Vardell's car had safely disappeared down the road and over a hill. Then she walked quickly across the grass to Willow's grave. She saw that he'd placed a small white envelope there with Willow's name written on it.

Theodosia shook her head. No, she couldn't read it. It wouldn't be right. Whatever Vardell had poured out to his dead fiancée in this letter was his business alone.

Then her eyes fell on the dirt surrounding the gravestone. In the dirt he'd traced a message—*I will always love you*.

Theodosia walked back to her car, tears sparkling in her eyes.

32

❧

"*Where have you* been?" Drayton demanded. "It seems like you've been gone for hours."

"Did you need me for something?" Theodosia asked. She felt a tiny wave of guilt seep in. Maybe she *had* been gone too long.

"Well, not really," Drayton said. "But we were worried about you nonetheless. How did things go with Timothy?"

"I gave him the long-lost book, and he seemed happy enough," Theodosia said. She decided to leave it at that. No need to tell Drayton about her side trip to the cemetery.

"Did Timothy want to know how we recovered it?"

"He asked, but I didn't tell him."

"I don't know if that's a good thing or not," Drayton said.

"Maybe we should just let the whole Claire episode play out and see where it goes," Theodosia said. "You think you can live with that?"

"For now, I probably can," Drayton said.

"I also arrived at Timothy's place, like, five minutes after Robert Vardell had left."

"What do you mean left? Is Vardell going somewhere?"

"Leaving town. Timothy thought he'd probably spend some time with his folks in Myrtle Beach, then move on."

Drayton narrowed his eyes. "That man's a skunk. I'm also not sure we've seen the last of him."

"I'm not, either," Theodosia said. "Trouble is, Timothy isn't furious enough at Robert Vardell."

"Even though Vardell is a murder suspect?"

"Timothy doesn't see it that way at all," Theodosia said. "Do you?"

"I'm not sure anymore."

Theodosia wandered into the kitchen where Haley was baking sultana raisin scones and making Brie cheese and cranberry pastries.

"How are you doing?" Theodosia asked her. "Need any help?"

"I'm a teensy bit nervous about getting everything done, but I expect I'll manage," Haley said. "Thank goodness Angie's chefs are handling the roast pork and the two side dishes. I hope they follow my recipes to the letter."

"I'm sure they will."

Haley cleared her throat.

"What?" Theodosia asked.

"I have a kind of confession," Haley said.

"You do?" *Why Haley and not the killer?* "What is it, Haley?"

"I adopted a cat. Well, more like took him in."

"That little brown-and-orange cat that's been hanging around out back?"

"He's been hanging around because I've been feeding him."

"Of course you have," Theodosia said. "Where is he now?"

"Upstairs. In my apartment. I love Teacake. I want to keep him."

"You've already named him?"

Haley nodded.

"Then I guess you have to keep him."

"Really?"

"Really," Theodosia said. She glanced around the kitchen. "Do you need me to pitch in on anything? Right now I mean?"

Haley thought for a moment. "Nope."

"Okay then. I'm going to get busy and pack up a couple dozen teacups and saucers. I doubt that Angie will have enough."

Theodosia wandered back out into the tea room where Drayton was deep in one of his contemplative moods, pulling down tea tins from his shelves and viewing them with his critical tea sommelier's eye.

Drayton saw her and said, "Did Haley tell you about Teacake?"

"She did."

"And you're okay with it?"

"I don't see why not, especially since he's already living here as part of the family." Theodosia glanced at Drayton's array of tins. "You're still deciding on a tea for tonight?"

Drayton nodded. "Vacillating between my witch's broom puerh and a Chinese black tea with cinnamon and cloves."

"It's Halloween. Doesn't that pretty much dictate your choice?"

"So the witch's broom?"

"It sure *sounds* perfect," Theodosia said.

"Oh, I think people will get a chuckle. Witch's broom, as you probably know, is an aged green puerh tea made from large, dried tea leaves that have been tied into bundles resembling a witch's broom."

"Remind me of the taste," Theodosia said.

"Slightly sweet, reminiscent of peaches or plums."

"Bingo. That's it."

"Now I'm wondering . . . will I have full access to the Featherbed House kitchen? Where exactly am I going to brew my tea?"

"Maybe in the breakfast nook," Theodosia said.

Drayton lifted a single eyebrow and let it quiver. "Please don't tell me I'll be working on a single hot plate."

"I'm sure Angie and her crew can do better than that."

They could. And they did.

With Drayton and Haley ensconced in the Featherbed House's large industrial kitchen along with two of Angie's regular chefs, Theodosia left them alone to check their entrées, prep the side dishes, and start brewing tea. Stepping out of the kitchen, she walked through the cozy breakfast nook and then out through a door that led to the Featherbed House's lobby.

The place was adorable as always, homey and comfortable with Angie's trademark geese scattered everywhere. There were quilted patchwork geese, plaster geese, carved wooden geese, and ceramic geese. Needlepoint geese decorated fat patchwork pillows that were propped against the backs of overstuffed chintz sofas and matching chairs.

Bottles of wine and sherry stood on a long, rough-hewn wooden side table, along with a wheel of orange cheddar cheese and baskets heaped with sliced French bread and crackers. A few guests milled about, enjoying the warmth and hospitality of the place.

"Theodosia?" Angie's voice tinkled merrily over the soft music that played on the sound system. And then she was skipping toward Theodosia across the planked wooden floor. Angie's hair was curly blond and shorter than ever; her lovely oval face held a wide smile. Tonight she'd traded her ruffled blouse and homey denim skirt for a long black velvet witch's costume.

"You look appropriately spooky," Theodosia said to Angie as they exchanged hugs.

Angie stepped back and did a little pirouette. "Don't I just? Tonight I feel more like Morticia Addams than an innkeeper."

"Maybe I should have worn a costume, too," Theodosia said. "But I figured a black apron over black slacks and a white blouse would be more appropriate for serving tea."

Angie held up an index finger. "But I have an extra costume if you're interested . . . if you dare!"

Theodosia was interested.

"What've you got?"

"Come with me." Angie grabbed Theodosia's hand and pulled her behind the reception desk and into her overstuffed office. She grabbed a cardboard box, rustled around inside it, and pulled out a long white shroud. "This is the first part." She handed it to Theodosia.

"Okay," Theodosia said.

"And here's the rest."

"Whoa." Angie had just handed Theodosia a tattered wedding veil and a rubber skull mask.

"Cool, huh?" Angie said. "It's a ghost bride costume."

"It's . . . interesting," Theodosia said.

The ghost bride costume had caught her slightly off guard. For some reason, an image of Willow French flashed through her mind. Then she fought hard to try to shrug it off.

"I've never seen this side of you before," Theodosia said.

Angie grinned. "You've never seen me at Halloween. Or hosting an Enchanted Garden Party." Then she got serious. "You remember my asking if you'd be part of our Pepper's Ghost illusion?"

"Sure."

"Well, that would be your costume."

Theodosia needed to know a few more details. "Why haven't you shanghaied your boyfriend, Harold, into being part of this magic trick?"

"Because he's upstate in Murrells Inlet looking at a possible vacation property for us."

"Okay, got it. So . . . Pepper's Ghost. Explain, please."

"Here's the thing. Pepper's Ghost is an old illusion that originated in Europe in the eighteen hundreds. At magic shows and what they used to call phantasmagoria performances."

"How's the trick work?" Theodosia asked.

"It's basically a kind of hologram prototype," Angie explained. "A reflective screen bounces a two-dimensional image of a person onto a see-through screen." She laughed. "You know, smoke and mirrors. In fact, that's probably where the term came from."

"And you've got this mirrored contraption all set up and ready to go?"

"It's sitting in the courtyard waiting for someone—hopefully you—to be part of the illusion. To scare the bejeebers out of my guests at the dinner's grand finale. Right before the music and dancing starts."

"And then what happens?" Theodosia asked.

"Ideally you go poof—and disappear into the night," Angie said. "So. Are you interested? Can I count on you?"

Theodosia stuck a hand inside the grinning skull mask, manipulated the rubber mouth, and said in a hoarse whisper, "We thought you'd never ask."

"You're going to die when you see what we did to the back patio," Teddy Vickers said. Teddy was Angie's manager, a thin man with thinning hair who favored a Charleston wardrobe of seersucker suits, silk cravats tucked into shirt collars, and pastel Ben Silver polo shirts. Always a trifle flamboyant and over-the-top, Teddy was dressed in a devil costume tonight—red sequined jacket, skinny black slacks, tiny white horns stuck on the side of his head—and carry-

ing a glittery pitchfork. Or, as he explained it to Theodosia, "Devils are so run-of-the-mill. Tonight I prefer to think of myself as Mephistopheles."

Teddy was also chomping at the bit to show Theodosia the decorations in their courtyard patio.

And when they walked out the French doors and stepped down onto the large brick patio, Theodosia was definitely impressed.

Teddy had hired a professional crew to decorate for Halloween, and they'd done an amazing job. Orange and white twinkle lights were strung in the trees, filmy ghosts dangled from branches, and enormous wrought-iron candle stands—like something you'd find in a church—stood everywhere, pillar candles blazing away. There were also dozens of white pumpkins clustered at the base of every tree, gnarly-looking tombstones, and gossamer cobwebs. A dozen large round tables were draped in black with centerpieces of silver pumpkins and white mums. The dishes were dark purple with black glass goblets.

"This is spectacular," Theodosia said as she took it all in.

"Isn't it fabulous?" Teddy was pleased that she was pleased. "And take a look at our little greenhouse."

Theodosia did. Orange lights backlit cutouts of ghosts and goblins as they capered across the large windows.

"I'm getting chills," Theodosia said.

"I know," Teddy said. "Isn't it grand? We've even got floating skulls in our little pond over there. Oh, and look, we've got Haley's raven cake set up on its own table. And when our jazz combo arrives we're going to tuck them right between the gravestones."

"It's all perfect," Theodosia said. "Couldn't be better." She glanced at her watch and decided she should probably run back into the kitchen and check on Drayton and Haley. See if they needed any help.

"When do the guests arrive?" Theodosia asked.

There was a sudden murmur of voices, and Theodosia

turned to see a half dozen costumed guests spill onto the patio.

"Right now," Teddy said.

Haley's dinner menu was spectacular. They started out with sultana raisin scones, then served a sausage apple soup along with miniature Brie cheese and cranberry pastries. The entrée consisted of roast pork with scalloped potatoes and brussels sprouts with balsamic vinegar and honey.

Theodosia figured there had to be at least a hundred people seated in the courtyard (all in costume, no less), so she was vastly relieved that Angie had hired extra help. She and Drayton took care of serving tea, Haley and two of Angie's regular chefs handled the plating, while six servers hustled out all the food.

As Theodosia wandered from table to table, refilling teacups and chatting with friends, she was thrilled by all the compliments.

"Delicious!"

"Might there be seconds on scones?"

"How about a doggie bag, even though I don't have a dog."

Theodosia had just poured a cup of tea for her friend Brooke Carter Crockett when her cell phone jingled in her pocket. She pulled it out, saw who was calling, and said, "Hey there," to Riley.

"Hey there, yourself," he said. "Am I still invited to tonight's big Halloween extravaganza?"

Theodosia stepped off the patio and tried to fade into the background so she could have a little privacy. "Absolutely, you are. As long as you're feeling well enough." She paused. "Are you? Feeling well enough?"

"Leaps and bounds, sweetheart. I just woke up from a catnap and feel like I'm growing stronger with each passing moment."

Are you really feeling better, Riley, or do you just want to keep tabs on me?

"That's great," she said. "When can you be here?"

"Take me five minutes at most. But the big question is, will there be any food left?"

"For you? Not a problem. I've got an in with the chef."

"Okay, see you soon," Riley said.

"Oh, hey!"

"What?" he asked.

Theodosia smiled to herself, thinking about the ghost bride costume and the optical illusion that was yet to come.

"Better hurry, because I've got a surprise for you."

"What is it?"

"You'll have to get over here and see."

Theodosia hung up, then headed back inside. The servers were clearing plates, and it was almost time to bring out dessert. She ghosted along the edge of the patio, smiling to herself.

And suddenly stopped dead in her tracks. And stopped smiling as well.

There, sitting at one of the tables, chatting amiably with another guest, was Ellis Bouchard!

33

❦

Theodosia's first thoughts were, *Bouchard? How on earth did Bouchard suddenly turn up here? Tonight of all nights?*

Somehow this didn't feel like a coincidence. Rather, it felt . . . eerie.

Goose bumps prickled Theodosia's arms as she hurried inside. When she saw Angie standing behind the reception desk, talking on the phone, she waved at her and mouthed, "We need to talk!"

Thirty seconds later, Angie hung up. "What?" she said.

Theodosia grabbed Angie and pulled her outside. Aimed a finger at Bouchard. "You see that gentleman sitting over there? Is he one of your guests?"

"That's Mr. Bouchard," Angie said matter-of-factly. "He's been staying here for the last two weeks, renting one of the rooms in our annex. Why? Is something wrong?"

"I hope not."

"What? Tell me," Angie said.

"He's basically a suspect in the murder of Willow French."

Angie's mouth pulled into an almost perfect oval. "Oh. I didn't know that. Do you want me to . . . what?" She shook her head. "Ask him to leave?"

"No," Theodosia said. "Let's just . . . let it go for now."

"You sure?"

"Yeah. I'll be okay."

Still, Theodosia felt jittery and on edge as she helped serve dessert. Okay, she knew why Ellis Bouchard was staying here, why he'd chosen this particular B and B. It was close to the mansion he was struggling to gain control of. And close to Timothy and the Heritage Society as well.

Too close for comfort?

Had Bouchard known that she, Drayton, and Haley would be serving dinner here tonight? Or was it just happenstance? Should she ask him? No. Theodosia dismissed that thought immediately. Better to wait until Riley showed up. Then he could ask the questions. After all, he was the one with official credentials.

The raven cake they cut and served for dessert proved to be a huge hit. Haley called her recipe the Blackout because it was basically dark chocolate cake with chocolate pudding filling and chocolate frosting and fondant. Sinfully rich and, judging from the way forks were scraping against plates, also quite delicious.

"Hey." Angie touched Theodosia's elbow. Lightly, but it had made her jump anyway. "You okay? Still feeling rattled?"

Theodosia shook her head. "Nope, I'm fine. Is it time for me to get into my costume?"

Angie nodded. "I'd say you've got about five minutes. What I'm going to do is thank my guests for coming tonight, introduce our jazz combo, then segue into a quick fun talk about Charleston ghosts and hauntings. You know, because every B and B, hotel, and church around here is reputed to be haunted."

"This place, too?" Theodosia asked.

Angie smiled. "Why do you think I chose the ghost bride costume?"

"Okay," Theodosia said. "Then I'll go change. What's my cue?"

"When you hear me say Clarice—that's the name of our ghost—that's when you should come wafting out."

"Got it."

Theodosia bumped into Drayton in the lobby. He was carrying a teapot in each hand.

"Would you believe I'm the ghost tonight?" Theodosia asked him.

"Seriously?" Drayton smiled. "I like that. What do your ghostly duties entail?"

"Nothing too tricky. I'm just supposed to float out and then disappear."

"Ah yes, Teddy Vickers mentioned the Pepper's Ghost trick to me. I know that many European magicians once used it. So did Harry Houdini. Best of luck with your disappearance. Take care you don't venture too far. I'm supposed to do my reading right after."

Theodosia went into Angie's office, pulled on her shroud, added the rubber mask, then placed the tattered veil on her head. She peered into a little oval mirror that hung on the wall and gasped. She really did look awful. The dreadful veil looked almost moldy while her eyes gazed out from darkened, hollow eyeholes. Oh well, it was Halloween after all. A time for ghostly, ghastly surprises.

Theodosia stood behind the French doors, listening as Angie give her little speech, nodding along as the guests clapped. She bounced on the balls of her feet, trying to get loose, trying to get into the mood.

Method acting?

Sure, why not? She snicked the door latch open, poised to make her grand entrance.

Then, when Angie uttered the name Clarice, Theodosia burst through the French doors and ran into the courtyard. She stretched her arms out wide, the better to show off her flowing shroud and veil. Then, when she hit dead center, she did a slow twirl and let out a ghostly howl.

The applause startled her. But Theodosia quickly regained her ghostly composure and spirited herself the rest of the way across the courtyard where Angie was holding out a hand to welcome what she called her "house ghost, Clarice."

Theodosia barely registered the rest of Angie's words as she glanced across the courtyard, taking in the laughter of the guests and the smiles on the servers' faces. Then, she saw Riley, his arm in a sling, standing next to Drayton. They were outside the French doors, their heads close together. Drayton was doing all the talking, as if he were explaining something.

Drayton just told him it was me.

Then Riley turned and looked across the courtyard, over the heads of the guests, and spotted Theodosia. A smile lit his face. He'd seen her, probably recognized her even with the crazy costume. Now he was watching carefully, waiting for the magic trick to happen.

Theodosia smiled inside her mask as Angie continued talking to her guests, explaining the wonderful illusion she was about to perform.

Then Teddy Vickers was standing behind her, whispering. Telling her to stand on her mark.

Theodosia moved into a beam of light that shone down from above. And stood there, still as a statue.

A hush fell over the audience. Then, out of the corner of her eye, Theodosia saw a mirror image of herself projected on a screen.

Teddy grabbed her by the sleeve and pulled her backstage as the audience began to cheer.

"Well done," Teddy whispered to her. "Just stay here, out of sight, and I'll be back in a flash."

Theodosia stood there, wondering what was going on, wishing she could have seen the expression on Riley's face when she disappeared.

There was another whisper. Off to her left. Off in the shadows. Soft and hushed.

"Theodosia."

Theodosia turned, hesitated, and took three steps toward the back of the stage. It was pitch-dark, and she couldn't see a thing.

"What?" she said. "What do I do now?"

"This way," the voice whispered.

"Teddy?"

Was it Teddy? A warning bell clanged in Theodosia's head. What was going on?

There was a quick flash of yellow, bright and sparkly, like sunbeams on water.

Bright eyes, was Theodosia's first impression. Then she turned and thought . . . *No, that's not quite right.*

In the instant it took for Theodosia's brain to form that singular idea, a crushing weight struck her on the back of her head. A galaxy of stars exploded before her eyes, followed by a dark and sickening image of a deep, wildly swirling whirlpool. Theodosia was falling, softly, almost floating ever downward, like gentle snow descending on aspen leaves.

And then Theodosia was truly gone, her mind a total blank, her body as helpless and compliant as a rag doll.

Which made it easy for her attacker to toss her hastily and carelessly into the van.

34

❧

Pain. Darkness. And a sickening sense of motion.

Theodosia regained consciousness little by little. Slowly, methodically, she became aware of the fact that she'd been struck on the back of her head. Struck hard. Maybe even concussion hard since she was having a terrible time gathering her thoughts and recalling what had just happened to her.

Gradually, as her memory came back in fleeting images and flashes, she realized that she was lying on her left side with her cheek pressed against some sort of prickly, smelly carpet. And that, wherever she was, it was swaying slowly.

Theodosia opened her eyes. Darkness but not a total blackout.

Where am I? Trunk of a car?

She forced herself to move, to reach out and explore the space around her.

No, there's lots of room. I must be in some sort of van.

Her knees were drawn up to her chest, as if she'd been haphazardly loaded into a vehicle.

Or pushed. I think I was pushed.

Theodosia rolled over slowly and eased herself up onto her knees. She was shaky at best. Unsteady.

Getting her balance now, Theodosia slipped off her shroud—the mask and veil had disappeared somewhere—and reached out tentatively. She felt something slithery. What was it? Her fingers touched it again. Something smooth and cool. Plastic? That's what it was. A thin sheet of plastic like you'd drape over a dress to keep it clean.

Theodosia sat bolt upright, her mind pinging with fear along with a smattering of remembrances. The faint odor of dry cleaning fluid that had lingered on the Sherlock Holmes costumes. The bit of plastic she'd found stuck to Earl Grey's collar. The smell of dry cleaning fluid right now.

She eased herself forward in the van, moving cautiously toward the faint light of the vehicle's cab. And saw that a grate separated the back of the van from the front. A crisscross piece of metal. Like you'd see in a prison van.

So what is this? I'm in the back of a dry cleaner's van? But why?

And then the reality of the situation came rushing at her.

Somebody's taken me prisoner? Who?

Frantically searching her memory for a sliver of a clue, Theodosia kept coming up blank. Until she finally remembered an insignificant conversation from a few days earlier. A conversation about paying the bills and . . . working for a dry cleaner?

"Sybil?" That single word came out as a dry croak.

There was no answer. Only faint road sounds coming from outside.

"Sybil?" Theodosia tried again. "Is that you?"

Again, nothing.

"What's going on? What's happening?" And then, in an almost plaintive voice, "Why am I here?"

Theodosia crawled toward the front of the van on her hands and knees, blinking rapidly to clear her vision, and stared through the metal grate.

Sybil was sitting behind the wheel, ignoring her as she drove. And she was wearing a pair of stunning yellow diamond earrings.

Willow's Hibiscus Diamond earrings. Oh, this is not good. This is so not good!

"Sybil?" Theodosia tried again. She knew she had to make a convincing appeal, somehow persuade Sybil that kidnapping her was all wrong.

Without taking her eyes off the road, Sybil said, "Shut up back there."

"Sybil, no. This is me, Theodosia. We know each other. We're friends. Don't you remember when you served tea with Drayton and me at the Heritage Society? You were so sweet and lovely to help us."

"I said shut up." Sybil's voice was like gravel. "You weren't supposed to wake up this fast. I should have hit you harder."

"What's going on?" Theodosia asked. "Will you please tell me what's going on?" Then, in a more demanding tone, "Sybil, you know this is wrong!"

"You know what's wrong?" Sybil shouted back. "Me working two jobs and being saddled by massive debt. Me playing gopher for everybody who snaps their fingers while Miss Fancy Pants natters on about her big fat wedding."

"I completely understand," Theodosia said. She didn't really but knew she had to keep Sybil talking, keep trying to communicate. "You were under pressure and you cracked."

"No, honey, I cracked the code. It's easy street from now on."

"You won't get away with this."

But Sybil ignored Theodosia's words. Instead of answering, she turned on the radio. Immediately, a blast of music filled the van, something with incoherent lyrics and a thumpity-thump beat that rattled Theodosia's teeth and made her aching head pound that much more.

As Theodosia tried to make sense of what was happening, what struck her as extremely peculiar was the fact that Sybil was wearing a white zip-front Tyvek jumpsuit. It was the kind of disposable uniform that workers in clean rooms wore.

Why would Sybil do that? Theodosia wondered. What was she up to that she had to protect her clothes?

Then the answer came to Theodosia in a terrible, unholy wallop.

Sybil wanted to protect her clothes from getting all bloody.

Bloody? From my blood?

Theodosia clamped both hands over her mouth to stifle her scream.

Oh dear Lord! How am I going to get out of this?

Theodosia knew she had to regroup. She needed to calm down, gather her thoughts, whisper a prayer, and figure out an escape plan. When nothing of particular brilliance struck her, she lay on her back and thumped the bottoms of her feet against the metal grate. Tried to kick it out.

All it did was rattle loudly.

"I have a gun, you know," Sybil said. "In case you go all ballistic on me."

Theodosia stopped kicking the grate. She rolled back onto her hands and knees and peered into the front of the van. Sybil wasn't kidding. There was a gun sitting on the seat next to her. An ugly matte-black pistol.

"You killed Willow," Theodosia said.

"Good girl. *Now* you figure it out," Sybil said.

"And Henry Curtis?"

"He was sniffing around, asking questions. He was getting way too close, just like you were. Then when he confessed—under some duress, I might add—that he was about to meet with you, well . . . he had to go."

"And now me?"

"Such a brilliant deduction."

"Did you steal Willow's computer, too?" Theodosia asked.

"Yup. It's called misdirection, in case you're interested."

"And now you're wearing Willow's earrings," Theodosia said in a dry voice.

Sybil actually smiled. "Nice touch, huh? Too bad I have to sell them." She shrugged. "But that's life. Easy come, easy go."

"And the matching pendant?"

"Got that, too. Although it took a little more work on my part."

Theodosia clenched her hands as a fiery red bomb seemed to explode in her brain.

She shot Riley. This is the crazy person who shot Riley.

Theodosia wanted to scream, gnash her teeth, and rip Sybil from limb to limb. But she couldn't right now because she was trapped. Theodosia took a deep breath and forced herself to swallow her anger. It tasted terrible.

"We could end this right now," she finally said. "You could simply pull over and let me out. We could both walk away from this."

"Hah!" came Sybil's sharp bark. "Like that's going to happen. Now shut up and enjoy the ride."

"Where exactly are we going?" Theodosia asked.

She pressed her face against the grille and saw they were flying down Tradd Street. Okay, they hadn't gotten all that far yet. This thing could still be resolved, right?

"Sybil?"

"I said shut up. Your chatter is annoying," Sybil said.

The van careened left, and they were suddenly flying down Concord. She reached a hand out and grabbed the pistol, clanged it against the grate. "Settle down."

Theodosia retreated to the back of the van. As her panic hit an all-time high, she searched around frantically. She needed something—a weapon, any kind of weapon—so she could fight back if the chance arose.

Her fingers fluttered across the stiff hunk of carpet, then onto a rubber mat.

Was there nothing at all?

No, she had to keep searching!

Theodosia's fingers finally touched a thin piece of metal that was half-hidden under the rug.

What's this?

She eased it out and found herself clutching a wire coat hanger.

Yes. This could work. No, it has to work!

Working as fast as she could, Theodosia straightened out the wire hanger, then pinched it together to form a long piece with a hook at the end.

If she could slide it through the grate and maybe snatch the keys from the ignition, then she could stop the van!

Still on her knees, Theodosia crept forward until one shoulder was pressed up against the grate.

Now all she had to do was slip the hanger through one of the slots and try to hook those keys! But she had to do it fast!

Theodosia drew a deep breath, then poked the hanger through, aiming for the keys.

"What are you doing?" Sybil screamed. "Stop that right now!"

Theodosia ripped the wire hanger back. As ridiculous and pitiful as the straightened hanger was, it was her only weapon.

Sybil turned, anger burning like red-hot coals in her eyes, and started to reach for her gun.

No!

Quick as a serpent's bite, Theodosia jabbed her hanger back through the grate and poked hard at Sybil's freckled little hand. The metal tip broke the surface of her skin and raised a thin line of blood.

"Ouch!" Sybil cried as she jerked her wounded hand back. "That move is going to cost you. I don't just have to shoot you in cold blood, you know. I can draw it out, make the pain last a lot longer."

An ice pick of fear stabbed at Theodosia's heart.

No, nada, not happening, Theodosia told herself. *I gotta get myself out of this mess. So I have to make this count . . .*

Theodosia pulled her weapon back and, like a fencer aiming a thin, deadly rapier, drove it directly at Sybil's face. The tip skimmed through a fluff of hair, caressed her cheek, and skittered into the corner of her eye.

Not hard enough to actually poke her eye out, but . . . well, maybe that hard. Because this was life and death after all!

Sybil let loose a piteous shriek. "Agggh! You stuck me, you crazy witch. It hurts! I can't see! I'm blind! You blinded me!"

Theodosia was more concerned with the immediate danger on the road than Sybil's visual acuity. The van was dipping and dodging drunkenly through all kinds of traffic.

"Put your foot on the brake!" Theodosia screamed. Signs flew by, red lights flashed up ahead, and she could see they were rapidly approaching a major intersection. "Do it now! Pump the brake!"

But Sybil was still screaming her lungs out, like a banshee whose wings had caught fire.

"Damn you, it hurrrrts!"

The van blasted right through the intersection. Horns honked, brakes screeched, angry drivers yelped at them. No matter, Sybil continued to scream at the top of her lungs as the van careened forward.

Now they'd just sailed past the public pier toward Waterfront Park!

"Owwww!" Sybil warbled. "My eye is *killing* me!"

"Sybil, you have to stop the van!" Theodosia cried. The van was rolling along at thirty miles an hour, then thirty-five. "You're completely out of control! We're going to . . ."

Sybil was spewing words, her voice entirely unintelligible, just a soundtrack of curses and moans as she pulled a hand from her face and made a half-hearted, one-handed grasp for the steering wheel. In doing so she caused the van to slalom hard right and cut across an entire lane of traffic. More horns blared as the van's right front tire bounced up and over the cement curb.

BUMP! BAP!

Seconds later, the entire van jounced up and over the curb. Now they were churning along on a level piece of grass.

A park? was Theodosia's first thought. *We've gone off the road and into a park?*

But the van's speed hadn't tapered off one bit!

With the Cooper River just to their right, Theodosia was suddenly in a blind panic. What if, in Sybil's crazed mental state, she decided to end it all and drive them right into the river? Theodosia could just imagine the van shooting over the edge of the precipice, then tumbling slowly, end over end, into that dark, cold water. In seconds they'd plunge below the surface.

Could I kick out a window and escape?

Didn't happen that way, thank goodness.

Instead, the van continued to roar down a patch of dry grass, churning up turf, kicking up sticks and stones in its wake. They were completely out of control!

Theodosia made a second try at hooking the keys, but Sybil was thrashing around so much she ended up poking her leg instead.

"Ouch!" Sybil's leg kicked out in a knee-jerk reaction, and

she grazed the brake pedal, helping to slow them down a touch. There was another terrifically hard BUMP and CRUNCH as the van sideswiped something—a park bench?—and then they slewed sideways with a sickening tilt.

Theodosia flew up, her head smashing against the ceiling of the van. Then they were rolling, tumbling, almost in slow motion. Until the van hit what felt like a brick wall—SMACK—and shuddered to a stop.

35

❧

Am I dead yet?

That was Theodosia's first thought when she opened her eyes.

Then she scraped herself off the floor—or was it the ceiling?—and stared at a windshield threaded with a galaxy of cracks.

Where am I?

DRIP. DRIP. DRIP.

The sound was loud and unmistakable.

What is that? Gasoline gushing out of the gas tank? Oh no, please don't tell me this stupid van is about to catch fire!

Theodosia was terrified. Something was leaking slowly into the van. There was a sense that the carpet beneath her was getting wet.

Then she heard a louder sound of cascading water.

Theodosia pulled herself into a kneeling position and stared out. Amazing! They'd landed in Charleston's famed

Pineapple Fountain. It was one of Charleston's major landmarks and meant to represent hospitality. Theodosia had never been so happy to see it in her life.

Water. Not gasoline. A lucky break.

Sybil was still moaning as Theodosia worked to pry the grate off—thank goodness it had come loose in the crash! She levered it away from its moorings, seesawing it back and forth as Sybil opened her eyes and suddenly scrambled for her gun!

Faster than a sidewinder rattlesnake, Theodosia tilted the grate and smashed it against her. Sybil's head snapped back, and she was rocked sideways. But only for a moment. With an angry grimace, Sybil struggled to free herself and lunged for her gun again.

Theodosia saw Sybil clawing toward the gun, so she swiped a hand out and batted it away. The gun skittered across the seat and landed on the floor. Or was it the ceiling? Theodosia still wasn't sure which way was up or down.

Sybil's arms flailed wildly, then she pulled her hands into claws and turned toward Theodosia, trying to scratch her face.

"Oh no you don't!" Theodosia cried.

She balled up a fist, cocked her arm, and let fly. As she connected hard with Sybil's nose there was a loud *crunch* and the girl's eyes crossed.

Sybil's mouth dropped open in shock. As if she couldn't believe Theodosia had fought back.

"You broke my nose!" Sybil shouted, her words sounding heavy and sluggish.

Blood streamed down her face as Sybil howled in pain. She doubled over, made a horrible gurgling sound in the back of her throat, and clutched her broken nose with both hands.

"You hurt me!" Her voice rose in a piteous, bubbling shriek, like she was talking underwater. And Sybil was not only angry, she sounded accusatory! "I thought you were a *lady*!" she screamed.

"A lady who's smart enough to get herself out of trouble," Theodosia said. She leaped into the passenger seat, kicked open the door, and bailed out.

Just as Theodosia squirmed from the wrecked van, two police cruisers swerved onto the grass, heading in her direction. Their light bars pulsed blue and red, sirens piercing the night. Had the officers seen the van careen through the stop sign? Had they heard the blaring of horns, the screeching of brakes? Were they out to give the crazy van driver a speeding ticket? Theodosia didn't care why they'd suddenly appeared; she was just overjoyed to see them.

"Help!" Theodosia cried as she half limped, half ran toward the police cruisers. "I need help!" She waved her arms frantically, hoping they'd see how disheveled she was, that they'd understand she was in serious distress.

Another car, an older model that was following them, drove up onto the grass and rocked to a hard stop some ten feet away.

"Please help!" Theodosia called again. Every muscle in her body ached, and she felt sick to her stomach.

Wait. Is that . . . ?

The passenger door of a Crown Vic suddenly burst open, and Theodosia was stunned to see Pete Riley jump out!

"Riley?" Theodosia's voice was a surprised, almost cautious squeak. Then she found her voice, cried his name with joy, and promptly sagged in relief. She'd never been so glad to see anybody in her entire life.

But the surprises didn't end there.

The driver's side door flew open, and Detective Tidwell climbed out. He stared at Theodosia, then grabbed for his belt and hitched up his pants.

Theodosia paid no attention to Tidwell. She couldn't care less. It was Riley she was laser focused on as he ran toward her, one arm still in a sling.

"Theodosia!" he cried. "You're hurt! What happened?"

Theodosia couldn't quite find the words.

Riley grabbed for her, fumbling one-handedly, and pulled her close. "*Are* you hurt?"

Theodosia slid into Riley's arms as carefully as she could and laid her head against his shoulder. Then she finally found the presence of mind to answer him. "I think I'm okay. Mostly bumps and bruises." Tears stung her eyes.

"You're really all right? Please be all right," Riley whispered.

"I am," Theodosia managed. Then she nodded, as if to reassure him as well as herself. "Now that you're here."

Riley's lips gently caressed her forehead, then moved down to kiss her full on the lips.

Theodosia, for the first time in her life, suddenly understood what an old-fashioned swoon was like.

So this is what it feels like. To practically faint with relief. And happiness.

Theodosia kissed him back, loving him, reveling in the feeling of being safe and cared for as Riley's good arm held her tight and made small, calming circles on her back. Finally, she pulled back, caught her breath, and said, "Now I *know* I'm okay."

Riley released her and held her out at arm's length. "Who . . . ?"

"Sybil," Theodosia said. Just saying her name made Theodosia feel ragged and fluttery, as if she'd escaped a terrible fate. Which she probably had. "It was Sybil all along."

"Who?" Riley's eyes bored into her, and his brow furrowed in frustration. He sounded as if he'd been caught completely off guard and never heard the name before.

"Sybil, the intern at the Heritage Society," Theodosia said. "She's . . . she's still in the van. Pretty banged up I guess."

Riley shook his head, not quite comprehending her words.

"There was no Sybil on our radar," he said.

"She wasn't on mine, either," Theodosia said. "That's why she was able to . . ." Her hands made twirling gestures, trying to fill in the words.

"Detective Riley!" Tidwell shouted. He was standing ten feet from them, looking crabby. Officially crabby. "Stop fooling around over there and have the uniformed officers check that crashed van. Start earning your pay grade!"

"I'm on it, sir," Riley said. He kissed Theodosia once more and then got busy.

36

❧

"How did you get here so fast?" Theodosia asked, once she was back in Riley's arms. "How did you know I was in trouble?"

"You went missing. What was I supposed to do?" Riley said. "I came looking for you and saw a van speeding down the alley. Then I found your mask lying on the ground and put two and two together . . ."

"And put out a call . . ."

"And guess who answered."

They both looked over at Tidwell, who was shaking his head and glowering at Sybil as one of his officers pushed her into the back of a cruiser. Theodosia was delighted to see she was securely handcuffed.

An officer drove Theodosia and Riley back to the Feather-bed House. Theodosia was worried that Drayton, Haley, and Angie would think the worst—that she'd actually disappeared into the netherworld. Or been abducted, which she actually had been.

They were stunned when she walked through the front door!

"Where did you run off to?" Haley demanded. "You missed Drayton's recitation."

"Thank goodness you're here!" Angie cried.

"We thought you were kidnapped by Pepper's Ghost!" Drayton cried.

Theodosia gave a nervous chuckle. "You're not going to believe this, but I kind of was."

She told them the full story then, scary parts and all. There were shocked reactions when Theodosia revealed that Sybil was the murderer, then a general cooing and fussing over her. Angie draped a shawl around her shoulders, Drayton handed her a cup of tea, and Haley just looked stunned.

Teddy Vickers interrupted their little confab when he crashed into the lobby and said, "I could use some help outside if you don't mind. We've got a party going on!"

"The guests!" Angie cried as she flew out the door. Before it closed, Theodosia could hear raucous voices and loud music.

"You two should stay," Drayton urged. "There's a wonderful jazz trio out on the patio. They're even playing some Miles Davis and John Coltrane."

"Wait a minute, you know jazz?" Haley asked Drayton. He'd grown suddenly cool in her estimation.

But Theodosia's eyes were beginning to droop, and she looked a little woozy. So it was Riley who stepped in and put his foot down.

"I think it's time to go," he said.

"But it's Halloween," Haley argued. "Not even nine o'clock yet. You're going to miss the dancing. And the drinks!"

"It does sound like fun," Theodosia said. Then she yawned. "But I am awfully beat."

"I think we both need to hit the pause button," Riley

said. He guided Theodosia to the front door where they waved a tired goodbye, then strolled slowly down the street, dappled in streams of moonlight, holding hands.

Riley smiled at Theodosia and said, "Your hair."

"Oh no." Theodosia reached up and patted it, thinking she must look awful.

"It looks angelic. Like you're wearing a halo."

Theodosia relaxed. Clearly, that comment warranted another kiss.

FAVORITE RECIPES FROM
The Indigo Tea Shop

Haley's Pumpkin Soup

2 Tbsp. olive oil
1 medium onion, finely chopped
1 can pumpkin puree (15 oz.)
2 Tbsp. fresh thyme leaves
½ tsp. ground cumin
½ tsp. salt
¼ tsp. pepper
⅛ tsp. ground ginger (optional)
2 cups vegetable broth
2 Tbsp. maple syrup
2 Tbsp. heavy cream

HEAT olive oil in a medium saucepan over medium heat, then add onion and cook for 3 minutes. Add the pumpkin puree, thyme leaves, cumin, salt, pepper, and ginger (if using). Cook for about 5 minutes. Add vegetable broth and cook for an additional 4 minutes, stirring constantly as mixture bubbles. Remove from heat and stir in maple syrup and cream. Serve warm. Yields 4 servings. (Note: This soup can be made ahead and refrigerated for up to 5 days.)

Tarragon Chicken Salad

2 cups diced cooked chicken
⅓ cup mayonnaise
1 Tbsp. tarragon, chopped
⅛ tsp. onion powder
1 Tbsp. fresh lemon juice
Salt and pepper to taste

MIX chicken with mayonnaise. Stir in tarragon, onion powder, lemon juice, and salt and pepper. Yields 2 servings if the tarragon chicken salad is served on lettuce as an entrée, 4 servings if served on bread as a sandwich, or 8 servings if served on crostini as an appetizer.

Chai–Flavored Cupcakes

1 pkg. white cake mix (2-layer size)
1¼ cups half-and-half
½ cup cooking oil
2 eggs
1 tsp. pumpkin or apple pie spice
½ tsp. ground cardamom

PREHEAT oven to 350 degrees. Line muffin tin (24 cup–size) with paper cups. In a large mixing bowl combine dry cake mix, half-and-half, cooking oil, eggs, pie spice, and cardamom. Beat with an electric mixer for 2 minutes on medium speed. Spoon batter into cups. Bake for 16 to 18 minutes or until toothpick inserted into center comes out clean. Cool cupcakes for 5 minutes, then remove from pan. Frost with your favorite frosting. Yields 24.

Crab and Avocado Tea Sandwiches

    3 Tbsp. mayonnaise
    1 Tbsp. fresh chives, chopped
    1 tsp. lemon juice
    1 cup cooked fresh crab or canned crab
    Salt and pepper to taste
    Butter
    8 slices thin white sandwich bread
    1 avocado, peeled, seeded, and sliced

IN a medium bowl, combine mayonnaise, chives, and lemon juice. Gently add in crab and stir to combine. Add salt and pepper to taste. Spread butter on 8 slices of bread. Arrange sliced avocado on top of 4 slices of buttered bread and top with crab mixture. Top sandwiches with remaining 4 bread slices. Trim the crusts and cut each sandwich into 3 equal pieces. Yields 12 tea sandwiches. (Note: Sandwiches can be made 1 to 2 hours before serving if you cover them tightly with plastic wrap and refrigerate.)

Southern Peach Crisp

    3 cups peaches, fresh or frozen (but thawed)
    1 Tbsp. lemon juice

1 cup self-rising flour
1 cup sugar
1 egg
6 Tbsp. melted butter

PREHEAT oven to 350 degrees. Place peaches in baking dish and sprinkle with lemon juice. In medium-sized bowl, mix flour, sugar, and egg together—mixture will be lumpy. Spread mixture over peaches, then pour melted butter on top. Bake for 30 to 35 minutes at 350 degrees. Yields 4 servings. (Hint: May be served with whipped cream or ice cream.)

Ham and Corn Muffins

⅓ cup soft butter
2 tsp. scallions, finely chopped
1 Tbsp. honey
6 corn muffins, partially split
6 slices of ham, very thin-sliced

IN small bowl, mix butter with scallions and honey. Gently spread butter mixture into partially split corn muffins and fill with sliced ham. Yields 6. (Note: This is a fun alternative to a traditional tea sandwich.)

Herbed Chèvre Butter

½ cup butter, room temperature
¼ cup goat cheese, softened

1 tsp. fresh dill, finely chopped
1 tsp. fresh thyme, finely chopped
⅛ tsp. salt

COMBINE ingredients in small bowl and chill. Serve at room temperature on tea sandwiches with sliced radishes, tomatoes, or cucumbers. Yields ¾ cup.

Haunted Hibiscus Cooler

2 cups ginger ale
1 cup brewed hibiscus tea, cooled
½ peach, sliced
½ cup rum (optional)
4 cinnamon sticks

IN a large pitcher, mix ginger ale, hibiscus tea, peach slices, and rum (if using). Pour into tall glasses filled with ice and garnish with cinnamon sticks. Yields 4 servings.

Charleston Apple Pudding

2 cups apples, peeled, cored, and chopped
⅓ cup pecans, chopped
1 Tbsp. rum
¼ cup flour
2 tsp. baking powder
⅛ tsp. salt
2 eggs

1 cup brown sugar, packed
2 tsp. vanilla extract

PREHEAT oven to 350 degrees. In large bowl, combine apples, pecans, and rum. In separate bowl, mix together flour, baking powder, and salt. In a mixing bowl, beat eggs with electric mixer for 3 minutes adding in sugar and vanilla. Slowly add flour mixture to egg mixture, mixing on low speed. Now fold in pecans and apples. Pour batter into a greased 8-inch square pan and bake 25 minutes at 350 degrees, or until top is bubbly and golden brown. Yields 9 servings.

Best Banana Bread Ever

⅔ cup sugar
½ cup soft shortening
2 eggs
3 Tbsp. buttermilk
1 cup mashed banana
2 cups flour
1 tsp. baking powder
½ tsp. baking soda
½ tsp. salt
½ cup chopped nuts

PREHEAT oven to 350 degrees. Mix together sugar, shortening, and eggs. Stir in buttermilk and banana. Sift together flour, baking powder, baking soda, and salt and stir in. Mix in nuts. Pour into well-greased 9-by-5-inch loaf pan. Let stand 20 minutes. Bake at 350 degrees for 50 to 60 minutes. Yields 1 loaf.

Haley's Pork Tenderloin

1 lb. pork tenderloin cutlets (4)
2 eggs, beaten
Bread crumbs, fine, about 1 cup
Oil for frying
8 slices bacon
2 Tbsp. butter
1 medium onion, chopped
1 can mushrooms (4 oz.)
1 Tbsp. oregano
1 cup beef broth

DIP pork cutlets into eggs and then into bread crumbs. Heat oil in skillet and fry cutlets on both sides until brown. Remove from pan and place in a baking dish. Fry bacon until crisp, crumble, and set aside. Melt butter in fry pan, then add bacon, chopped onion, mushrooms, and oregano. Sauté for 2 minutes, then pour mixture on top of pork cutlets. Then pour beef broth over pork also. Bake at 350 degrees for 45 minutes. Yields 4 servings.

TEA TIME TIPS FROM
Laura Childs

French Cottage Tea

Turn your dining room or patio into a quaint and charming
French cottage. Think creamy linen tablecloths and napkins, country crocks brimming with fresh flowers, and
bunches of French lavender. Put on the music of Édith Piaf
and you're ready to go. Start your tea with lavender scones
served with jasmine white tea. Mushroom turnovers and
Brie and tomato tea sandwiches would make fabulous savories. As would tea sandwiches of country French pâté or
Gruyère cheese tarts. Be sure to add French cornichons as
a garnish. For dessert serve chocolate-dipped strawberries
or elegant French macarons that you buy at your favorite
patisserie.

Agatha Christie Tea

Channel England's mysterious moors and mysteries with
an Agatha Christie tea. This calls for a traditional British
theme, which means your guests should dress in their finest
tweeds, hats, berets, jeweled stickpins, and sensible shoes.
Forget the delicate china; this tea calls for hearty crockery,

pewter candleholders, and a stack of well-read Agatha Christie novels. Start with cream scones and Devonshire cream or buttermilk scones with lemon curd. Serve a hearty English breakfast tea. Serve smoked salmon and cream cheese on brown bread, or sliced ham with mustard on a hearty country bread. Perhaps a Victoria sponge cake for dessert. If you're a die-hard Agatha Christie fan, perhaps an Agatha Christie trivia contest?

Pretty in Pink Tea

If you're having a princess party, bridal shower, or Mother's Day tea, why not do it up in pink? We're talking bold-pink tablecloths, napkins, flowers (pink tea roses would be fabulous), candles, and even pink china if you have it. Start with cherry scones and Devonshire cream along with a hearty and slightly malty Assam tea. Crab salad tea sandwiches would be delicious, as would traditional cucumber and cream cheese sandwiches. A red pepper and onion quiche would make a delicious entrée. For dessert serve strawberry shortcake. Oh, and you can always up the ante by serving pink champagne!

Crystal Tea

Pull out all your best crystal—crystal stemware, crystal plates, crystal glasses—and set it up beautifully on a white tablecloth. Decorate with white tapers in crystal candleholders and white flowers in crystal vases. For a first course in this elegant tea start with cranberry-orange scones with Devonshire cream and a lovely Darjeeling tea. Your savories might include deviled eggs with asparagus tips, smoked salmon mousse on rye bread, chicken salad on sweet Hawaiian rolls, or classic cucumber and cream cheese sandwiches. Oh, you want dessert? How about a sinfully rich coconut cake?

Under the Tuscan Sun Tea

Ladies, grab your red-checkered tablecloths, then decorate your table with Italian pottery, bottles of olive oil, baskets of grapes, breadsticks in pots, and crocks filled with fabulous sunflowers. Start with savory cheese or pistachio scones and serve a classic black tea or an herbal tea flavored with anise. Your first course might be baked mozzarella bites, then on to cream cheese and sun-dried tomato tea sandwiches or mortadella and cheese sandwiches. Small pieces of lasagna would be a fabulous entrée, and glasses of pinot grigio would not be out of the question. Wow your guests with a classic Italian dessert like tiramisu or Italian gelato, and don't forget to put on an Italian opera.

Family Reunion Tea

Get the gang together, but instead of having a barbecue, make it an outdoor tea. Set up your patio or picnic table with baskets of summer fruit, mason jars full of flowers, and gallons of sweet tea or iced tea. Make place cards using little pictures of all your gang. Start your tea off right with deviled eggs and buttermilk scones. Your tea sandwiches might include turkey and Gouda cheese on hearty potato bread, Cubano sandwiches of hot pork and melted Swiss cheese, or biscuits with ham and apricot mustard. For a heartier entrée consider lobster rolls. Dessert might be ginger cake or blueberry crumb cake. While everyone's busy getting reacquainted, get a jug of sun tea brewing. And for tea-totalers, don't forget the mint lemonade.

TEA RESOURCES

TEA MAGAZINES AND PUBLICATIONS

Tea Time—A luscious magazine profiling tea and tea lore. Filled with glossy photos and wonderful recipes. (teatimemagazine .com)

Southern Lady—From the publishers of *Tea Time* with a focus on people and places in the South as well as wonderful teatime recipes. (southernladymagazine.com)

The Tea House Times—Go to theteahousetimes.com for subscription information and dozens of links to tea shops, purveyors of tea, gift shops, and tea events.

Victoria—Articles and pictorials on homes, home design, gardens, and tea. (victoriamag.com)

Texas Tea & Travel—Highlighting Texas and other Southern tea rooms, tea events, and fun travel. (teaintexas.com)

Fresh Cup Magazine—For tea and coffee professionals. (freshcup .com)

Tea & Coffee—Trade journal for the tea and coffee industry. (teaandcoffee.net)

Bruce Richardson—This author has written several definitive books on tea. (elmwoodinn.com/books)

Jane Pettigrew—This author has written thirteen books on the varied aspects of tea and its history and culture. (janepettigrew .com/books)

A Tea Reader—By Katrina Avila Munichiello, an anthology of tea stories and reflections.

AMERICAN TEA PLANTATIONS

Charleston Tea Plantation—The oldest and largest tea plantation in the United States. Order their fine black tea or schedule a visit at bigelowtea.com.

Table Rock Tea Company—This Pickens, South Carolina, plantation is growing premium whole leaf tea. (tablerocktea.com)

The Great Mississippi Tea Company—Up-and-coming Mississippi tea farm about ready to go into production. (greatmsteacompany .com)

Sakuma Brothers Farm—This tea garden just outside Burlington, Washington, has been growing white and green tea for over twenty years. (sakumabros.com)

Big Island Tea—Organic artisan tea from Hawaii. (bigislandtea .com)

Mauna Kea Tea—Organic green and oolong tea from Hawaii's Big Island. (maunakeatea.com)

Onomea Tea—Nine-acre tea estate near Hilo, Hawaii. (onotea.com)

Minto Island Growers—Handpicked, small-batch crafted teas grown in Oregon. (mintogrowers.com)

Virginia First Tea Farm—Matcha tea and natural tea soaps and cleansers. (virginiafirstteafarm.com)

Blue Dreams USA—Located near Frederick, Maryland, this farm grows tea, roses, and lavender. (bluedreamsusa.com)

TEA WEBSITES AND INTERESTING BLOGS

Destinationtea.com—State-by-state directory of afternoon tea venues.

Teamap.com—Directory of hundreds of tea shops in the U.S. and Canada.

Afternoontea.co.uk—Guide to tea rooms in the U.K.

Teacottagemysteries.com—Wonderful website with tea lore, mystery reviews, recipes, and home and garden.

Cookingwithideas.typepad.com—Recipes and book reviews for the bibliochef.

Seedrack.com—Order *Camellia sinensis* seeds and grow your own tea!

Jennybakes.com—Fabulous recipes from a real make-it-from-scratch baker.

Cozyupwithkathy.blogspot.com—Cozy mystery reviews.

Southernwritersmagazine.com—Inspiration, writing advice, and author interviews of Southern writers.

Thedailytea.com—Formerly *Tea Magazine*, this online publication is filled with tea news, recipes, inspiration, and tea travel.

Allteapots.com—Teapots from around the world.

Fireflyspirits.com—South Carolina purveyors of Sweet Tea Vodka.

Teasquared.blogspot.com—Fun, well-written blog about tea, tea shops, and tea musings.

Relevanttealeaf.blogspot.com—All about tea.

Stephcupoftea.blogspot.com—Blog on tea, food, and inspiration.

Teawithfriends.blogspot.com—Lovely blog on tea, friendship, and tea accoutrements.

Bellaonline.com/site/tea—Features and forums on tea.

Napkinfoldingguide.com—Photo illustrations of twenty-seven different (and sometimes elaborate) napkin folds.

Worldteaexpo.com—This premier business-to-business trade show features more than three hundred tea suppliers, vendors, and tea innovators.

Fatcatscones.com—Frozen ready-to-bake scones.

Kingarthurflour.com—One of the best flours for baking. This is what many professional pastry chefs use.

Californiateahouse.com—Order Machu's Blend, a special herbal tea for dogs that promotes healthy skin, lowers stress, and aids digestion.

Vintageteaworks.com—This company offers six unique wine-flavored tea blends that celebrate wine and respect the tea.

Auntannie.com—Crafting site that will teach you how to make your own petal envelopes, pillow boxes, gift bags, etc.

Victorianhousescones.com—Scone, biscuit, and cookie mixes for both retail and wholesale orders. Plus baking and scone-making tips.

Englishteastore.com—Buy a jar of English Double Devon Cream here as well as British foods and candies.

Stickyfingersbakeries.com—Scone mixes and English curds.
Teasipperssociety.com—Join this international tea community of
   sippers, growers, and educators. A terrific newsletter!
Melhadtea.com—Adventures of a traveling tea sommelier.

PURVEYORS OF FINE TEA
Plumdeluxe.com
Globalteamart.com
Adagio.com
Elmwoodinn.com
Capitalteas.com
Newbyteas.com/us
Harney.com
Stashtea.com
Serendipitea.com
Marktwendell.com
Republicoftea.com
Teazaanti.com
Bigelowtea.com
Celestialseasonings.com
Goldenmoontea.com
Uptontea.com
Svtea.com (Simpson & Vail)
Gracetea.com
Davidstea.com

VISITING CHARLESTON
Charleston.com—Travel and hotel guide.
Charlestoncvb.com—The official Charleston convention and
   visitors bureau.
Charlestontour.wordpress.com—Private tours of homes and gar-
   dens, some including lunch or tea.
Charlestonplace.com—Charleston Place Hotel serves an excel-
   lent afternoon tea, Thursday through Saturday, 1 to 3.
Culinarytoursofcharleston.com—Sample specialties from Charles-
   ton's local eateries, markets, and bakeries.

Poogansporch.com—This restored Victorian house serves traditional low-country cuisine. Be sure to ask about Poogan!

Preservationsociety.org—Hosts Charleston's annual Fall Candle-
light Tour.

Palmettocarriage.com—Horse-drawn carriage rides.

Charlestonharbortours.com—Boat tours and harbor cruises.

Ghostwalk.net—Stroll into Charleston's haunted history. Ask
them about the "original" Theodosia!

Charlestontours.net—Ghost tours plus tours of plantations and
historic homes.

Follybeach.com—Official guide to Folly Beach activities, hotels,
rentals, restaurants, and events.

ACKNOWLEDGMENTS

Special thank-yous all around to Sam, Tom, Elisha, Brittanie, Stephanie, Sareer, Talia, M.J., Bob, Jennie, Dan, and all the amazing people at Berkley Prime Crime and Penguin Random House who handle editing, design, publicity, copywriting, social media, bookstore sales, gift sales, production, and shipping. Heartfelt thanks as well to all the tea lovers, tea shop owners, book clubs, bookshop folks, librarians, reviewers, magazine editors and writers, websites, broadcasters, and bloggers who have enjoyed the Tea Shop Mysteries and helped spread the word. You are all so kind, and you help make this possible!

And I am forever filled with gratitude for you, my very special readers and tea lovers, who have embraced Theodosia, Drayton, Haley, Earl Grey, and the rest of the tea shop gang as friends and family. Thank you so much, and I promise you many more Tea Shop Mysteries!

Keep reading for an excerpt
from Laura Childs's next
Tea Shop Mystery . . .

TWISTED TEA
CHRISTMAS

*Available now from
Berkley Prime Crime!*

'Twas the week before Christmas and all through the house, a Victorian Christmas party was stirring in a genuine Victorian mansion at one of the swankiest addresses in all of Charleston, South Carolina. The original owner of the mansion had been a signer of the Declaration of Independence, and the current resident, a certain Miss Drucilla Heyward, was signatory on a bank account that contained more money than the GDP of a small European country.

Picture it this way: a group of well-heeled women in St. John Knits and low-heeled Manolos, wearing stacks of bangles, diamond stud earrings, and subtle hints of Chanel No. 5. All quite tasteful and genteel as they sipped Lapsang souchong from bone china teacups.

The men at the party leaned toward portly and were beginning to get ruddy faced from nipping brandy. The rent-a-bartender in his snug, red rent-a-jacket was pouring Hennessy XO tonight, so that's what they were drinking. Talking stock markets and sailboats and business and family, dressed in conservative Corneliani suits from M. Dumas & Sons on King Street, here and there a few of them sporting tartan plaid vests or Christmas bow ties.

And down the hallway, in the palatial dining room . . .

Theodosia Browning would never consider herself a member of this well-heeled, fairly insular clique. But she knew what they liked. Which is why she'd orchestrated a spectacular buffet menu for tonight's party. Rare roast beef on rye with dabs of horseradish, steamed blue crabs pulled fresh from local tidal creeks, Capers Blades oysters on the half shell, goat cheese crostini, and spicy chimichurri steak bites.

And then there were the tea sandwiches.

"I hope the guests love these little sandwiches as much as I do," Theodosia said as she arranged her offerings on polished silver trays.

"The crab salad on brioche?" Drayton asked. As Theodosia's tea sommelier at the Indigo Tea Shop he was also her partner in crime for tonight's catering gig.

"And lobster salad accented with fresh tarragon. Haley whipped up both fillings using her famous homemade mayonnaise recipe—or receipt, as she calls it."

"Yum," Drayton said. "No wonder Miss Drucilla asked us to serve champagne along with Lapsang souchong." He paused. "I do love that tea. The gently twisted leaves impart such a delicious smoky flavor."

"I'd say it's all rather perfect," Theodosia said.

She stepped back to admire their buffet table, an amazing amalgam of food, flickering candles, crystal vases filled with red and white roses, and some silver angel figurines that had somehow snuck their way in. As proprietor of the Indigo Tea Shop on Charleston's famed Church Street, Theodosia was used to serving cream teas, luncheon teas, and afternoon teas. But anytime she could land a fancy catering job—and this one sure was fancy—it was a happy addition to her shop's bottom line. Theodosia also knew that happy, satisfied guests often led to new bookings, which led to more business for her tea shop. And, really, wasn't that a good, no-brainer kind of marketing?

Theodosia normally wore T-shirts, khaki slacks, and a long black Parisian waiter's apron. But tonight she was glammed up in a red velvet hostess skirt and pink ruffled blouse that set off her complexion to perfection. Her English ancestors had blessed her with fair peaches-and-cream skin, startling deep blue eyes, and an inquisitive face. And some distant-distant relatives (from perhaps even farther north?) had gifted her with masses of curly auburn hair. In her mid-thirties now, Theodosia had worked in marketing, traveled a bit, dated enough men to know what type she preferred, and set up her own tea shop. In other words, she knew enough to be dangerous.

Drayton Conneley, also a born and bred Southerner, was sixty-something, a tea fanatic, and most definitely a world traveler. Drayton was smart, stylish, droll, and exacting (some might say demanding) in everything he did. His tastes ran from Shakespeare and Dickens to Baroque music, and he lived in a historic old house—in the Historic District, of course—that had once belonged to a Civil War doctor. Tonight he wore black slacks, a Brioni jacket, and a red-and-green-plaid bow tie.

"Can you believe this place?" Drayton asked, glancing around the dining room. "It's like something out of *Architectural Digest*. Only the castle and manor house version."

"If the Great Gatsby lived in Charleston," Theodosia said.

And who could argue with her? Given that they'd arranged their buffet on a twenty-foot-long antique Sheraton table in a dining room where a marble fireplace occupied most of one wall, a domed ceiling and crystal chandelier hung overhead, and walls were hand-painted with colorful Venetian scenes. Lavish garlands entwined with red roses, greenery, and fairy lights highlighted the tall, narrow windows that looked out over the back gardens, and an enormous fifteen-foot-high gilded Christmas tree sat next to a glass-fronted cabinet that held silver and crystal treasures.

"You hear that?" Drayton asked.

Theodosia stopped to listen for a moment. A string quartet had begun to play a rousing rendition of "God Rest Ye Merry, Gentlemen" in the front parlor.

"That's our cue," Theodosia said. "When the music starts we're supposed to light the candles and pop a few champagne corks."

"Happy to oblige," Drayton said. He grabbed a bottle of Moët & Chandon, twisted off the metal cage, placed a towel around the cork, and eased it out. There was a gentle, resounding POP.

"I'm thinking we should open four or five bottles," Theodosia said. "Once the music concludes and the guests come streaming in . . ."

The rest of her words were drowned out by a loud, unpleasant buzz that seemed to blast out of nowhere. The sound not only startled her, it filled her ears like a hive of angry bees.

"What's that?" Drayton asked. Only the noise was so loud Theodosia wasn't able to hear him; she could only read his lips and see the consternation on his face.

Suddenly, Miss Drucilla fluttered into the room wearing a coral silk caftan and dripping with diamonds. She held up a finger, darted around a corner, and then, mercifully, happily, the buzzing stopped.

"What was *that*?" Drayton cried.

Miss Drucilla returned, and her laughter filled the room.

"Oh, don't worry, kittens, it's only my crazy security alarm. Sometimes it pops off for no reason at all."

At eighty-four, Miss Drucilla Heyward was still a force to be reckoned with. Tiny as a bird, pixie white hair cut short to show off her favorite Tiffany Victoria earrings, she was spirited, fun loving, and social to the max. She served on the board of directors of the Charleston Opera Society and the symphony, and contributed money to dozens of charities. She was also known to occasionally join the men after dinner to smoke a cigar and enjoy her whiskey straight.

"Thank you," Drayton said. "But what an awful sound."

"Kind of gets your attention, doesn't it?" Miss Drucilla said.

Though she was still, technically, Mrs. Everett Heyward, she was generally addressed as Miss Drucilla. That's how it was done in the South. Women of a certain age and charm often had the moniker Miss added to their first name. Miss Kitty, Miss Abigail, Miss Drucilla. Like that.

Miss Drucilla surveyed the buffet table. "I love it," she said, clapping her hands together. "Everything's perfect."

"Thank you," Theodosia said. "And I sure do love—I mean *really* love—your jewelry."

Miss Drucilla brandished an arm. "Look here, I even wore my Verdura cuff tonight. Took it out of the vault just for this special occasion."

"Gorgeous," Drayton said. "A showstopper."

"That's not all you took out of the vault," Theodosia said. She couldn't help but notice the array of diamond rings that glittered on Miss Drucilla's tiny fingers.

"Oh, these?" Miss Drucilla fluttered her hands to show off her rings, sending brilliant flashes of light everywhere. "Tonight I'm wearing five diamond and gold rings in honor of Christmas—you know, like the song." She giggled as she half sang, "Five *gol*-den rings." Then she folded her hands to her chest and added, "All were gifts from my dearly departed husbands, Gerald, Charles, and Everett. All three of whom I've managed to outlive, knock on wood."

"Love the manicure, too," Theodosia added.

Now Miss Drucilla studied her fingertips. "Jolene over at Fantasy Salon did them. Kind of trendy, don't you think? Tipped my nails with fourteen-carat gold."

"Fun," Theodosia said.

"But not all that expensive. Anyway, enough with my tiny indulgences." Now she leaned forward and said, in a conspiratorial whisper, "I've decided to part with some of my money. That's why, along with a bunch of friends and neighbors, I invited executive directors from six of my favorite charities tonight. They're all going to be getting a wonderful Christmas present."

"That's fantastic," Theodosia said. She served as a board member for Big Paw Service Dogs and knew firsthand that nonprofits were constantly on the lookout for funding.

"Okay, you two open a couple more bottles of champagne and, in a few minutes, I'll start herding my guests in," Miss Drucilla said. And she hurried off in another quick burst of energy.

"She's amazing," Theodosia said to Drayton. "I hope I have that much energy when I reach her age."

"You will," Drayton said. "Look at your aunt, Libby. How old is she now?"

"Eighty-seven," Theodosia said.

"And she still gets up at five every morning to feed the birds."

"I guess that's called commitment," Theodosia said as a loud bray suddenly filled the air for a second time.

"There goes that annoying alarm again," Drayton shouted, pursing his lips in dismay. "I hope Miss Drucilla punches in the code before the security company gets nervous and sends an armed response." He touched his bow tie and fidgeted. "That's all we need, a couple of rent-a-cops rushing in to upset our lovely buffet."

"Everyone going head over teakettle," Theodosia said. But even as she tried to make herself heard, the alarm continued its terrible buzz.

"Can't they *hear* that in the parlor?" Drayton asked.

"Apparently not. Probably because the quartet's still playing."

Drayton walked around the table to shout in Theodosia's ear. "Well, that noise is driving me batty!"

"I'll see what I can do," Theodosia said. She nipped around a corner, intending to run down the wide center hallway that served as a sort of art gallery and led to Miss Drucilla's front parlor.

But Theodosia had taken only a single step when she saw a crumpled body sprawled halfway down the hallway on the marble tile floor. Then she recognized the filmy coral caftan and cried, "Oh no!" running as fast as her high heels could carry her.

"Miss Drucilla!" she cried, bending over the small body. But the woman lay ghostly still.

Is she breathing? I don't think . . .

Theodosia sprinted back to the music room.

"Drayton!" she cried. "Miss Drucilla's fallen down and I'm afraid she might have had a stroke or something!"

"Dear Lord!" Drayton went running while Theodosia stepped into the butler's pantry, located the security system panel, and hit a couple buttons. That seemed to do the trick, thank goodness, and stop the noise. Then she rushed back out, shouting for help as she ran down the hallway, dropping to her hands and knees next to Drayton. And poor Miss Drucilla.

"What do you think? Did she have a stroke? Is it her heart? Is she even breathing?" Theodosia asked.

"I don't know," Drayton said. "She's facedown and all crumpled up. I'm afraid to move her."

Theodosia's cries had alerted a dozen or so guests and now they poured into the hallway, one man immediately pulling out his phone and calling 911, directing the dispatcher to hurry up and send an ambulance.

Thank goodness. Theodosia breathed a huge sigh of relief. At least help was on the way.

"Passed out," another man behind her said. He spoke

with a high voice and sounded concerned, but calm. "Probably too much excitement."

"Let's try to turn her over, make sure she's breathing," Theodosia said. She was keenly aware of the buzz of voices behind her and realized that more party guests had spilled into the hallway.

"Theo?" a woman's voice called out. "What happened?"

Theodosia allowed herself a quick glance over her shoulder and saw her friend Delaine Dish, her brows puckered, expression solemn, eyes scared and jittery.

"I don't know," Theodosia said. "She just collapsed. She's . . ."

"Slide your hands under her shoulders," Drayton said. "We'll try to change her position and see if we can make her more comfortable."

"Okay," Theodosia said. Miss Drucilla was hunched up and still facedown. Not moving a single muscle.

Drayton was deeply shaken but still gamely hanging in there. "Okay. Ready?"

Theodosia nodded. She tried to gather Miss Drucilla up gently, like you would a sleeping child, then turn her over carefully.

"Oh my, I'm not sure about this." There was a momentary hesitation as panic flared in his voice. "We'd best be careful."

"Let's try to shift her very gingerly," Theodosia said. She knew something had to be done—and fast. But as she started to move Miss Drucilla, the woman's head lolled heavily onto one shoulder and her eyes remained squeezed tightly shut, as if she'd experienced some terrible horror.

"Okay . . . easy." Drayton was trying his best but Miss Drucilla's face was a washed-out pale oval, and there was a terrible finality about her.

"Drayton!" Theodosia cried as they began to slowly turn Miss Drucilla. "Look at . . ." Theodosia's heart lurched crazily, and she gasped, words logjamming in her throat. Finally, she lifted a trembling hand and pointed.

Reacting to the shock on Theodosia's face, Drayton's eyes widened with worry. Then he saw what she was pointing at.

"Oh no," he groaned.

Someone had plunged a bright-orange syringe deep into Miss Drucilla's throat!

NEW YORK TIMES BESTSELLING AUTHOR

LAURA CHILDS

"Murder suits [Laura Childs] to a tea."

—*St. Paul (MN) Pioneer Press*

For a complete list of titles,
please visit prh.com/laurachilds